REBECCA OF PROVIDENCE, RHODE ISLAND

REBECCA OF PROVIDENCE, RHODE ISLAND

1605–1683

Bonnie L. Schermer

iUniverse, Inc.
New York Lincoln Shanghai

Rebecca of Providence, Rhode Island
1605–1683

iUniverse, Inc.

For information address:
iUniverse, Inc.
2021 Pine Lake Road, Suite 100
Lincoln, NE 68512
www.iuniverse.com

ISBN: 0-595-30392-7

Printed in the United States of America

Contents

Preface

I wrote about Rebecca because I wanted to know more about what sort of woman would choose the life path of an early emigrant to New England, and what would happen to her personality once she got there. Unfortunately for me, there are very few records about my ancestress Rebecca, wife of John Throckmorton.

Therefore, this is FICTION, based on research I did into the lives of others who lived at the same times and places as did Rebecca. I think that I came to understand her well, and have tried to present her in an interesting way.

From the records consulted, I know that the Throckmortons interacted with many of the famous people named in this book. The nature of that inter-action is mostly my invention.

The events described are as close to fact as I could make them; For the times I got carried away by my story, I can only plead insanity...

Bonnie L. Schermer
1994

The *Lyon*

Rebecca straightened her back, clutching the ship's wooden rail, trying desperately not to be sick any more. Breathing the cold sea air deeply, slowly, she dominated the nausea which had been her constant companion for the last two months. Since the *Lyon* had cleared Bristol Harbor, England, on December first, 1630, heading for Massachusetts, Rebecca had endured more sustained misery than she thought possible. One storm after another had ravaged the vessel mercilessly. The odor of human waste and illness below deck was indescribably bad; the icy wind above, intolerable. Even Rebecca's heavy woolen cloak, hood, and fur muff did not begin to keep her warm. A too familiar, despised voice sounded in her ears:

"'Thou hast swallowed down riches, and shall vomit them up again.'"

Rebecca wiped her mouth on a kerchief and looked up into Roger's icy blue eyes. Controlling her temper with an effort, she responded:

"I have repented; may God grant us respite from these storms."

"Woman, it is not seemly for you to remain alone on deck; I will assist you below."

Wanting to remain above, but lacking the energy to oppose him, she murmured, "You are too kind, Master Williams."

Grasping his proffered arm, long skirts swaying, she gracefully stepped to the open hatch. Turning, she backed down the rough wooden ladder into the main quarters, where the passengers ate, as Roger steadied her arms from above. The stench of unwashed bodies closed around Rebecca once again.

Goodwoman Noakes handed Rebecca a spoon and a wooden bowl, half filled with hot barley water. She had nearly summoned the courage to taste it when she heard Roger's grating voice proclaim:

"Blessed be the Lord, who giveth us his bounty!"

From a dozen throats all around her came, "Amen!"

Losing her appetite completely, Rebecca cautiously carried the bowl toward a bench occupied by her closest friend, Roger's wife. Rebecca gently smoothed a few wisps of once beautiful black hair which adhered to the twenty-one year old woman's face.

"Did he release you yet?" she whispered.

"Yes. I may eat now, but he will not pray with me until he is sure I have repented."

"Monster."

Rebecca was thoroughly tired of Roger's constant badgering of his wife's soul. It seemed that he could not tolerate any woman, especially his own, being relaxed and happy. According to him, women were impure, the vile instruments of Satan's temptation. He was forever identifying their sins, then declaring days of prayerful fasting to purge them.

"Have some gruel; it will strengthen you."

Her friend made a face, but did manage to eat most of the barley. Feeling better herself, Rebecca fetched them each a flat, dry biscuit, eating hers quickly. She followed this by sipping a mug of ale, which Rebecca especially needed in order to produce milk for her three month old daughter, Mary.

Turning to the end of the table occupied by her own family, Rebecca encountered a warm smile in the eyes of her husband. His bowl was empty, but he was feeding the contents of a second one to their adored one year old daughter, Joan. The child had a bottomless appetite, and, thank God, an immunity to the motion sickness which plagued nearly all the other passengers.

Lifting baby Mary, who was beginning to whimper, Rebecca carried her up a short, steep flight of steps and through a door into her own family's cabin. She loosened her bodice in order to nurse the child. Lying in her bunk, she began the feeding. Then she heard the wind pick up and felt the ship begin to roll harder.

"Here we go again," she thought.

Leaning against canvas bags of their softer belongings, which served as bunk cushions, Rebecca let her mind drift back to the coast of Essex, England, to the carefree days of her girlhood. Every night she prayed that she would be able to provide as happy a home for her own dear little ones.

England: Bradwell

Rebecca Cornell's earliest memories included the seashore. She recalled running along the beach near her native village of Bradwell, picking up pieces of colored rock and weathered wood. Sometimes, she and her older sisters trod the sandy marsh paths, gathering wild bird eggs for the family's supper.

It was during long walks by the shore that Rebecca's father taught her about God. Each Cornell child, when he or she turned five years old, was entitled to turns walking and talking with Papa alone. In this way, their characters were studied and moulded. They learned the basic tenets of their faith, which was Anglican strongly leaning toward Puritanism.

When Rebecca, as a young girl, first absorbed the idea that she was a sinner, bound for Hell, she responded with terror. She alarmed her family with screaming nightmares for a week, until her father was able to make her understand that Christ's redemptive work at Calvary guaranteed believers access to heaven.

"But how do I know I'm one of the predestined ones?" Rebecca quavered.

"If thou hast faith, and continually confess and repent thy sins, then thou mayest be saved," came her father's answer.

The Cornell family was doubly glad when Rebecca's conversion was accomplished. They expected to be able to sleep better thenceforth, without interruption from her.

Rebecca's new understanding of her faith made her quite insufferable. She preached to the local dogs, cats, and younger children, and was most disappointed to learn that women were not permitted to become ministers of the Gospel. She felt she could do a much better job than Parson Ashby.

When she was older, Rebecca learned her Catechism with ease, and was confirmed in the church where she had been baptised as an infant.

Chelmsford

Early in 1625, when Rebecca was fifteen, the Cornells relocated westward, inland to the growing town of Chelmsford, Essex. Her father, Edward, a master scrivener, took over the larger shop of a fellow guild member who had died there. In the shop, letters were written for a fee, legal documents were copied and notarized, and money was collected to be lent out at interest. Edward Cornell's skill at this last was the source of his considerable wealth. He and his family were members of the expanding middle class, the gentry, which did not earn its living through manual labor. Therefore, he was eligible to use the title, "Gentleman," after his signature, and was addressed as "Master Cornell."

The Cornell family at that time consisted of Rebecca, her father and mother, her troublesome brother Thomas, seventeen, and Joseph, the youngest at thirteen. Job, Rebecca's favorite sibling at twenty-three years old, was apprenticed to a merchant, in Norwich. Rebecca's four older sisters had all by then made good marriages, her father having provided each with a substantial dowry.

Rebecca, her parents, and her two brothers moved temporarily into three cramped rooms over the Chelmsford shop, while Master Cornell supervised the construction of a new wattle and daub, wood framed, thatched house. ("Wattle and daub" meant that spaces between wooden timbers were filled with a clay made from mud, straw, and twigs.)

One March morning shortly after their arrival, Rebecca was looking out one of the upstairs windows. An elegant carriage, silver shield of arms upon its doors, pulled by four black horses drew up to the shop door below. The liveried footman assisted an expensively dressed lady, who looked to be in her late sixties, from the coach. Rebecca could hear the woman's authoritative voice talking to her father, but could not distinguish the words. After half an hour, the lady emerged from the shop, smiling. Rebecca then could hear her father's voice clearly.

"Lady Joan, if there is anything further I can do to help settle this matter, just let me know…"

The Lady paused, then said, "Since thou hast been so kind, perhaps there is something I can do for thee. Hast thou any daughters of an age to be my companion and maid? I am losing my current maid to marriage, which I confess I arranged, and so far have been unable to find anyone to replace her who has been gently brought up. I need not tell thee that a position such as this in my household is a very great advantage to any girl wishing to make a good marriage."

Edward spread his hands in a deprecating manner, and shook his head.

"My older daughters are all married, and I'm afraid that Rebecca, at fifteen years, may not yet be ready to leave home. She is an obedient child, however, and learns quickly."

Lady Barrington replied, "Why not give this matter some thought? I have successfully taken in maids younger than that. In fact, my granddaughter, Johanna, has a fifteen year old maid right now. At least when I get them young I can train them properly! I shall return to sign those papers in seven days, and will interview the girl. If thou art agreeable, have her ready to go with me. I assure thee that she will be kindly treated."

As the carriage pulled away, Rebecca heard her father's footsteps on the wooden stairs. He took her hand, patted her thick chestnut hair, smiled down into her lovely sapphire eyes, and asked,

"'Becca, heardest thou what Her Ladyship just said?"

"Yes, Papa, I could not help but overhear."

"Art thou willing to live at Hatfield Broad Oak? It should be a great opportunity for thee."

"How far away is that?"

"Only about fifteen miles."

"I should miss you and Mama terribly."

"Yes, but thou knowest we cannot be with thee forever. This could be thy chance to advance in the world, perhaps to meet and marry a fine gentleman."

"I will do whatever you think best, Papa."

"Let me convince Her Ladyship to give thee a six month trial. After that, if thou art unhappy, thou mayest return home to us."

The following week, Lady Barrington conducted Rebecca's interview as if she were buying a horse. She checked the girl's hands for cleanliness, her teeth for soundness, and grimaced to discover that Rebecca could read and write.

"Education for women is not the fashion today," she pronounced. "King James has said, 'To make women learned and foxes tame has the same effect: To make them more cunning.' His prejudice has influenced the younger men. Perhaps it would be advantageous to conceal that skill until thou art well married."

Rebecca did not respond. She had always been proud of her abilities with pen and paper, and thoroughly enjoyed showing up her older but slower brother, Thomas. Once she had been made to confess her sin of pride to God...

At the end of their discussion, Lady Barrington announced, "She is a beautiful child. I shall try her for six months, as we discussed. If she seems honest and biddable by the end of that time, she may stay on. What sayest thou, Rebecca?"

"Yes, My Lady, I'll try hard to please you."

Hatfield Broad Oak

Rebecca's first few weeks at Hatfield Broad Oak were difficult because every-thing was so strange. Homesickness plagued her, both a longing for her own family and for the seaside village so recently left behind. She felt landlocked, trapped.

Rebecca's duties were light, and mostly involved accompanying her mistress everywhere, reading the Bible to her, fetching and carrying. Lady Joan prom-ised that eventually the maid would be trained to maintain her extensive ward-robe, as well as to help her dress and arrange her hair.

"And," she said to Rebecca, "since thou canst read and write so well, thou mayest help me review the manor accounts. Just don't tell any of the young men what we're up to!"

It took Rebecca a week to learn her way around the great house, a former priory, with its fifty-three rooms and numerous outbuildings. Nearly every-thing needed by the residents of the house and surrounding village was pro-duced on site. The place functioned as a tightknit community, with each person dependent on the others.

The members of the immediate and extended Barrington family required more study before Rebecca could identify them all. There were Sir Francis and Lady Joan, of course, and their four sons. Sir Thomas resided at Barrington Hall, several miles to the north with his wife and children. Robert, with his family, lived across the road in a house called Barrington Bury. Francis, a bach-elor, occupied the family's London town house. John, with his wife, used a suite of rooms in the great house itself.

The five daughters were all married, and had left home. Winifred, with hus-band Sir William Meux, had gone to the Isle of Wight, where the family owned property. Joan was the wife of Sir Richard Everard. Ruth, unhappily paired with Sir George Lamplugh, was considering returning to her parents' home. Mary had married Sir Gilbert Gerard of Harrow on the Hill, Middlesex. Eliza-beth, first widowed, married second Sir William Masham, and lived at Otes, three miles south of Hatfield Broad Oak.

In addition, living in the greathouse at Hatfield Broad Oak were Lady Johanna Altham, Lady Joan's granddaughter from Lady Elizabeth's first mar-riage, and Lady Joan's niece, Lady Jane Whalley.

Because Sir Francis had been a Member of every Parliament during the past twenty-three years, regular visitors to the manor included many important religious and political figures, as well as many figures who longed to become important. In this category was Lady Joan's nephew, Oliver Cromwell, with wife Elizabeth and their three young children, Robert, Oliver, and Bridget. Rebecca was pleased to see how Master Cromwell doted on his wife and children.

What Rebecca did not yet realise was that the Barringtons were THE power among the gentry of the County of Essex, and that their numerous relatives and associates comprised a hotbed of Puritan politics.

On her first morning at Hatfield Broad Oak, Rebecca met Mary Barnard, personal companion and maid to Lady Barrington's granddaughter, Lady Johanna, or "Jug," as she was nicknamed. Mary, just Rebecca's age, was endowed with both a sweet nature and striking beauty. The only daughter in a poor parson's large family, Mary had been taken on by Lady Joan after Mary's mother died. Tall for a woman, she had thick black hair and large, brown eyes set in a bewitching face. Thin, unlike Rebecca, whose body curved generously, she moved hesitantly, the effect always being that of a lovely bird poised for instant flight. The two maids quickly became fast friends. When they were dismissed from duty, they would meet in one of the empty chambers or, in good weather, wander down to the bank of the stream. Together they would discuss their dreams:

"I want a man like my father," said Mary. "He must be perfect as the day. Tall, blue eyes, I think."

"A perfect man? You don't ask for much!" teased Rebecca. "My man need not be perfect, but he must be kind. I could not abide being treated as some of the women in Bradwell were. I don't care what he looks like, as long as he's not TOO ugly."

"Blue eyes or brown?"

"It does not matter. But I did meet a man once…He had the most lovely, kind brown eyes I ever saw!"

"Tell me about him!"

"He is apprenticed at my uncle's scrivener's shop, in the same town as my brother Job. You should meet my brother. He is not perfect, but very attractive, I assure you!"

"But the man with the brown eyes…what is his name?"

"John, I think. John Throckmorton. And he kissed my hand, bowed to me so elegantly. I think I could like him. Brother Job is apprenticed to his father, and has always spoken well of him!"

"Throckmorton, Throckmorton. I know I've heard that name. I must ask Lady Jug."

"Well, leave my name out of it. I only said he has kind eyes."

A few days later, the two met again, and Mary's eyes were round with excitement.

"Your uncle's apprentice is one of the Throckmortons of Norfolk County? Lady Jug says they are from an ancient noble family. In addition, they have much money. They are grocers and woolens merchants of Norwich town!"

Rebecca yawned.

"I care not for any of that. My man must be one who treats me well!"

Mary agreed, "Money and pedigree mean little to me. I have not the dowry to attract a rich gentleman, anyway. But I must have a man who walks with God."

One afternoon in July, the girls were working together in the folding chamber. Looking out of the window, Mary pointed her finger.

"Look there! Who's that in the stable yard?"

Rebecca turned carelessly, saying, "Must be more visitors...Great heavens! It's Job, my brother, and his friend John Throckmorton!"

Rebecca dashed down the staircase before remembering that she must obtain her mistress' permission before leaving the greathouse. She ran back up the stairs. Slipping her feet rapidly over the polished floors, she skidded to a halt outside Lady Barrington's door. Tapping softly, she entered the chamber after hearing Her Ladyship's voice. Her eyes dancing, Rebecca struggled to contain her excitement.

"Visitors, M'Lady!"

"Someone thou knowest?"

"My brother, My Lady, Job, and Master John Throckmorton. They must have ridden from Norwich."

"Thou hast permission to greet them. And thou art free from duty until bedtime."

"Oh, thank you, My Lady!

Rebecca raced down the back stairs and out the side doorway. She encountered her brother at the opening of the tall hedge which separated the house and gardens from the stables. Job did not speak, but bent his knees, catching his sister in a hug. Kissing her cheek, he set her down, and took her hand in his. He led her to a nearby bench, where they sat, and he asked, much too somberly,

"Have you been well, 'Becca?"

"Very well, thank you, Job. Is something amiss?"

"It is fortunate you have found this place to live. Are you content here?"

"I have been a little homesick, but the lady is very kind."

"If you are content, you must consider this your only home. Our parents..." He stopped, losing his voice.

"...and our brother Joseph have succumbed to plague, about three weeks ago. Thomas is still gravely ill, but expected to recover."

Rebecca stared at him as this information soaked into her consciousness. Then she covered her face with her hands and cried. Job gathered her into his arms and held her until the sobs slowed. Rebecca heard as from a distance the voice of Lady Barrington addressing Job,

"Master Cornell, is there anything I can do? John Throckmorton has acquainted me with thy family's misfortune."

"Lady Joan, I am already indebted to Your Ladyship's care for preserving my sister alive. I am grateful. If Your Ladyship continues to shelter her, it will be of great help to me, as I have yet to complete my apprenticeship."

"What is the status of her dowry?"

"It is being held in escrow for her by our uncle, the scrivener, Robert Debney."

"Then I shall continue to bring her up gently, as befits the station she may someday occupy."

"Thank you, kind Lady!"

"It is my pleasure to help such a good family as thine in its time of trouble. And thy sister is not only a lovely child, but also obedient and usually cheerful. Already I am receiving inquiries from young men who want to court her."

Because her face was still red from weeping, Rebecca did not go in to supper, nor vespers, with her brother. He, having already mourned his family for weeks, soon was involved in political discussions with the Barringtons. Rebecca mourned alone as she paced the halls of the greathouse, then prayed in the manor chapel, and finally sought the solace of the darkened garden. Sitting, sobbing quietly on a bench, she was surprised to be addressed by John Throckmorton, who approached her softly and took her hand.

"Let me offer my condolences, Miss Cornell."

"Thank you, Master Throckmorton."

"This loss has been difficult for you," he began, sitting beside her. "I lost my mother, eleven years ago, when I was thirteen. There are so many aspects to grieving...it seems that just as one conquers a part of it, another part leaps up to add to the misery. I knew your family slightly, and thought it might help you to talk about them a little."

Rebecca could not resist his kindly tone, so began to tell him of Bradwell, and of the walks on the beach with Papa. She spoke of learning to sew and spin from Mother, and of little brother Joseph, always pestering and teasing.

"I forgot to ask Job…where is my brother Thomas? What will become of him?"

"It is my understanding that your sister Elspeth is caring for him, and that when he recovers, he will be brought to live with us, at Debney's in Norwich."

"Is my uncle a good master?"

"I never would have been apprenticed to him if he were not, even though he is a cousin of my stepmother. My father is most particular about the training I receive, as it may affect the entire family's fortune someday. In addition to possessing great skill in the 'art and mystery' of the scrivener, your uncle is a demanding teacher, very strict, but fair."

"I am glad to hear it. If only Thomas recovers, he may yet find a bright future. But surely not as a scrivener. I am better at such things than he. Oh! I'm not supposed to brag so, nor to reveal that I can use pen and ink."

John chuckled.

"I'll keep your secret, Miss. But truly, you must control your prideful tongue!"

"Yes. I would go inside, now. Lady Joan will be looking for me."

He gravely offered his arm, and escorted her to the foot of the staircase.

"Your brother and I are staying in the guest wing, so I'll say good night here. I know you will still grieve for your family. But do you remember that 'all things work together for good, to them that love God.'"

Impulsively, Rebecca squeezed John's hand and ran up the stairs. As she fell asleep in her bed in Lady Joan's dressing room, she imagined that she saw John's kind brown eyes once again, and that she heard his deep, gentle voice.

The next day, after morning prayers, she bid her brother and her friend goodbye. She did not see them again for a long time.

During the next year, Rebecca noticed increased numbers of visitors attending her mistress' husband, Sir Francis Barrington. Since the ascent in 1625 of the abusive King Charles, the Puritans had gained a focus for their discontent. The King, diplomatically and militarily inept, mismanaged wars with both Spain and France. When he quickly became financially insolvent, he imposed new taxes and ignored basic rights held by the English for centuries. Essex County, and especially Barrington Manor became a center of dissent. Opposing the king being the English definition of treason, the gentlemen of Essex were then walking a kind of tightrope. They balanced their actions and words against patriotism, their sacred honor, and their religious convictions. Rebecca overheard enough hellfire and brimstone from the men whenever she came near them to make her ears burn.

More and more often, the unmarried among them took time out from their debates to pursue the lovely Essex maiden with the huge sapphire eyes. They were invariably disappointed, for she saw nothing in any of them to spark her interest.

The issues they discussed seemed inconsequential to Rebecca until she heard in late October, 1626, that Sir Francis Barrington had been imprisoned at Marshalsea, in Southwark, London. His son in law, Sir William Masham, was sent to the Fleet Prison simultaneously, for the same crime. The two of them were the only ones to refuse the king's command to sit, at Romford, on the illegal Commission in Essex for the Forced Loan to the Crown, which would have impoverished the County. Attending as her mistress mourned Sir Francis' misfortune, Rebecca heard Lady Joan announce:

"Then I'll join him!"

Thinking she had not heard correctly, Rebecca turned to see Her Ladyship commencing to pack her clothing. Hurrying to help, the girl found her own eyes welling with tears. She knew that wives could accept imprisonment with their husbands, but few did so. Prison very often meant illness and death for those incarcerated there.

Lady Joan turned to Rebecca, patting her shoulder.

"Do not cry for me, Miss, nor for thyself. Cry rather for England, where men and women of good will are forced to serve such tyrants as our king."

On the day Lady Joan Barrington left for Marshalsea, every inhabitant of the manor and village lined the road to do her honour and bid farewell. Lady Joan had ordered all her daughters and younger son to remain at home.

"I won't have thee mewling and puling over me!" she exclaimed.

Rebecca, as always, accompanied her mistress. They had ridden only a short way, however, when the Lady Ruth, who had recently separated from her husband, caught up with them on her horse.

"If I lose both you and Father, I don't want to live. Please let me go with you!"

Lady Joan, alarmed and touched at this speech, reluctantly let her join them in the coach. The journey to London took two days. Lady Barrington's mood varied during the journey, but the inspiring memory of her grim determination and raw fortitude remained with Rebecca forever. Lady Joan told Rebecca that she considered some ideas more valuable than life itself; that among these was the preservation of ancient freedoms for which so many patriots had already sacrificed themselves.

"If we fail England now," she asked, "who else will find courage to limit abusive royal power, and how long will it take? Better to fight it now, in this small way than to wait for war."

London

Lady Joan's coach had stopped one night on the way, near Loughton, with cousins, who commiserated tearfully and angrily. Once in London, it proceeded over the narrow, cobbled streets to young Francis Barrington's tall, wooden town house on King Street in Westminster. He warmly greeted his mother and sister, but it was obvious to Rebecca that he feared for their lives. Rebecca overheard him pleading with his mother to reconsider, to support her husband from outside rather than inside the prison.

"You have heard what the place is, Mama. All the prisoners are thrown in together: male, female, murderers, debtors, the insane, the brain damaged, all scrambling through filthy, verminous straw for scraps of rotten food. There is no heat, no ventilation, no water for washing. I rode over there yesterday, to see Father. Mama, it is no place for you!"

"Francis, my dear son, do not attempt to dissuade me from my chosen course. Thou art not married, and so do not understand the bond thy father and I share. We are part of each other. I could no more live away from him than thou couldst live separated from half thine own body. He and I will see this trial through together, or not at all."

Sir Thomas and Robert Barrington, who had been in London attempting to have their father's sentence suspended, arrived at the house later. They added their pleas to those of young Francis, but received the same stolid response.

The next morning, Rebecca helped the ladies dress, encouraged them to eat, even though it was not a regular meal time. She rode with them and young Francis in the carriage, escorted by Sir Thomas and Robert on horseback.

Half an hour later, after crossing the Thames by the Westminster Bridge into Southwark, they arrived at Marshalsea. The entrance to the grim, coal smoke blackened building put Rebecca in mind of descriptions she had heard of the gates of Hell. Rebecca clung to Lady Joan's hand until the last second, forbidding her own tears to begin.

"Farewell, little Miss. When I am released, whether alive or dead, wilt thou come to fetch me home from this place?"

"Yes, it would be an honour for me, My Lady!"

The lady kissed Rebecca's brow, embraced her sons, and departed with her daughter. Rebecca's eyes then filled with tears. She only caught blurred glimpses of the heavy prison doors swinging outward, the Barringtons marching stalwartly in, and the doors banging shut. Young Francis, likewise overcome with sadness, sat next to Rebecca in the coach. As turned toward his house, he took her hand and began to pray earnestly that God would protect his family in this dark hour. Together, the two recited psalms and the Lord's Prayer. Somewhat comforted, the young man urged Rebecca to dine with him and his brothers. When the meal was over, she began the long journey back to Hatfield Broad Oak, alone in the elegant carriage.

Hatfield Broad Oak

Rebecca felt lost in her mistress' absence. She found plenty to occupy her, for the work of such a large manor never ceased. And every day, she added to a continuing letter, or journal to Lady Joan, installments of which she sent whenever someone was going to London. But she missed the personal interest taken in her by the indomitable Lady Joan. If not for Mary Barnard's companionship, Rebecca would have felt quite lonely.

One late afternoon in July, 1627, the two women sat embroidering in the slanting rays of the sinking sun. When Mary stopped speaking in mid sentence, Rebecca looked up, then followed the direction of her friend's gaze to the chamber doorway.

"Job! Master Throckmorton!"

The two young men bowed low, large smiles lighting their handsome faces. Each kissing Rebecca's hand in turn, they looked expectantly toward lovely Mary, who blushed charmingly.

"This is my good friend, Mary Barnard," offered Rebecca, when at last she found her voice.

"Pleased to meet you," murmured John.

"Enchanted," added Job.

Each kissed her hand.

"We were just completing our needlework for the day," continued Rebecca. She stood, holding up a man's gold embroidered sleeve for them to admire. "Perhaps you two will be fortunate enough to wear something as fine someday!"

"Perhaps you will be fortunate enough to sup tonight with two gentlemen of Londontowne!"

"Job, are your apprenticeships completed?"

When he nodded, Rebecca hugged him, then delicately touched John's sleeve.

"Congratulations, both of you!"

Since reaching the doorway, except for greeting Mary, John had neither spoken nor taken his eyes from Rebecca's face. Presently, he recollected himself.

"Shall we go to the dining hall?" he asked, offering Rebecca his arm.

She looked up into his eyes, liking very much the admiration she saw there. Glancing back, she noticed a similar expression on Job's face as he offered his arm to the beautiful Mary.

The four entered the great dining room, where the young men were welcomed by the Barrington family. Supper, served at five o'clock P.M., consisted of bread, butter, cheese, eggs, milk, a thick meat soup, and partridge pie. All this was washed down with tankards of ale.

During the meal, John explained to Rebecca that he and Job were enroute to Lincoln Inn, London, where they would follow an abbreviated course of legal studies considered necessary for gentlemen who wanted to improve their family fortunes. After vespers, John and Job bade the women goodnight, then turned to the young master, John Barrington. They wanted to know the latest in the effort to free Sir Francis, who had fallen ill at the prison. A formal request for pardon and early release had been sent to King Charles. John's father, an old friend and distant cousin of Sir Francis, was circulating petitions on his behalf among the various guilds of Norwich.

Rebecca and Mary retired to the chamber they shared, adjacent to Lady Jug's rooms, in order to discuss the afternoon's events. Rebecca's mood was one of calm satisfaction, Mary's of wistful uncertainty.

"Do you think your brother knows that I have no dowry? Surely he would not be interested in such a poor maid as I."

Rebecca reassured her: "When Job is interested in anyone, he finds out all there is to know about that person. I'll guess that he will ask Lady Joan. From her, he'll learn more about you than you know, yourself. Another thing: With Job, I think a love match might be possible. Because our parents are gone, he has more money and more freedom than most young gentlemen to choose his own wife. Of course, Uncle Robert will have something to say about it. But why are we talking about dowry and such? Surely you realise that Job is not a perfect man, nor especially called of God. I thought those were your requirements."

Mary said, "You're right. I am losing sight of my convictions. But when your brother looks at me, I have the most peculiar feeling inside...Did you notice that during the grace, Job took my hand? Why did he do that?"

Rebecca smiled.

"I don't want you to misunderstand. In my father's house, our family as well as guests all held hands during the grace. It had the practical aspect of keeping the children's hands still, but also gave us a feeling of unity."

"How charming! But when the chaplain finished, Job did not let go my hand until I looked into his eyes. I must confess that what I saw there made me blush. Then he smiled. It was most embarrassing! But what think you of Master John?"

"Actually, he asked me to meet him in the manor chapel in a few minutes. Do I look all right?"

"Here, let me fix your collar. If you don't return soon, shall I send out the bloodhounds?"

Rebecca tossed a pillow at Mary and left the room. Her heart beat faster as she entered the small stone church, burial place of the Barrington family. It had been built adjacent to the house, and was a refuge for those needing privacy for prayer. No effort had been made, however, to heat or ventilate it. The chapel, as a result, was perpetually cold and dank, though it was always lit with candles at night.

John was kneeling, at the polished wooden prayer rail, facing the old altar with its embroidered cloth and candles. As she drew nigh, Rebecca saw his lips moving in prayer. She knelt beside him, folded her hands, closed her eyes, and tried to pray. Gently, John's large right hand closed over her small ones. Rebecca trembled, and opened her eyes.

"Miss Cornell, I do not intend to frighten you."

"Of course not, Master Throckmorton. I think that uncertainty and the damp chill of evening made me quake just now. Why have you bidden me to this place?"

"I shall not have time to speak to you alone in the morning, before we depart. Your brother and I are beginning a difficult course of training, and I am not sure when we will return. In the few times you and I have been together, I have begun to care for you particularly. It is important to me to find out if you feel able to return my affection, or if I am just imagining that a special attachment between us may be possible."

"Master Throckmorton, I hardly know you. What I do know, I admire. I consider you a true and gentle friend. Is that what you need to hear?"

"Not quite. Miss Cornell, I am trying to say that I love you, and hope that you care a little for me in return."

After looking deeply into her eyes, which appeared navy blue in the candlelight, John pulled Rebecca close, kissing her cheek. When she did not resist, he kissed her mouth. After a moment, she found herself kissing him back, then pulling away. Waiting for her heart to slow, she finally spoke.

"I believe you have your answer, Master Throckmorton. I shall not run off with the stableboy while you are at Londontowne!"

She left the chapel swiftly, running up the darkened staircase to her room. Entering the chamber, she beheld Mary, who clutched a small envelope.

"Look what I found under the door! It has my name, I see that. Oh, please, read it to me. I cannot read script..."

Rebecca unfolded the note and read, "I have never before enjoyed a meal so much with such a lovely maid. The memory of our time together will always occupy a special place in my heart. Job."

"I knew he would find you irresistible!" exclaimed Rebecca. "We could be sisters someday if things work out."

"You haven't told me about John."

"Well...I let him kiss me."

"What!"

"Only a little, and then I ran away. But I gave him reason to hope that I am interested in him."

"I hope he doesn't think you behave this way all the time."

"I doubt that he does. It would be easy enough for him to ask Her Ladyship about me, anyway."

After morning prayers, the two women accompanied Job and John to their horses, which were standing, packed and ready, in the stable yard. Rebecca first embraced her brother, and then offered John her hand.

Curious, she watched her brother bid Mary goodbye as she murmured to John, "You see your rival over there..."

She nodded toward the well built stable boy, Dudley.

"Hurry back to me so that I'm not tempted..."

"Wicked girl!" he exclaimed. "Now I shall worry every minute we're apart!"

"Worry not, just come back!" she told him as he kissed both her hands.

Mary and Rebecca stood in the yard together for a long time after the men had gone. In his saddlebag, Job bore Rebecca's latest letter to Lady Joan.

London

In September, 1627, news reached the manor that the Barringtons were to be released from Marshalsea Prison. Accompanied by Sir Thomas and Robert, Rebecca rode in the carriage dispatched to carry them home. According to plan, they proceeded to Francis' house. He greeted them at the door.

"You are faithful, as well as lovely!" exclaimed Francis as he kissed Rebecca's hands. "Thank you for writing to my mother every day. You helped sustain her spirit during these months."

Later, when they arrived at Marshalsea, the three Barrington sons approached the great gate. After an interminable wait, the doors creaked outward, and three filthy, ragged skeletons staggered out. Rebecca leaped from the carriage, ran to Lady Joan's side. Sir Thomas and young Francis finally had to carry Sir Francis to the coach, while Rebecca and Robert supported Lady Joan and Lady Ruth, walking slowly.

Rebecca asked Francis, "Have you arranged for a doctor to call?"

Francis shook his head.

"They need one, and quickly."

Turning to Sir Thomas, who had ridden his horse, she sent him to fetch a physician.

The carriage wended its way toward Francis' house. Sir Francis and Lady Joan seemed barely conscious, and Rebecca was alarmed.

As they bundled the Barringtons into the house, Rebecca saw that the sons had no idea what to do next. Assembling the servants, therefore, she began giving orders:

"Stoke the fires in these two bedchambers. Fetch two wooden bathtubs, and fill them with warm water. We'll need the mildest soap you can find, scissors, razors, sponges, and large towels. Later, we want any kind of meat broth, strained. Also get some bread, and whiskey."

As soon as the first tub was filled, she ordered Sir Francis carried into that bedchamber.

Turning to young Francis' manservant, she told him, "Cut off all his clothing and burn it, then place him in the tub. Cut his hair off and shave his head completely, disposing of all the hair. Clean him as well as you can without chafing his skin. Then warm the bed thoroughly, dry him, and get him into bed without chilling him. Try to get him to eat a little. And do it all quickly, gently, because he is very weak."

Since the housekeeper was the only other female besides the cook in this bachelor's household, Rebecca made her help with Lady Joan and Lady Ruth. As soon as the ladies were asleep, Rebecca changed her own clothing and wandered downstairs. Completely exhausted, she entered the sitting room, and dropped into a chair. Burying her face in her hands, she heard Francis' voice, asking,

"Will they be all right?"

"I hope so. Lady Joan hasn't spoken yet, but kept patting my hand as if to thank me. She ate well, which is a good sign."

"I didn't realise she was so sick…she's been holding up, caring for Father until today."

"When will the doctor be here?"

"Soon, I think. I hear someone knocking, now."

In a moment, the butler announced, "Master John Throckmorton, to see Miss Cornell."

"Show him in, Jackson!"

Francis was on his feet, exclaiming, "John! How good to see you! I'm afraid we are all at sixes and sevens, but Miss Cornell has set everything right."

Robert, standing to greet John, added, "Thank you for delivering the Norwich petitions to the palace. I'm sure they influenced the king to hasten the release of my family."

John replied, "I only wish I could have done more."

Jackson was back, saying, "Doctor Mayerne is here. Would you like to speak with him?"

Francis said, "Of course. Show him to my father's room first. I'll be there in a moment."

To John, he added, "Please excuse us."

Francis left, followed by Robert.

Rebecca stood up. John opened his arms and she walked wearily into them, and stayed there. After a gentle kiss, he guided her to a couch, where they sat. She related the afternoon's events, briefly, and he shook his head.

"The Barringtons are lucky to have you."

"I am glad to be able to serve in this way, because I owe her ladyship my life, and something more. Because of Lady Joan's example, I am beginning to think about the effects of tyranny on the human spirit in a very personal way."

"You are not alone. The notion of divine right is being tested before our eyes."

"Indeed. The brave actions of patriots such as the Barringtons will do more to stoke the fires of liberty than a thousand angry speeches."

"Perhaps. Many noble actions such as theirs have accomplished little in the past."

"That is true; God forbid that they have suffered in vain."

"I cannot stay longer; I see that you are tired, and I have obligations later today. I shall call again tomorrow morning."

"I'll see you tomorrow."

Rebecca started toward the door, but John caught her hand, drawing her back.

"There's only one problem—I don't want to leave you."

Gathering Rebecca into his arms, John kissed her lingeringly.

"Heart's Lady," he whispered. "I want to stay…"

Rebecca was up all that night, tending Sir Francis and the ladies. By offering them small amounts of broth and bread frequently, she was able to get a reasonable amount of nourishment into each.

In the morning, when Jackson told her that Job and John were downstairs, Rebecca looked at herself in a mirror and moaned, distressed at how tired her face appeared. Carefully, she washed in cold water, brushed her hair, and slipped into a fresh gown. As she reached the foot of the stairs, she turned toward the open sitting room. Then she realised that five men, three of them the Barrington sons, had risen and turned toward her with looks which ranged from grateful admiration to undisguised love. She hesitated, then quickly embraced Job, who swung her off her feet.

"They tell me you are an angel of mercy!" he said.

When Job set her down, John took her hand and pulled her round to face him. Tipping her chin up, and looking into the bloodshot eyes, he said, "She's a tired angel—looks like you after final exams, Job!"

Possessively, he slipped an arm around her waist and held her at his side, asking, "Is there any plan to fetch another maid for tonight? We don't want Miss Cornell to wear herself out."

Francis answered, "Yes. The housekeeper will care for my parents and sister today, and the housekeeper's daughter is coming for tonight."

"Excellent!" said John. "'Becca, I want you to go straight to bed, and we'll be back tomorrow to see you."

Returning to her patients upstairs, Rebecca conferred with the housekeeper.

"They seem stronger than when we brought them home, but I still think they should take a little nourishment every three hours. Did Cook get any fresh milk for them? Ask her to bake some egg custard, and to sweeten it well. Stewed, sweetened apples would be good for them, also. I will be resting in the next chamber; call me at any time if you need my assistance."

Rebecca did not know that young Francis overheard this. As soon as she retired, she found out later, he instructed the housekeeper not to wake her unless there were an emergency.

After sleeping all day and night, Rebecca woke before the rest of the household the next morning. She washed and dressed, then checked the Barringtons, who were sweetly sleeping under the watchful eyes of the housekeeper's daughter, Mabel. After motioning the woman into the hall, and questioning her, Rebecca determined that all three were improving. Thanking Mabel, Rebecca dismissed her until that night, taking over the responsibility for their care once more. Later, because the housekeeper assisted, Rebecca was able to run downstairs, receiving Job and John enthusiastically when they returned as promised.

After greeting Rebecca, Job asked, "How fare the lord and ladies?"

"It is still too soon to tell, but they seem to be better. Their ladyships respond more and are able to sit up in a chair. Sir Francis is quite weak, but no longer feverish."

Seeing young Francis passing through the hall, John called to him, "We are going to kidnap Miss Cornell this morning, as we discussed. I'll also want her tomorrow afternoon if things are going well here."

"What are you two plotting now?" asked Rebecca.

Job said, "We want to show you around London. John borrowed this fantastic turnout from a friend of his father. The friend is Richard Chambers, Alderman of the Merchant Taylors, no less, and it seems a shame to waste the opportunity..."

John asked, "What say you? Will you favour us with your company?"

"Let me find out what Jackson did with my cloak. Yes, I supposed I must see a little of London besides one house and a prison."

As soon as Rebecca was warmly wrapped against the cold, John led her quickly out to the carriage. A liveried footman opened and closed the door for them. Job had remained in the house, talking to Francis. For the briefest of moments, Rebecca wondered if the two men had engineered this, as John began kissing her ardently. Then she decided she did not care. John released her as Job entered the coach.

Noting Rebecca's blushes, Job reproached her saying, "You at least could have brought Mary Barnard to London with you. That way, I wouldn't be left out!"

Off they rolled, on a whirlwind tour of London. Since they were already on King Street in Westminster, they drove through slums past the palace reserved for the Houses of Parliament, past Westminster Abbey, where kings are crowned and buried. Turning west to Hyde Park, they took a brisk turn around the Serpentine Lake. There were deer in the park, and people exercising their horses. From there, it was not far east to St. James Palace, London home to His Royal Majesty. Driving farther east toward the Thames, they came to Whitehall Palace, containing the government offices, which hugged the river for half a mile. From Whitehall, they drove north to Charing Cross, then proceeded east along the Strand. Turning north, they passed Lincoln Inn where John and Job read the law every day. Then they cut back south and east to enter the ancient City of London through Tempull Bar Gate.

Arriving at St. Paul's Church, the coach stopped, and John pulled Rebecca from it.

He explained, "I have arranged for the caretaker to let us climb into the church tower; from there you can get an excellent view!"

Rebecca said, "It's a good thing there is little chance of lightning today; it looks as if the tower has not recovered from the last strike. Do they intend to restore the spire?"

Job answered, "I understand that the cost is too high. Perhaps someday…"

After admiring the interior of the building, the three climbed one hundred fifty wooden stairs to look out the narrow slits in the walls at the top platform of the tower. Rebecca could see the charred wood where the fire begun by the lightning had been extinguished. Looking north, they saw verdant hills in the distance, some topped by Dutch style windmills used to grind grain.

Turning west, Rebecca said, "That's where we just were. Oh, it's all so lovely from up here, despite the coal smoke."

Job added, "The wind is blowing hard enough today to keep the air cleaner. When it dies down, and the fog comes in off the river, it's hard to see anything at all."

South across the Thames was Southwark, which Job informed her contained all the seamier entertainments not allowed in the City proper:

"The Bear Garden is there, the new Globe Theater, Miss Marple's Academy for Young Women…"

John choked.

Rebecca wrinkled her brow.

"What academy?"

Job continued as if she hadn't spoken, "If you squint, you can just make out the Marshalsea Prison."

Rebecca said, "That's one sight I'd as soon never see again."

Looking east down river, they saw London Bridge, with its tall buildings and gates. Straight to the east sprouted a multitude of churches.

John directed her attention, "That is Guild Hall, where the Lord Mayor presides. Within the City, he is, by law, above even the king. I have an invitation to a formal reception and dinner there tomorrow afternoon. If the Barringtons are still improved, would you care to attend? I should welcome the chance to show you off!"

"I, I don't know, John. My clothes are not suitable for such an occasion."

"We'll take you around to Mistress Chambers, the lady whose coach we are using, for dinner today. She said she'll be happy to fix you up, because of your kindness to the Barringtons. All of London has been concerned about them."

"Very well, John, we shall see."

Job led the way back down the stairs and into the coach. They then passed the open air market of Petticoat Lane, and the approaches to London Bridge. Rebecca saw several oceangoing vessels at the wharfs. Next, they drove past Billingsgate and the fish market, beyond which loomed the grounds of the Tower. John pointed out the ravens circling it.

"They say that when the ravens leave the Tower, Britain will fall. I think the jailors are paid to feed them."

They drove out toward Tyburn Gate, with its gallows for twenty-four, and its channeled wooden floors, blood stained from executions.

Before Rebecca expected it, the coach pulled up to an imposing wooden house on the City's northeast side. John and Job escorted Rebecca to the door, where they were bowed inside by a somber butler, who took their wraps.

The three were soon greeted by Mistress Chambers. She asked anxiously after the Barringtons while making them all welcome. It was obvious that the woman knew John well. Rebecca was reminded that she, Job and John all belonged to this society of guild members, with which she had lost touch. These people were of the same class, but had differing lifestyles from the landed gentry she lived among.

Master Chambers soon arrived for dinner, and they all sat down in the formal dining parlour. There they were treated to a truly elegant meal of salad, several meats with boiled vegetables, bread, fruits, and wine. They ended with little cups of cold chocolate.

Mistress Chambers took Rebecca upstairs to find clothing for the next evening.

"My daughter is staying with her sister's family in Herts for a month, but left all her best things here; they never really dress in Knebworth, you know.

Let's see, I think blue is your best colour; it brings out your eyes. Here are three that may work—this one's too small in the bust for you, but this is looser, and my maid can baste in a tighter waist to show off your figure—you'll be quite alluring!

And here are white kid gloves and a darling little headpiece; almost a cap, but not quite—it will show off that wonderful hair without upsetting the mad dog Puritans in the group.

It's too bad not much jewelry is being worn these days—I have a diamond pendant left from the days of Good Queen Bess (now *there* was a woman who knew how to dress!) which would simply glow on your bosom. Never mind, we'll use this plain gold chain, and you'll be simply stunning! Now, don't worry about a thing—my carriage will collect you at three o'clock, and we'll dress here, all travel to the reception together—you'll be my protege, the toast of the aldermen!"

In the coach, riding home, Rebecca was very quiet.

Noticing this, John asked, "Is everything all right, Miss Cornell? We have tried to show you a good time."

"I think I'm just tired, and a bit overwhelmed. Mistress Chambers is determined to dress me very elegantly, and I'm afraid I can't carry it off."

John said, "From what I've seen of your steady spirit lately, I feel sure you can. It would give me great pleasure to have one evening out in London with you. But I will not be responsible for making you unhappy; the choice is yours."

Rebecca said, "I'll go if you will protect me from pushy types; I won't want to do much talking."

He smiled.

"But of course. You'll come across as lovely and mysterious!"

Rebecca attended Lady Joan all evening, and the following day she made Her Ladyship smile a little by describing the lovely blue dress she was to wear to the reception. John arrived with the carriage at three in the afternoon, and they rode alone in it, taking the long way to the Chambers' house. Being embraced and kissed by John for an hour was rather more sustained excitement than Rebecca had ever known. She began to wonder about the mysteries of marriage, and whether married women felt this way all the time.

"How could they?" she asked herself.

By the time she was dressed and ready for the reception, Rebecca had a hard time recognising her reflection in the glass. Her posture, always erect, had become regal, mostly because her body was still tingling from being so close to John during the afternoon. Her hair had been elegantly arranged by Mistress Chambers' maid, and the dress now fit to perfection. The V shaped waistline showed off her narrow waist and flaring hips. The gloves set off her shapely arms, and the low cut neckline emphasised her full bosom. Feeling naked, she would have protested, but saw that Mistress Chambers' gown was even more daring.

"This is London," explained her benefactress. "There is quite a French influence here, even though we don't like to admit it. London Puritans wear things that rural Puritans never would. I assure you that your outfit will appear demure next to those worn by most of the young women you will see tonight. Trust me. And there is another advantage to being dressed as you are. You do want to keep John for yourself, right?"

Seeing Rebecca's telltale blush, she continued, "Once he sees you in this dress, he will remember you this way forever. He will be enchanted."

Mistress Chambers was right. John reacted almost with shock at first, never having seen Rebecca dressed formally. Later, though, she noticed that his chest expanded with pride at the reception when it became apparent that he led on his gold embroidered, velvet sleeved arm one of the loveliest and most tastefully dressed gentlewomen in London.

Rebecca looked around the ancient Guild Hall with interest. Pike men were strategically placed around the walls in uniforms of scarlet; their helmets and breastplates were of burnished metal. On the walls were displayed the banners of the twelve great companies, each with its own colours and symbols: Mercers, Grocers, Drapers, Fishmongers, Goldsmiths, Skinners, Merchant Taylors, Haberdashers, Salters, Ironmongers, Vintners, and Cloth workers.

Rebecca and John sat with the Merchant Taylors, and John was constantly being approached by friends who wanted to meet Rebecca. Rebecca sensed that she was being evaluated; apparently some of the women present were dying of curiosity and envy. When dinner was nearly over, the Toastmaster introduced the guests sponsored by each guild. When Rebecca's name was read, all the men at their table said loudly, "Hear, hear!" Rebecca blushed, but graciously acknowledged their toast with a nod, as she had seen the other ladies do. The last event of the evening was the presentation of all guests to the Lord Mayor and his Lady. Rebecca executed an elegant curtsey, and received the Lady's salutatory kiss on her cheek. Then it was time to go. They returned to the Chambers' house, where Rebecca changed into her own clothing. She hugged Mistress Chambers and thanked her for a glorious evening.

"I'll never forget your kindness!"

Then she and John rode to Francis' home in the carriage, the long way, for another magical hour together.

At the door, Rebecca said, "John, I know I shall never have another evening like this. Thank you. You have made me feel very special."

"You ARE very special, Heart's Lady, to me!"

Inside, Rebecca automatically checked the Barringtons. Lady Joan was awake, and quite alert. Rebecca sent Mabel into her own chamber to rest.

"I am too excited to sleep," she explained, "and I want to tell Her Ladyship everything that happened."

When her tale had wound down to repetitions of how wonderful John was, Lady Joan spoke her first words since leaving Marshalsea.

"We mustn't let him get away! I'll help thee."

Rebecca, tears of joy springing to her eyes, kissed Her Ladyship's cheek.

In the morning, Rebecca dressed the ladies, covering the shaven heads with caps, and brought them downstairs for the first time.

Lady Joan talked a little more, saying, "It is such a blessing to be clean and warm and safe!"

Sir Francis was able to sit in a padded, leather covered chair for an hour, and Rebecca was pleased with her patients' progress.

Rebecca ate dinner alone with young Francis. As she sat, she noticed a small envelope by her plate. She quickly slid it into a pocket.

Francis asked, "Aren't you going to open it?"

"I may do something silly if I do."

"I'll never tell."

She slit the paper with a knife, pulling out a card bearing the symbol of the merchant's guild, surmounted by a large, embossed "T." She smiled.

"What does he say?"

"He says, 'Dudley doesn't stand a chance.'"

"Does that mean anything?"

"To me, it does."

"You two definitely have something started between you. I hope it works out."

"Me, too."

Hatfield Broad Oak

Rebecca stayed with the Barringtons in London for two more days. Each day she saw John and Job, and every day her patients grew a little stronger. At last they began the journey home, slowly, making frequent stops with friends and relatives for rest. When they were five miles from Hatfield Broad Oak, a special messenger galloped ahead to call the manor's inhabitants once again to line the road, welcoming their lord and lady.

The carriage pulled up to the main entrance, and the Barrington family members surged forward. Lady Joan walked, holding onto the arms of her older sons, Sir Thomas and Robert. Rebecca assisted Lady Ruth. A litter had been prepared for Sir Francis, and he was carried into the house. Rebecca saw many heads shaking, and tears being shed among the onlookers. Rebecca took Lady Ruth to Lady Joan's room, which had been decorated with roses.

The Lady swept into her chamber with some of her former energy, then seemed to lose it. Surrounded by her five daughters, three daughters in law, her oldest granddaughter, her niece, and all their maids, her shoulders slumped. She sank into a chair, and allowed a few tears to escape her eyes.

"I prayed every day, sometimes every hour to be reunited with thee, my dear girls, but I did not think God would permit…I am a very great sinner, but I have paid dearly for my sins, and repented. There are those in England who do not repent, and they shall pay yet more dearly than I…I would lie down now."

Seeing Rebecca, Lady Joan called, "My dear child, come to me." She told the group, "Miss Cornell was an instrument of God to restore my health and strength."

Rebecca said, "It is an honour for me to serve Your Ladyship again."

Rebecca adjusted the bed curtains and removed Lady Joan's slippers as the daughters helped the frail woman climb into the tall, canopied, carved oak bed.

Looking at Rebecca, Lady Joan asked, "What didst thou while I was away? I received a letter concerning thee from a certain young gentleman…"

Her eyes twinkled.

"Look in my case, Winifred, perhaps I put it in there…No? Well, no matter, I know thou sawest him in London, too…He formally seeks permission to court thee in my household, and says his family is requesting verification of thy marriageable status and dowry from thy uncle."

She glanced around the room.

"Do we all know the gentleman in question? He is one of those who worked so hard to secure our release from prison."

Seeing several negative responses, Lady Joan continued, "God willing, within a short time we shall be announcing the engagement of our dear Rebecca to Master John Throckmorton of Norwich!"

Excited, some of the women began offering their congratulations.

"Wait! We have not asked Rebecca. If the Throckmorton Family approves the match, wilt thou accept Master John's suit for thy hand?"

Blushing, Rebecca looked at the stone floor, uttered a barely audible, "Yes."

"Speak up, my dear! We'll never be able to hear thy vows in church if thou whisperest!"

Looking up with a trace of the pride she tried so hard to control, Rebecca said, "If Master Throckmorton will have me, I shall accept his suit."

"Well now! Elizabeth, fetch us some wine! We ladies will toast Rebecca's happiness!"

Rebecca shyly accepted the toasts, good wishes, and kisses of the group.

At last, Lady Mary said, "Our mother must rest now. Let us all leave her."

Taking up her customary job of tending the chamber door, Rebecca was the last one remaining inside. Seeing Lady Joan beckon to her, she closed the door and approached the bed.

"The Throckmortons, as well as the Barringtons, carry royal blood in their veins, from King John through one of the Henry Bohuns of three hundred years ago. If thou marriest John, we shall become distant cousins, if indeed we are not already through some other line.

I have always been impressed with John Throckmorton. I watched him develop from a remarkable youth into a splendid gentleman. He has some unusual aspirations which thou wouldst do well to explore before thou pledgest thyself irrevocably to him.

I received another letter. It seems thy brother is interested in Mary Barnard. I must write to tell him she has no dowry, no status as a gentlewoman. How dost thou think he will respond?"

"Job wants what he wants. If my uncle agrees, Job will probably take Mary anyway. And I believe he would be very good to her. It's just…"

"What?"

"Job is not a pious person, at least not called of God. Mary once told me she is looking for a man like her father, the parson. Once she gets used to Job's fine looks and flattering attention, will she be happy with him?"

Lady Joan answered, "That would be up to the two of them. Before I reply to thy brother, I will interview Mary. Perhaps we can turn up a suitable man of the cloth for her…as well as a suitable gentlewoman for thy brother. I am too weary now, but when I am back on my feet, we'll do some splendid matchmaking! I must say, however, thou didst well for thyself without my help!"

Rebecca left her, but guarded the door so that no one could disturb Lady Joan's rest.

During the following months, the lord and ladies of the manor made slow recovery from the damage done to their health by imprisonment. England, however, did not recover. King Charles' fist tightened around the land, continually squeezing more money from his subjects.

The Barrington family seat remained a meeting place for Puritans who vehemently opposed the Royalists in London. The main issues Rebecca heard being discussed involved the arbitrary laws imposed to raise money. These came under such categories as forced loans, taxes on the weight of all goods sold, exported, or imported, tax on the use of harbors, and the forced sale of knighthoods. What enraged the Puritan gentlemen of Essex most were what they perceived as the king's pro-papist leanings, inspired by his French Queen, Henrietta Maria.

By the time King Charles' third Parliament opened in March, 1628, the House of Commons included at least ten members of the extended Barrington family, including, as M.P. representing Huntingdon, Oliver Cromwell. Sir Francis, Sir Thomas, and Robert also served, representing different areas where the family owned land. By late May, Parliament issued a statement of its position, titled the Petition of Right, demanding the redress of two main grievances, these being the arbitrary arrest of subjects without trial and arbitrary taxation. Both categories of the king's actions violated Magna Charta.

The king's response to the Petition varied from day to day. At first, he delayed even looking at it, and refused to accept the accompanying "Remonstrance." Then, because he lacked the finances to wage war on the powerful members of his government, he made concessions, agreeing to redress the grievances. He claimed he was merely confirming "the ancient liberties" of his subjects. But he also reaffirmed the concept of divine right of kings, saying he owed account of his actions to God alone. Then, on June 26, Charles temporarily suspended, or "prorogued" Parliament.

It was at this juncture, in mid summer, that Sir Francis Barrington died. Severely weakened by his illness in the prison, his heart had never recovered its former strength.

Rebecca, so near the widow's inner circle, was struck by the undercurrent of anger beneath the grief. Lords and Ladies, M.P.s, respected Puritan ministers, many in mourning cloaks, gathered from miles around. Some traveled for two days in order to attend the funeral.

Rebecca, out early on the day of the funeral, gathering flowers for her lady's chamber, was accosted by a handsome, plump young gentleman.

"Miss Cornell. My name is John Winthrop, Jr. Perhaps you know my father, who is attorney to the Barringtons and Mashams."

"I have seen his signature, I believe. We have never been introduced."

"A pity. I bring greetings from Lincoln Inn, where I read the law."

"Are the greetings from my brother, Job?"

"Yes, and from my good friend, John Throckmorton."

"Is Master Throckmorton in good health?"

"Yes."

"One would never know it from the frequency of his correspondence...I thought perchance he had died."

"Is there any message you would like me to convey?"

"Perhaps you could tell him I am considering the benefits of a simple life, such as that enjoyed by wives of stable hands."

"I beg your pardon?"

"A joke. But John will understand it if you be sure to say, 'stable hand.'"

"I understand it not, but I do see what he meant when he described you to me in such glowing terms. I wish the two of you all the best."

"Thank you, Master Winthrop! Good day."

After the interment, the undercurrent of anger among the mourners swelled into open hostility. Every group of people Rebecca passed on the grounds of the estate, in the halls, even in line waiting to use the privy had at its white hot center a furious preacher of the rights of Englishmen.

Rebecca remembered one group of young men discussing revenge, and quoting scripture to show how God could work through a man to accomplish it. She shuddered whenever she recalled their bloodthirsty words and faces. At the end of August, when the king's favorite, the Duke of Buckingham, was assassinated, she speculated privately which one of the group she had seen could be responsible. Soon after, one of them, John Felton, was executed for the crime. But by then Rebecca's world had changed.

In July, Rebecca had received a note from Job saying that he and John would soon visit, their course of study complete. Miffed by the infrequency of John's letters to her, she weighed different effective ways to greet him. When Rebecca got word that they had arrived at Hatfield Broad Oak, she put her plan into action. Slipping into an old, worn dress, ragged bonnet, and a torn cloak borrowed from a scullery maid, she took a roundabout route to the stable. Once there, she began working earnestly, forking hay into mangers, even currying one of the more gentle horses. Finally she heard an exasperated sigh from the stable door. Turning, she saw John, who was doing his best to remain serious. Hands on hips, he shook his head.

"I'm looking for Miss Rebecca Cornell."

"I think she ran off with Dudley…"

Rebecca found herself unable to speak as John, taking two long strides, picked her up, kissing her.

"Fair maid, whatever your name, you have won my heart! Please, please marry me!"

He kissed her.

"John!"

"Yes?"

"What did you say?"

"I said, 'Marry me!'"

"I meant the part about me being fair."

He kissed her.

"'Behold, thou art fair, my love, behold, thou art fair; Thou hast doves' eyes.'"

"Aren't you going to set me down?"

"Not until you promise to marry me."

He kissed her.

"Oh, all right, I'll marry you! Now put me down!"

Brushing the hay from her clothing, Rebecca gracefully stepped to the door, asking, "Are you going in to supper, Master Throckmorton?"

"Only if you go with me."

"I must change my costume. Lady Joan is not accustomed to dining with stable girls."

Offering his arm, John walked her to the great house. "Then I shall wait. I do not want Dudley to make off with you while I am at table."

Rebecca raced up the stairs. She washed her face and hands, then changed the old clothing for a becoming gown and slippers of deep blue. She arranged her hair, wrapped herself in a warm shawl, then headed back down the steps to find Job, John, and Mary waiting.

Job hugged her, kissed her cheek, and whispered, "Stable girl?" in her ear. Rebecca blushed becomingly, then took John's arm as he led the way toward the dining hall.

Once inside, they encountered Lady Joan on the arm of Oliver Cromwell. John and Job bowed, offering their sympathy to the still grieving widow.

"I thank thee. Art thou acquainted with my nephew?"

"Of course, My Lady," replied Job turning towards Cromwell. "Things are still rather warm among the M.P.s, I understand."

Cromwell responded, "Our sovereign had best think twice before he attempts to rule without Parliament!"

"The less often he thinks, the more comfortable I am," said John.

Cromwell chuckled, saying, "I like that. His thinking is causing me a great deal of trouble. His Majesty's religious Declaration, being prefixed to the Book of Common Prayer, is loaded with papist views. In January, I will be sitting on a new Committee of the House of Commons on Religion. We will make recommendations for an official response to the Declaration."

Job said, "Sounds like more fireworks ahead."

Cromwell agreed, then asked, "How long are you staying here? Are you men free to follow the hounds tomorrow at dawn? Some of us expect to have fine sport."

Job nodded, and John said, "I should enjoy that. We anticipate remaining here several days, as we have important business…"

Glancing at Rebecca and Mary, Cromwell commented, "Rather important, I'd say! Do you women realise that you have monopolised two of the most eligible gentlemen of London? Many gentlewomen of that town remain mystified as to their elusiveness. But, seeing you, I understand."

Rebecca said, "Master Cromwell, you flatter us. Tell us how you are feeling. I heard that your health has been impaired recently."

"You heard correctly. My stomach has been giving me much trouble, and I still experience severe bouts of melancholy. I am taking greater care with what I eat, and taking more time for recreation. God has yet to give me peace."

Lady Joan interjected, "Shall we sit down? They are waiting for us."

Near the end of the meal, Lady Joan rose and announced, "We will now toast the future of Master John Throckmorton and his bride to be, Miss Rebecca Cornell."

There were cheers as the family and guests rose to their feet for the toast. Rebecca blushed, but felt better as John's hand stole into her lap to claim her hand. When he released it, she found that he had surreptitiously placed a small golden ring, engraved with a "T" upon her finger.

Lady Joan continued, "I have been negotiating with a corporation of scriveners based in Colchester to diversify our family investments. Master Throckmorton, being multi-talented, has agreed to represent us to them, as well as to market our wool and other manor products. Therefore, he will be joining our community in the near future."

There were more cheers, and, as the meal had ended, John and Rebecca were deluged with well wishers.

After vespers, Rebecca kissed her brother goodnight, and was escorted to her staircase by John.

"Miss Cornell, I will see you at dinner tomorrow, after the hunt. Perhaps, if the weather is clear, you would care to go riding afterwards."

"Perhaps. Master Throckmorton?"

"Yes."

"I am glad you have returned."

"So am I."

He kissed her rather more insistently than before, and she was quite breathless when he released her.

"Goodnight, Master Throckmorton!"

She slowly walked up the stairs, wishing she could remain below.

At midmorning, Rebecca was going over the manor accounts with Lady Joan, when a commotion was heard in the hall. Bridge, the steward of the manor, stood in the doorway.

"My Lady, there has been an accident. Could you please come downstairs?"

"Of course." Lady Joan swept out.

As she tried to follow, Rebecca found her way blocked.

"Pray do not become excited, Miss," said Bridge. "Promise me you will remain in this chamber. I will send someone to you in a moment."

He left. A cold fear clutched Rebecca's stomach. She sat, going over the previous page of accounts in order to control her thoughts. Mary entered the chamber, tears in her eyes.

"Someone has been killed during the hunt. I saw them bearing the body in, but I could not see…"

Next in the door was Lady Joan, followed closely by John.

"No," moaned Rebecca, guessing the truth from John's face.

"It's Job," said Lady Joan. "He fell from his horse…it wasn't anyone's fault…there wasn't anything they could do for him. I'm so sorry, girls. Catch her!"

Without thinking, both Rebecca and John responded to Lady Joan's command, lowering the unconscious Mary gently to the floor. Rebecca sat, weeping, with Mary's head in her lap, until someone passed her a wet cloth. Dampening Mary's face, then her hands, Rebecca was able to restore her to consciousness. At last Lady Jug appeared with Bridge, who lifted Mary, carrying her toward the women's chambers.

Rebecca discovered that John had stepped behind and was gently helping her stand. When he found that she was too shaken to walk, he swiftly gathered her up, following Lady Joan. Soon they were in the lady's private sitting room, John holding Rebecca in his lap. The lady brought them each a shot of whiskey, and made them drink it. Then she left them alone, with orders that no one disturb them.

During that afternoon, Rebecca learned what a fine memory John possessed. He recited from the Book of Common Prayer to her for hours, including the entire psalter. He also told her about his childhood and his training in Norwich. John had completed the equivalent of two apprenticeships, one as a merchant, working for his father, the second as a scrivener. He spoke of the routine of the past year at the Inn of Court in London. Through it all, he tried to avoid mentioning Job, in order to divert their minds from the overwhelming grief which assaulted them both. A supper tray appeared for them at the appropriate time. They ate a little bread and cheese, drank all the ale. After that, the two wandered down to the chapel, hand in hand, to pray.

"They have laid him here," John said. "Are you ready to go in?"

Rebecca looked at John, wanting desperately to be stronger than she felt.

"Will you help me?" she whispered.

Together, the two approached Job's open coffin in an agony of dread. Rebecca stood there for a long time, trying to comprehend that this handsome, strong, young body no longer contained her brother. At last, comforting words began to flow through her mind, words she had heard many times, but which she had never needed so much.

"I am the Resurrection and the Life," she quoted. "He that believeth in Me, though he were dead, yet shall he live. And whosoever liveth and believeth in Me shall never die."

She and John knelt at the prayer rail for a time, and then left the chapel. It was then that Rebecca realized that she could endure anything with John at her side.

Rebecca found it more wrenching to leave John that night than anything she had yet experienced. She felt as if part of her body were being removed, and almost turned back down the stairs to find him.

"No," she ordered herself. "You have already crossed the bounds of propriety today by staying alone with him so long. Do not shame yourself by displaying weakness."

John was waiting for Rebecca at the entry to the chapel next morning. He had kept vigil there with Job's body all night, and then attended Rebecca constantly for the next two long days.

Mary had proved inconsolable. Lady Jug, following Lady Joan's instructions, kept the girl sedated with repeated doses of whiskey.

For Rebecca, the morning funeral was a blur. Two of her sisters attended, but Rebecca felt them to be strangers. They were duly impressed with John, whose impeccable manners and dark good looks, Rebecca noticed, turned most women to jelly.

Rebecca was surprised to see her brother, Thomas, whose face reminded her so much of their mother. He had been visiting with Rebecca's sister when the news came, and traveled to Hatfield Broad Oak with her. Thomas was understandably distressed at his brother's death, and disoriented in his new role as head of the Cornell family. He was, however, quick enough to do and say all the right things. He displayed an easy rapport with John, with whom he had lived at Debney's.

After the burial, Rebecca was able to spend an hour alone with Thomas, and to enlist his support for her betrothal to John.

"If you oppose my marriage," she threatened, half seriously, "you may end up having to support me as an aging spinster."

"Don't worry, 'Becca. I should never pass up a chance to have someone else take care of you. That should limit your opportunities to annoy me as you used to do."

"You were the one who annoyed me!"

"You've got it wrong, obviously."

The two ended the mock quarrel with an embrace dampened by tears.

"Truly, brother, we have been apart too long. I have forgotten how to stay angry with you."

"I'm sure it will all come back to you."

After dinner that noon, John led Rebecca to an alcove off the main hall.

"I intended to ride on toward Norwich tomorrow, to make preparations for our wedding. Your uncle is in poor health, unable to travel here. Therefore, he and Thomas would like you to be married in Norwich, from their household. The banns must be read for three Lord's Days in that city, and there are papers to be signed…"

"John, I want to go with you."

"I was about to say that I cannot bring myself to leave you. Let us talk with Lady Joan, seek her advice."

They were admitted to Her Ladyship's sitting room, and presented their situation.

"Oh, my dears, the weather at this time of year can be simply beastly! I fear thou wilt have a miserably uncomfortable journey, unless…how long does it take thee to ride home, Master Throckmorton?"

"Four days by horseback, five by coach. I usually stay one night with my mother's family at Bury St. Edmunds, two with merchants who are family friends. This time, though, I thought to stop another night at the family seat, Bungay, where my cousin, Sir Robert, and my brother Thomas will welcome us. From there it is an easy journey to Norwich."

"I shall lend thee my carriage; Dudley shall drive. I can always use one of the other vehicles if I want to go out. And Mary Barnard—you'll want her as maid of honour, of course. The change will do her good, poor dear."

"Bless you, My Lady!"

Rebecca ran to find Mary. Then the women packed their things into wooden trunks. Rebecca included the clothing she had made as her trousseau.

The Journey

Early next day, after morning prayers, the party started for Haverhill, their first destination. At first, Thomas and John rode their horses before the carriage. But when the cold rain began, midmorning, they joined Mary and Rebecca inside, tying their horses onto the back of the coach. Even wet, Rebecca thought, John was the best looking man she had ever seen. And his damp arm around her in the roughly bouncing, swaying carriage was the best comfort she had ever know. The merchants' alderman at Haverhill was most accommodating, and his family saw to it that they spent a comfortable night.

Bury St. Edmunds

They proceeded northeast all next day, still eating food packed by the manor kitchen, and arrived at Bury St. Edmunds just at dusk. Rebecca felt suddenly shy while being introduced to John's mother's family. There were his aged grandfather, Master William Hill, and his grandmother Joan. John's eldest uncle, Myles, with wife Elisabeth and their three youngest, teenaged children completed the group. The house was large, made of wood, thatched, and much warmer, less drafty than the greathouse at Hatfield Broad Oak. Rebecca and Mary were quickly shown to a chamber by John's cousin, Alice, and made to feel welcome. After washing and changing their gowns, they joined the family for supper. Rebecca ate little, feeling quite exhausted, but was content sitting at table next to John. The family prayed, sang, and read scripture together after clearing the carved oak dining table. Then all retired, Mary and Rebecca sleeping quite comfortably in the feather bed with Alice.

Next morning, after prayers, they said their goodbyes, promising to come back on the return trip. Again heading northeast, the party rode all day, reaching the tiny village of Eye. Once again, a merchant put them up, this time in rooms over his shop.

Rebecca was disconcerted to discover that the men and women were to sleep in adjacent rooms, and that their hosts lodged in another building entirely. Still in the throes of emotional turmoil from losing her brother, she had found herself seeking more and more the comfort of John's touch during the past few days. Before tonight, she had depended on the need to maintain appearances to protect her honour. Now there was nothing, really, to prevent her spending the entire night in the sitting room with John. Mary and Thomas were not the sort to interfere.

Sure enough, soon after their host left them, Rebecca found herself in John's arms.

Huskily, and with obvious effort, he said, "'Becca, I want you more than I want to breathe. But to make things right for us, I must leave you tonight. I am going for a walk. When I return, please be asleep with your door locked."

He left.

"So that's what it is to be a gentleman!" she thought.

Rebecca locked her door, but she did not sleep for a long time.

Bungay

Late next day, they arrived at Bungay as the sunlight faded. John and Thomas were riding their horses, since the weather was dry. Rebecca peered out one of the coach windows as they swung into a tall gateway beside a stonework lodge. The fading light showed stone beasts crouched upon the posts, each holding the Throckmorton shield of arms, which featured an elephant. An old man hurried out of the lodge.

John called out, "Hullo, Jenkins!"

"Good evening, Master John! It has been too long since ye stopped with us. Are ye come from Londontowne?"

The gates swung slowly outward.

"Yes, and from Bury St. Edmunds. We've had a long ride this day. Is your family well?"

"Doing first rate, Master, thank ye. They'll be proud to see thee up to the house."

He waved them through.

The party rode through the park, up a wide avenue of beech trees for a mile. Rebecca saw deer among the trees, peacocks on the lawns. Soon they arrived at the greathouse, its stonework looming grey in the sunset. The carriage stopped under a wide, roofed passageway at the main entrance. John, having alerted the servants to their arrival, with Thomas helped Mary and Rebecca from the carriage. As the group entered the narrow foyer, they were graciously received by John's first cousin, Sir Robert Throckmorton and his wife, Lady Anne. A few moments later, John's next older brother, Thomas, appeared with his wife, Margaret. All welcomed them warmly. When they learned how far the visitors had ridden that day, the ladies immediately led the women to private rooms.

Thanks to Lady Anne, Margaret, and their maids, Mary and Rebecca felt at home right away. Their gowns changed, they tripped in to supper looking perfectly splendid. Many toasts were drunk to their beauty, and to John and Rebecca's bright future.

That night, sharing a huge, canopied bed with Rebecca, Mary was finally able to talk about Job.

"What has bothered me most, 'Becca, is the feeling that Job's death was my fault. Perhaps, if I had listened to God's voice and obeyed His will, instead of wickedly trying to advance my social station, Job would still be alive."

"We must not play at guessing the motives of the Almighty, Mary. There were simpler ways for God to keep you from Job, or even to teach you a lesson than to smite my brother dead. You are needlessly tormenting yourself. You'll see! I'm sure that Lady Joan will have a selection of young men from which you may choose by the time we get home!"

"I can't even think about marriage anymore. I must obtain God's forgiveness for turning my back on His will. I shall spend my life in service to Him, and to others. If only England still had nunneries, that's where I belong."

"Nonsense, Mary! Do not denigrate yourself like this. You have done nothing deserving of a lonely, sequestered life."

"Nevertheless, at this point, that is all I desire."

The next morning, before prayers, as the luggage was carried out, Rebecca managed a moment alone with John and Thomas.

"I am worried about Mary. She is quite melancholy. We must do and say anything we can to cheer her."

Thomas squeezed her hand, and John kissed her cheek in reply. Then the three joined their hosts for prayers and goodbyes.

Norwich

By noon, they approached the outskirts of Norwich, crossing the River Yare, and headed for the east side of town. Rebecca had visited here once, as a child, but did not remember how crowded and dirty the place was. Because of the cold, rainy weather, the air was thick with black coal smoke from two thousand chimneys.

Mary had never been to a large city, and she stared out the coach window, taking it all in. Before long, they pulled up before a row of tall, narrow, half timbered buildings. Rebecca recognised one of them as the home of her uncle. As Thomas opened the front door, John helped the women from the coach. An austere servant, Manfred, led them in. Rebecca could tell that he was pleased to see John and Thomas, but it was in his nature to be reserved.

Offering them seats in the vestibule, Manfred left them.

"Watch out for cousin Sarah," warned Thomas. "She has grown teeth as well as claws since you saw her last."

"Whatever do you mean?" asked Rebecca.

"You'll see."

First in the door was cousin Henry Debney with his wife, Mary. For several minutes, they all shared their grief at losing Job, who was as much a son to this house as to any other. As they were yet seeking comfort in each other's presence, a lovely vision in blond curls and lace floated into the room.

"John!" she murmured. As if he and she were alone in the moonlight, the young woman took both his hands and gazed raptly into his face.

John, refusing to acknowledge her inappropriate behavior, said, lightly, "Miss Debney, you must greet your cousin, Rebecca. She and I are to be married very soon, as you know. And this is her close friend, Mary Barnard."

Rolling her eyes at Rebecca and Mary, Sarah sniffed, saying, "My dears, you look simply exhausted! We must find you a place for a long rest. Thomas!" she continued, "Tell me about your trip. Did you miss me?"

Thomas replied dryly, "I am continually amazed that I can get along without you."

Mary Barnard, thoroughly disgusted by the wench, said, "Perhaps, Miss Debney, if you show us where to retire, you could talk with Masters Throckmorton and Cornell at length."

John, seizing the opportunity, interjected, "I must report to my father, immediately."

Thomas said, "I must direct Dudley to the stables, and see to the luggage and horses."

Reading uncertainty in Rebecca's eyes, John slid an arm around her shoulders, turned her away from the others, and spoke softly:

"I shall collect you and Mary tomorrow morning at nine; my family is eager to meet you. We will all spend the day in my father's house. Heart's Lady," he continued loudly enough for Sarah to overhear, "I shall miss you."

He kissed Rebecca tenderly and left.

Turning past the spiteful Sarah, Rebecca asked Henry's wife, Mary, "Is there somewhere we may change out of our traveling clothes? I want to see Uncle Robert."

Mary Debney soon made them quite comfortable in the guest room.

"You'll have to forgive my sister in law, Sarah," said she. "The poor dear has been convinced for ten years that John Throckmorton was her private property. He was ever too courteous to tell her he was not interested. She was too full of herself to notice."

Rebecca and Mary swiftly changed and were led in to dinner, an elegant daily occasion at her uncle's fine house. Although Sarah sulked and was silent, Henry and Thomas chatted amiably. Uncle Robert sat at the head of the table. Glad to see them, he nevertheless spoke and ate little, apparently not feeling well.

After dinner, Mary and Rebecca sat with Uncle Robert as he reclined on a couch.

"Such a shame to lose Job," he said, eyes watering. "He was like my own son." Turning to Mary, he asked, "Art thou the young lady of whom he wrote to us?"

She nodded uncertainly.

"Thou wouldst have been welcomed here as a daughter. The will of the Lord remains a mystery to me. Hast thou met Basingbourne, yet?" he asked, looking at Rebecca.

"You mean John's father? No."

"The old curmudgeon will do his best to frighten thee. It's his way of scaring weakling spouses away from his children. I suppose thou art aware that his wife is a cousin of mine. I happen to know that most of the time he is bluffing—most of the time. It's up to thee to know when he is not."

"I, I will meet him tomorrow, I think."

"Thy wedding will take place only if thou hast what it takes to charm him. I hope that thou posessest character as well as a lovely face!"

Not wanting to pursue this daunting topic, Rebecca lifted a Bible from a table.

"Would you like me to read to you, Uncle?" she asked.

After about an hour, he fell asleep, and the women made their way upstairs to find Mary Debney. She showed them where to leave their laundry so that the servants would take care of it. Then they helped her with some sewing, while discussing wedding plans until suppertime. The day had passed slowly, but ended peacefully with family prayers.

Up at dawn the next morning, Mary and Rebecca washed and dressed quickly, blessing the warmth of a house heated by coal. They had scarcely finished with prayers when John came in. Thomas was needed that day at the scrivener's shop, so John offered each woman an arm.

"No one," he told them, "has ever brought such lovely ladies to my father's house as I do today. I shall be famous in the chronicles of the family!"

The Throckmorton carriage, with the Merchant's Guild symbol and a large "T" in silver on the doors, bore them swiftly northeast. As they turned into a secluded cul-de-sac, Rebecca could see that these houses must be among the finest in town. She turned to John, her eyes wide.

"I thought your father was a grocer, a merchant..."

"He is Alderman of the Merchant's Guild," replied John. "He's always worked hard, done well..."

The entire Throckmorton family, richly dressed, was assembled to greet them. Eldest brother and heir, Lyonell, bowed and kissed the women's hands. Sisters Mary, with husband William Rawlie and Elizabeth with hers, John Layer, were effusive with their greetings, as were their children. The two youngest brothers, Myles, twenty-four, and Robert, nineteen, unmarried, gracefully bowed and kissed the women's hands. Rebecca could tell they were awed by Mary Barnard's unusual beauty. Lastly, the lady of the house, John's stepmother, Hester, came forward. Kissing each woman upon the cheek, she took Rebecca's hand.

"I have been wanting to meet you for a long time," she said. "I loved your brother Job as a son, and I knew you would be as remarkable as he. You must be very special indeed to have caught our John; many women have broken their hearts over him."

Seeing Rebecca's blush, John interjected, "It was I who caught her, thereby breaking every male heart at Hatfield Broad Oak!"

A servant approached, saying, "He will see you now, Master John!"

John put his arm round Rebecca.

"Will the rest of you entertain Miss Barnard? She is particularly fond of music; perhaps you will open the clavier and get out the lute for some songs."

He guided Rebecca up a steep set of wooden steps to a landing surrounded by openwork, carved railings.

"Father may seem gruff to you, but he is soft compared to some of the characters you've met in Essex."

John tapped softly at the heavy door.

Rebecca heard a bass rumble, "Come!"

They entered the most spacious office Rebecca had ever seen. It was at least ten times the size of the small chamber where she had helped Lady Joan with manor accounts, and had five big windows. Six large oak tables were arranged in rows, strewn with open ledgers, papers, charts, quills and inkstands. The upper walls were covered with maps of England, Europe, and the world, with trade routes traced in varying colours. Heavy cases lined the lower walls, stuffed with more thick ledgers. Framed behind a carved wooden desk hung various commendations from mayors, earls, even Queen Elizabeth. Although she would have liked to examine the entire room slowly, Rebecca had only a second to scan the whole, because the imposing figure sitting behind the desk was rising to his feet.

He was huge, perhaps six and one-half feet tall, weighing two hundred fifty pounds. He was dark as John, but, unlike his son, his lined face showed his character. Rebecca instantly read there great pride, determination, and constant struggle.

Trying to remain calm, she thought, "I feel like David facing Goliath!"

"Miss Cornell!" he thundered.

Guessing correctly what to do, she approached him without curtseying, extending her hand and looking directly into his eyes.

Shooting piercing glances at her, he thoughtfully kissed the tiny, steady hand.

"Master Throckmorton," she said clearly, "I am quite pleased to meet you!"

Looking away, then back at her closely, he growled, "Leave us, John. I have somewhat to say to this young woman."

Noting that Rebecca appeared serene, John turned, leaving the room, closing the door.

"I wanted to make sure thou knowest what thou art agreeing to by marrying my son," Basingbourne began. "To explain better, I shall speak of my family in ancient times, and of England. This is a curious land, where people are free, yet chained. We have rights, yet most of us are locked into social and economic compartments beyond which we may not stray.

Since 1066, every Englishman has been serving, under the system of primogeniture, the first born son of the first born son, of the first born son, and so on, of the strongest and luckiest Bastard that Normandy ever produced. There were even a few daughters, and their descendants, of that line on the throne, as thou well knowest.

The Throckmortons were Saxon commoners who waited at Fladbury, Warwickshire, to greet William the Bastard. They survived only because they guessed correctly how best to serve him. For six centuries, my family has been luckier than his; our line produced enough sons to ensure that our name continued. We were even clever enough to marry some of the Bastard's progeny, to serve them well, and to remain in the top ranks of the gentry. There were a few branchings of the family; nevertheless, my father was lucky and energetic enough to earn a knighthood.

But I fell from grace; I am a third born son. In England, Miss Cornell, as thou knowest, every son after the first one is usually cast out upon society to seek his fortune. It is sink or swim. And I have swum so far…I have accomplished more for my family name than my older brothers ever dreamed. But my nephew, at Bungay, retains the lands, the crest, the knighthood, all the honors that descend on first sons. All I possess is the creation of my own brain…

And thou, Miss Cornell, have accepted the suit for thy hand in marriage brought by a third born son. Able as he is, trained as he is, handsome gentleman though he be, my beloved son, John, has no real claim in life beyond that which he creates with his own brain. Understandest thou this?"

Rebecca nodded. This much was a fact of life.

"In this century our sovereigns have seen fit to choke the merchants of England with arbitrary and overwhelming taxation. My ships are taxed, my imports and exports are taxed, even Great Yarmouth Harbour is taxed so that I must pay to use it…my profits are cut to a small fraction of what they used to be. This makes little difference to me. I can easily live out my days in comfort on what I have accumulated during the good years.

It is my sons who will suffer. First son will suffer little. Second, third, fourth and fifth sons will suffer much…my heart bleeds for them. Would that they had been daughters! I could send them off with a large dowry and a clear conscience. But sons! I owe them more.

So I trained each of them to take part in and expand my business, perhaps across the seas, whenever the timing should be right.

One day, when the boys were very young, the six of us played a game in which we divided the world. At least I thought it was a game. But recently, in listening to John, I discerned that he never gave up the game. He has dreams of claiming his portion—in New England, of the Americas!

Young woman, hast thou the slightest idea where that is?"

Rebecca glanced at the maps on the walls, correctly located the western hemisphere, Virginia, then Plymouth, Massachusetts, and pointed to it.

"If thou agreest to marry John, thou shouldst entertain the very real possibility that he will ask thee to accompany him there, and soon. For the situation of my family can only get worse now, in England, with the damned Stuarts on the throne. In New England, my dear Miss, it may very well get better.

And now, the questions I most wished to ask thee: How strong is thy commitment to my son? Over how many miles will it carry thee? And what will this mean to the unborn children who may come from God through thee? Most of all, hast thou the courage to see this commitment through?

I knew thy father and, of course, thy brother Job. They were good men, of excellent courage. In these evil days, the same courage is required of Englishwomen as of the men. Dost thou possess it? Speak!"

His last word sounded as a thunderclap.

Rebecca, never having been in a situation quite like this, turned her back, walked to a window, thinking of Lady Joan. How would her benefactress answer this overbearing man? Speaking softly at first, she turned to face him.

"Master Throckmorton. I did not choose nor pursue your son; rather, he found me. It is his judgment that I am a worthy partner in whatever course he should take."

Speaking more firmly, she went on:

"John has not spoken to me of ocean voyages. But that makes little difference. Is not every marriage a voyage, every mating a risk to the woman of an early grave from childbed? If the women refused to yield to their men out of cowardice, or lack of faith in God, would not the earth soon cease to be populated? My answer to your questions is this: My courage is untried. I do not yet know of what I am capable. But my faith is strong. It is strong enough that I would follow John anywhere, into any circumstance, knowing that God will either preserve me alive or call me home to Himself. Is that what you need to know, Master Throckmorton?"

Basingbourne made the floor shake as he advanced upon Rebecca. Sinking to his knees before her, he kissed her hands and said:

"Miss Cornell, if I were a single man, I should marry thee, myself!"

Smiling, she replied, "Master Throckmorton, if you were single, I believe I could not resist your suit!"

She kissed his cheek.

He stood up slowly, then strode to the door, flung it open, and motioned Rebecca to the landing.

"Family!" he bellowed. They all stopped singing, startled. "Make Miss Cornell welcome, for she is worthy to bear our ancient name!"

Later, in the carriage, in front of the Debney's, John sent Mary inside with the footman, ordering the coachman to wait.

"What ever did you say to him? My father cordially hates every spouse chosen by my siblings, but he adores you!"

"Just pray that your stepmother lives for three more weeks. I told your father that if he were single, I'd marry him."

"You didn't!"

"I did. And what's more, I think I meant it. HE never would have sent me into an ogre's den like that, unprepared. What could you have been thinking?"

"I didn't want to frighten you; I would rather die."

"You at least could have told me about New England."

"He knows about that?"

"Of course. And now I do, too. But it makes no difference, John. As I told him, I have the faith to follow you anywhere, through anything. Now I'm wondering if it is faith, or just stupidity."

"'Becca, I'm sorry. I had no idea what he would say to you."

"Do you remember that first time we met in the manor chapel?"

He nodded.

"You told me something that night which I have longed to hear you say again. I especially need to hear it tonight, because I am very weary."

"'Becca, I love you."

"And I love you. I shall never tire of hearing you say it. God be with you, John."

She kissed him goodnight.

The next three weeks passed rapidly. Rebecca found herself the toast of Norwich. It seemed that everyone wanted to ingratiate him or herself with the formidable Basingbourne by entertaining the fiance of his brilliant son, John. During this time, Rebecca met many of the young women who, according to Hester Throckmorton, had "broken their hearts" over John. Most of them were silly wenches such as cousin Sarah, but several were gentlewomen to reckon with, beautiful and intelligent. Rebecca could not understand why John had bypassed them for her.

"Perhaps their dowries were not in order," she postulated to Mary. "Or maybe they had legal entanglements…"

"Perhaps he simply fell in love with your sapphire eyes, as everyone else does!" exclaimed her friend. "Why second guess him?"

At last came the private, formal wedding ceremony at St. Paul's Church. Both families attended, with a few close friends, and Uncle Robert gave Rebecca away. John Winthrop, Jr. served as best man. Mary cried after the service, as she kissed her friend's cheek. The two women embraced, and Rebecca left the church on John's arm, his forever.

Basingbourne had purchased a comfortable wooden house in the town, furnished it, and staffed it with servants.

"My younger sons have been wanting their own lodgings," he explained. "When thou art gone back to Essex, they may use it."

Rebecca found the privacy heavenly. She and John spent a glorious week exploring each other, learning each others' more subtle language, starting the lifetime process of becoming one. She found John to be as gentle, yet insistent in private as he had ever been in the fish bowl atmosphere of Hatfield Broad Oak.

"When we get back," he told her, "Lady Joan will have prepared our own cottage. It is to be her wedding present to us, so act surprised."

"John, I have never been so happy!"

"Nor have I, Heart's Lady."

Hatfield Broad Oak

The five day return journey to Essex was accomplished early in September with a minimum of trouble. Two of Basingbourne's servants drove an extra, enclosed wagon, loaded with household furnishings they had received as wedding presents. The weather was mild and miraculously dry. Rebecca's only worry was Mary's emotional health. There were moments when her friend would brighten and seem to be perfectly normal. But most of the time she remained inside an impenetrable shell of gloom. Mary did little beside pray and recite scripture. The verses chosen seemed indicative of her mental state; they spoke of the wrath of an angry, punitive Jehovah.

Rebecca's heart was lifted at the sight of Hatfield Broad Oak. She and John at once sent Mary to Lady Jug, then went in search of Lady Joan. At the end of the narrative of their journey, Rebecca confided her fears about Mary.

Lady Joan's brow wrinkled with concern.

She said, "It's not made any better by the fact that Jug and Mary will be moving to Otes soon, to live with Jug's mother and stepfather, the Mashams. I will alert them to be especially careful of her."

Lady Joan insisted on immediately showing off the new cottage she had ordered built and furnished for John and Rebecca. The place was a typical wood frame, wattle and daub, thatched house. The rooms included a bedchamber, a dining parlour, lodging parlour, kitchen, study, and storage chamber. It was thoroughly furnished with a canopy bed, chairs, tables, cupboards, candlesticks, tableware, brass and iron cookware, bookcases, as well as with linens for windows, bed, tables and kitchen. Lady Joan had taken special care that all drafts were stopped, and that the place was warm and snug.

Rebecca struggled not to cry for joy, then gave it up and wept as she thanked Her Ladyship.

All through the fall and winter, Mary Barnard continued her self destructive retreat into religion. Lady Jug confided to Rebecca that the maid often prayed all night and that once she had been caught whipping her own back with a leather strap. Mary did not eat enough to keep a chicken alive, and the women feared for her life.

By mid November, Rebecca and Lady Joan suspected that Rebecca had become pregnant soon after the wedding. They decided, however, to say nothing to John for the time being. According to Lady Joan, the early portion of first pregnancies were uncertain propositions, no concern of the menfolk.

One morning in early March, 1629, Rebecca was at the great house, as she often was, assisting Lady Joan with the accounts, when Bridge appeared at the chamber doorway, an odd look on his face.

"An emissary from London to see you, My Lady."

"What sort of emissary, please?"

Lady Joan did not like being distracted from her inventory sheets.

"His name is Master Roger Williams, My Lady. He says that Your Ladyship's son, Sir Thomas, sent him here with a message."

Lady Joan sighed.

"Very well, send him in, but don't leave us. If I give the usual signal, show him out at once!"

"Very good, My Lady."

Rebecca offered, "I can withdraw, My Lady…"

"No, don't be absurd. I trust thee with my life's secrets!"

Rebecca inhaled sharply as Master Williams entered the chamber. He was a small man, dressed in a plain doublet and knee breeches of black worsted cloth, and long black stockings, with heavy leathern shoes. His cuffs and collar were white. His face was composed of sharp angles, with a pointed nose, chin, and sharp jawbones. He was clean shaven, except for a thin mustache. The features were otherwise unremarkable except for his intense, ice blue eyes. He smiled, but that frosty grimace struck more terror in Rebecca than all the thunderings of Basingbourne Throckmorton. She looked down at the ledger and shuddered slightly.

Master Williams, observing her, intoned, "'In the day when the keepers of the house shall tremble…then shall the dust return to the earth as it was, and the spirit shall return unto God, who gave it.'"

Lady Joan was irritated.

"State thy business, my good man. wherefore art thou at my door with such dire warnings?"

"Hold thy peace, woman. I am sent by thy son to give eyewitness account of the recent events at Parliament."

"Indeed. I find it difficult to believe that my son would wish such an impudent messenger upon me."

"Dost desire to hear the news, or not?"

"If thou canst impart the information without consigning us to dusty death, do so!"

Coldly, mechanically, the odd little man began to recite:

"I was at Westminster on the second of March, attending my patron, Sir Edward Coke. The House of Commons was about to be presented with a resolution by Sir John Eliot, condemning popery and illegal subsidies not granted by Parliament.

A message reached the chamber that emissaries were coming immediately from His Majesty to adjourn the session for eight days. Sir John Finch, the Speaker of the House, began to rise from his chair to declare the session ended. At that point, madness descended. Denzil Holles and Benjamin Valentine seized Finch by the arms and forced him back into the chair.

Holles cried, 'Zounds! You shall sit till we please to rise!'

The doors to the chamber were then barred.

Eliot, not wanting to be the cause of a riot, withdrew his resolution, throwing it into the fire. But Holles, who has what I deem to be a remarkable memory, quoted it to the House, word for word. the essence is that anyone who pays illegal taxes imposed by the Crown is traitor to England. A voice vote was taken, and the resolution passed. The House then voted to adjourn, as the king's men were pounding upon the doors.

Thy son, Sir Thomas, bid me advise thee that dissolution of Parliament, and possibly the arrest of some members by His Majesty seem imminent."

"Well now! These are news indeed. We are beholden to thee, Master Williams, for this succinct account of events which affect my family closely. Is there somewhat I can do to repay thee? Where art thou lodging?"

He smiled his icy grimace again, and Rebecca recoiled, turning to look out the window rather than watch him.

"Thy son has already done much for me, as he and Sir Edward Coke recommended me to Sir William Masham as private chaplain at Otes."

Rebecca pressed her hands over her mouth as the man continued.

"I now bear responsibility to God for thy daughter's and grandchildren's souls, as well as those of the rest of that household. Neither do I shrink from assisting the spiritually weak wherever I find them, noon or night. For I am a reliable conduit through which God's messages flow to true believers."

Lady Joan had been giving Bridge the signal all through this last gush of information, but Williams had refused to be interrupted.

Now that he was finished, he intoned, "'Riches profit not in the day of wrath, but righteousness delivereth from death'!"

He turned on his heel and left.

Rebecca and Lady Joan looked at each other in stunned silence.

"My horse…" said Her Ladyship. "I want my horse!"

Rebecca knew better than to try to follow Lady Joan on horseback when either of them were in such a state. Besides, she should not ride horses until her child was born in June. She stood instead at the window, until Lady Joan thundered out of the stable yard at a gallop, heading for Otes.

"Bridge," she said absently to the steward, "make sure they sent someone to attend Her Ladyship, as usual."

"Yes, Mistress Throckmorton."

As she left the manor house for home, Rebecca was astounded to glimpse Roger Williams in the garden, apparently deep in conversation with Lady Joan's unmarried niece, Lady Jane Whalley. The young woman's face wore an expression of awe. Rebecca was sure nothing good was about to come of this man's presence in Essex.

That night, when John came in for supper, Rebecca was still agitated by the afternoon's news and events. She held her peace, eating little, until John was lighting his after dinner pipe.

"Did you hear what passed in Parliament the other day?"

"Yes. Sir William told me while I was at Otes this morning."

"Then did you meet Roger Williams?"

"The new chaplain? Yes."

"He upset Her Ladyship this afternoon, quite unnecessarily. I hope to have no further dealings with him."

"Are you sure her reaction was warranted? He seemed to me an odd sort, but harmless."

"Did he consign you and Sir William to an early grave?"

"Not at all. He was quite witty and charming."

"I wonder if we are referring to the same person. This fellow was the prophet Jeremiah incarnate."

"It is my experience that you ladies discern more of a man's true nature in a few minutes than I do in years. I trust your judgment. Therefore, Master Williams need not trouble to ingratiate himself with the Throckmortons; We have him pegged as the devil in disguise!"

"You are making fun of me again. Forget I even mentioned it. Tell me about the price you negotiated for the manor's wool."

Pulling Rebecca into his lap, John's face relaxed into a satisfied smile.

"As I thought, the outbreaks of hoof and mouth disease elsewhere last fall killed enough sheep to send the prices high this spring. Because I was among the first to show up at Colchester with high quality fibers, the Barringtons and the Mashams realised much more than expected from their cash crop. I sold it all at half again last year's price. Sir William is paying me a large bonus, and you, my own lady, shall have a new gown!"

Rebecca slid her arms around his neck.

"I'm glad things worked out so well, because I'm going to need a new gown."

He looked at her, puzzled at her tone.

"A much larger gown, until sometime in June…"

Still not comprehending, he shook his head.

"I'm with child, Master John Throckmorton, and you are most definitely the father!"

"Oh, 'Becca. I did not expect, so soon, I mean…"

"You're disappointed?"

"No, I'm awestruck. And thankful. 'Becca, I love you!"

A week later, Rebecca was again with Lady Joan when Bridge brought in a packet of messages for Her Ladyship. Rapidly flipping through them, the Lady stopped, pulling out an envelope addressed to herself in an unfamiliar hand. The writing was inordinately large, the letters flamboyantly formed. Lifting her silver dagger, Lady Joan slit the envelope to extract a single sheet of paper. Reading it quickly, silently, Lady Joan shrieked as if the page had bitten her. She threw it toward Rebecca.

"Read it!" she cried, "And tell me if I'm only imagining that evil is stalking Hatfield Broad Oak!"

Gingerly, Rebecca picked up the epistle to read Roger Williams' brief demand for the hand of Lady Jane Whalley in marriage. The last part of the message was a furious exhortation for Her Ladyship to fear God and to obey His commands as interpreted by Master Williams.

Lady Joan angrily started for the chamber door, saying, "Where is that wench? I gave no one permission to court her!"

Rebecca quickly said, "My Lady, let me find her for you. I will bring her to your sitting room."

"All right, but hasten. My son in law may do as he likes over at Otes, but I'll not have the peace of Broad Oak wrecked by his parson!"

Rebecca had a difficult time locating Lady Jane. When she did find her, sitting alone in the buttery, she saw that the girl had been crying. Sitting beside her, Rebecca wrapped an arm around Lady Jane's shoulders.

"Tell me about it."

Piecing the story together between the girl's sobs, Rebecca was able to discern that Williams had attempted to completely destroy Lady Jane's feeling of self worth. He had begun by admonishing her to purity and holiness, then convinced the young woman that she was hopelessly inclined to evil impulses. To prove his point, he had kissed and fondled her, all the while castigating her for tempting him. Now he demanded that she marry him.

"You agreed to do that?"

"No; when I told him I needed Aunty's permission, he struck me."

"*What?*"

Lady Jane turned her face toward Rebecca, who then saw that the skin beside one of Her Ladyship's eyes was bruised. Beginning to cry again, Lady Jane added,

"He said I was defying God's will. I ran from him, but now I feel so ashamed...the things he said were true; I *am* sinful."

Rebecca held Lady Jane and let her cry for a time. Then she wiped the girl's face on her kerchief and admonished her:

"Your Ladyship is not at fault in this matter. That Williams is a sorry excuse for a chaplain. Your Ladyship has ever been the brightest sunbeam God has shone on Broad Oak. Do not let this cloud dim Your Ladyship's light!"

The girl smiled, and asked, "Do you mean that?"

"I do. We are now going to Lady Joan. Her Ladyship will set everything right. If My Lady seems angry, Your Ladyship must remember that none of this is Your Ladyship's fault."

Lady Joan's first impulse was to murder Roger Williams. Rebecca was gradually able to talk her down to merely having him flogged, then to being hounded from Otes, then to simply being denied access to Lady Jane. Suspicious, Her Ladyship turned to Rebecca.

"Why art thou protecting him?"

"I'm not. I'm protecting Lady Jane. If any hint of this gets out, the resulting scandal could wreck Her Young Ladyship's chance of a good marriage to someone else. Lady Jane must appear blameless to all the men. Therefore, Your Ladyship should write a letter giving some other excuse why Williams is unsuitable for Lady Jane, and bidding him abandon his suit for Her Young Ladyship's hand."

Lady Joan's eyes narrowed.

"Thou art a clever woman, Rebecca. I daresay Master Williams has little enough money. I shall accuse him of seeking to rise above his station, of being unable to adequately support my niece, the daughter of a baronet! In the meantime, I shall send thee, Jane, to visit my daughter, Mary. No one will

know where thou hast gone. That way, thou shalt be safe from his depredations."

So it was done. Days later, when Rebecca visited Lady Joan in her sitting
room, Her Ladyship tossed her another envelope from Williams. With a laugh,
the Lady said,

"This is one of the most entertaining letters I have ever received. It seems
Master Williams doesn't approve of me!"

Rapidly scanning the message, Rebecca protested, "But this is outrageous!
He says:

> If euer (deare Madam) when there is but the breadth of a few gray haires
> betweene you & your everlasting home let me deale vprightly with you.
>
> I know not one professor (of Christianity) amongst all I know whose
> truth & faythfullnes to Jesus Christ is more suspected, doubted, feared, by
> all or most of those that know the Lord...
>
> If euer (good Madame) cry hard, & the Lord helpe me to cry for you...I
> beseech you lay to heart these few Considerations.
>
> 1. First *Job* 34:[1]9. He with whome we deale excepteth not the persons
> of princes nor regardeth the rich more then the poore: for they are all the
> Worcke of his hands...
>
> 3. The Lord will doe what he will with his owne. he owes you no mercy.
> Exod. 33:19. I will be gracious to whome I will be gracious, & will shew
> mercy to whome I will shew mercy...
>
> 6. Remember, I beseech you your Candle is twinckling & glasse neere
> run the Lord only knowes how few minutes are left behind.

...the man is a raving lunatic!"

Lady Joan twinkled.

She said, "I know. But he doesn't blame Jane. I've won! Now I shall marry
her off quickly to another parson, William Hooke of Upper Clatford, Hants.
He has been begging for her hand, and is a truly kind and good man. With
Jane's dowry, they will afford a pleasant life. And I shall recommend Hooke as
chaplain to my nephew, Oliver Cromwell."

Within a week, they received word from Lady Elizabeth Masham that Roger
Williams had fallen desperately ill at Otes. He was feverish, pining for Lady
Jane. Was there any possibility that Her Young Ladyship could visit him? It was
doubted that he would survive.

Lady Joan replied with a one word message: "*No!*"

To Rebecca, she commented, "If that foul pestilence dies for love of Jane, it
will be the best thing ever to befall him!"

Rebecca fervently hoped she had heard the last of Roger Williams.

The beautiful spring of her first pregnancy floated toward a lovely summer.

In the words of John Milton, writing in that year of 1629, "The wanton earth offered herself up to the sun's caress."

Rebecca was able to spend time at Otes with Mary Barnard, who seemed a little more stable by then, suffering only occasional bouts of melancholy.

John was busy seeking ways to improve the economic situation of the Barringtons. They themselves had always been too bound up in politics to properly cultivate their many assets. By means of the simplest financial management techniques, John was able to avoid some taxes and significantly increase cash income to the manor. Since he received a percent of all moneys realised, he was able to make investments of his own. The future seemed bright. Yet Rebecca was aware that John still sought a more worthy direction for his many talents; She did not expect he would remain at Hatfield Broad Oak for long.

Too large to do much, Rebecca sat by her fireside, sewing, during most of May. A village maid came in daily to do the work, and a wet nurse and midwife had been lined up for the baby.

One morning in early June, Rebecca awoke feeling quite ill. She moped through the day, drinking a little broth, nibbling at a biscuit, restless. At mid afternoon her labor began, and she sent her maid to fetch the midwife as well as to inform Lady Joan.

When John came home that evening, Her Ladyship met him at the door.

"Go up to the greathouse for supper, and don't come back until I send for thee. And say a prayer in the chapel for thy wife and unborn child, for both must cheat death before they can be with thee."

Distressed at this speech, John pleaded to see Rebecca, but was firmly refused.

"It will not cheer her to see the author of her misery. Remember her as she was on her best day, and pray God to restore her to thee as she was then."

Lady Joan sat with Rebecca, tending her with love. When Rebecca tried to express gratitude, Lady Joan said,

"We owe each other our lives once. If I serve thee today, perhaps thou wilt save me again tomorrow."

As the evening wore on, Rebecca's discomfort increased, until, a little before midnight, she gave birth to a healthy daughter. The child was carefully cleaned, warmed before the fire, and swaddled, then given to her nurse, Annie, who would watch over the infant all night. After Rebecca's bleeding had slowed, and she had been gently washed and wrapped by the midwife, Lady Joan tenderly fed her hot broth and bread. Then Her Ladyship poured out a glass of rum, setting it at the bedside.

"When thou dost desire sleep, drink that!"

Throwing her cloak around herself, Lady Joan prepared to leave, saying:

"God has blessed this household tonight. I shall thank Him fervently before I sleep. And I'll send John home. After what I told him earlier, he should grovel at thy feet for bearing his child."

Rebecca smiled wanly.

Her Ladyship was right. John reached Rebecca's side sooner than she thought possible, looking quite distressed, and smelling of whiskey. He threw himself on his knees, clasped Rebecca's hand, and begged her, brokenly, to forgive him for causing her pain. Feeling rather smug by then, Rebecca tousled his hair as if he were a child.

"The Almighty held me in His hand tonight. Do not distress yourself. Don't you want to see your daughter? Annie! Bring John's baby to him."

It was love at first sight.

"We'll call her Joan," he said, "and have the baptism in a few days."

Colchester

The birth of John's first child apparently motivated him to take action toward improving his little family's fortunes. Since he was doing more and more business for the Barringtons and Mashams at Colchester, he moved Rebecca and baby Joan there in July. Because he then spent less time traveling, he was able to accept more clients, bring in more money. Already a member of the local merchants' guild, John bought part ownership in their fleet of vessels. This enabled him to transport his clients' goods at a lower cost, keeping more of the profit himself. Prices were beginning to catch up with taxes, and merchants were prospering again. Rebecca, her baby and Annie were quite comfortable in the town house John had purchased. Several other servants ran the place, freeing Rebecca for the gentle life to which she had been reared.

In mid July, John came home for dinner one noon, and drew Rebecca into a fond embrace.

"I'm afraid I must leave you for about three weeks; There is an important conference in Lincolnshire which I must attend."

"What sort of conference?"

"It concerns the planting of a colony in New England."

Rebecca's eyes widened, but she did not otherwise respond.

"Sir Thomas Barrington seeks my opinion on the advisability of investing in this endeavor. Many important Puritans will attend; the conference is being sponsored by the Earl of Lincoln, at Sempringham Castle. The contacts I make, alone, will cause this to be a worthwhile journey."

John did not return until early August, but had much to relate.

"One of your favorite people was there; he had everyone who has not yet given up use of the Book of Common Prayer in turmoil."

"Who could that be? He sounds like no friend of mine!"

"I was jesting. The man was Roger Williams. He seems not to know when to keep silent."

"The last I heard of him, he was at death's door, for love of Lady Jane Whalley. It's a pity he survived."

"My dear and gentle wife!" John kissed her, and continued, "I never knew such cruelty could lurk behind lovely eyes."

"There is more than cruelty behind Roger Williams' eyes. I believe him to be a man in conflict with himself and everyone else."

"I have come to agree with your estimate of him, although he does have lucid moments during which he very nearly makes sense."

"Did you meet anyone else of interest?"

"I became better acquainted with John Winthrop, Sr. I worked for him when he secured Sir Francis' release from Marshalsea."

"Oh? I believe I saw him when he attended Sir Francis' funeral."

"Yes. He has been disbarred for his Puritanism, and is quite eager to plant a colony for Puritans, governed by Puritans, in New England. He seems a wise and good man; I should have no trouble dealing with him in future. Many others were there; you know Thomas Hooker of Chelmsford. But I don't believe you know John Cotton of Boston, Lincolnshire. Cotton is as famous a preacher in Lincoln as Hooker is in Essex. Both were deep in debate with Williams every time I saw them."

"So what was the upshot of the conference?"

"There will be a Puritan colony planted, and soon. Winthrop is at work gathering several hundred people and arranging transport for them all. Sir Thomas is in favor of the project; He wants me to accompany them, to further his interests."

"And have you agreed?"

"Not yet. I wanted to discuss the matter with my father, and most of all, with you. 'Becca, being away from you for three weeks has made me realise that I could never go to the Americas alone."

"I would never send you to the Americas alone. John, I trust your judgment. You may make whatever decision you think best for our family; I will not oppose you."

"'Becca, this will mean great hardship, possibly death for us all."

"I know. I have faced death for you once already. I am not afraid."

All remained serene until late spring of 1630. Rebecca was again pregnant, expecting in late October. Baby Joan was adorable in her tiny, lace edged gowns as she crept about the house.

The worst problem faced by the family was caused by weather. For four years, nature had smiled upon English farmers, giving good harvests. But this spring remained too wet and cold. No one could plow or plant until very late. Then temperatures rose, but no rains fell. Drought conditions threatened the fall harvest.

Sheep were doing better than other livestock, because they browsed as well as grazed, and were able to eat woody plants which cattle could not. Therefore, John's woolens market was among the few agricultural concerns which looked promising for the fall. As the national supply of wheat and other grains was used up, the family began eating more fish, shellfish, and mutton. Vegetables were very scarce, but some fruit was available. Famine stalked the land, affecting the poor first.

It was early July when Rebecca received a letter sealed with Lady Joan's signet. Horrified, she dropped the paper and began to cry, covering her face and moaning. John, passing her sitting room, heard, dropped the papers he was holding, and knelt beside her.

"'Becca, what's wrong?"

"That monster, that villain..."

"Who?"

"Roger Williams." She blew her nose into a lace edged kerchief, and added, "He's wed Mary Barnard."

"Egad! Is that all? You women are so emotional!"

Rebecca looked daggers at him.

"The match is totally unsuitable. He will destroy what's left of her personality. She needed someone kind and gentle, like you, like Job..."

She began to cry again.

John, having just been called kind and gentle, and realising the depth of Rebecca's concern, wrapped strong arms around her. He pulled her to the floor, to sit on his lap and be comforted.

"Remember that 'all things work together for good,'" he murmured. "Mary is as much in the Almighty's hand as are you. 'Be ye not overcome with evil, but overcome evil with good.'"

"I never should have left her behind at Otes...She cannot even read if I write to her...I must see her! John, can you manage without me for a week?"

"Actually, I need to speak to Sir Thomas Barrington personally about the timing of our move to the Massachusetts Bay Colony...I don't trust the mails for this. I shall escort you, but I think we should leave the baby here. Annie is reliable, and the child need not be exposed to the hardships of the journey."

Hatfield Broad Oak

Rebecca reluctantly agreed. After packing, and giving Annie a hundred unnecessary instructions, she joined John the next morning in her coach for the journey to Hatfield Broad Oak. Because John had, the previous evening, thoughtfully sent a team of horses ahead to Braintree, they changed teams and continued traveling into the night, arriving at about nine o'clock. The household was asleep, but Bridge showed them to a guest chamber, where they gratefully collapsed.

Rebecca rose with the dawn, waiting on Lady Joan as if she had never been away.

"My dear! How lovely to see thee! Didst thou get my letter?"

Rebecca's face told Her Ladyship that she had indeed received it.

"Lady Joan, what ever shall we do? He will destroy her!"

Her Ladyship looked sad.

"There is little that can be done. The wedding was legally performed in December at High Laver, and since there was no dowry involved, no legal process was violated. To make matters worse, Mary's father is very ill, not expected to live. Her brothers have never seemed interested in their sister's welfare. How I wish I had been here, instead of running off to my daughter's in Middlesex!"

"I must see her."

"I was afraid thou wouldst say that. I tried to visit her, myself, but her husband would not permit me. My daughter, Elizabeth Masham, says that no one sees Mary except at church, and that she speaks to no one."

"Where do they live?"

"In a rude cottage about a mile this side of Otes."

"And he goes out without her?"

"Ah, I follow thy thinking. Yes. I believe we could manage to keep Master Williams busy at Otes chapel while thou seeest Mary. But thou shalt take Dudley with thee—for protection!"

"Are you sure I need that?"

"Most definitely. If riled, I think Master Williams may tend to violence."

The two finished their plans before nine that morning, and Lady Joan set out in her light buggy for Otes, to arrange for an all morning prayer service. The excuse would be that Lady Joan had beheld the devil in a dream, and was frightened for her soul's salvation.

Not wanting her identity or her mission known to anyone she might encounter, Rebecca thought it prudent to wear a disguise. A large, floppy bonnet hid her face, and the scullery maid lent a clean but ragged cloak, which hid her clothing completely.

Lady Joan had taken Dudley with her, but left him a half mile beyond the village to wait for Rebecca, in order that no one would see the two together. He led Rebecca on another mile and a half to the Williams cottage. Nearby, they found a suitably screened, forest hiding place from which they could view the side of the building, unobserved. The only signs of life were the puffs of smoke coming from the chimney. Soon, they saw a messenger arriving on a horse from the direction of Otes. He pounded on the door at length before it opened. Rebecca could hear Williams' grating voice responding to the boy's summons.

"Why didn't they send a horse for me?" he wanted to know. "Let me ride yours, and you walk back, since they need me quickly!"

Rebecca smiled. The horse would bear him away swiftly, giving her more time with Mary. As soon as the man had put on a cloak, he stepped out of the cottage, then locked the door with a heavy brass key. Rebecca heard him ordering someone inside to put up the oaken bar. Apparently, no one was to go in or out until his return.

"What if there's a fire?" Rebecca wondered.

As soon as Williams and the boy had gone, she ran to the door and beat on it with her fists.

"Mary, it's me, Rebecca!"

There was no response.

"Mary, please! Answer me!"

Rebecca stopped, on the verge of tears. "Use your brain," she ordered herself.

"Dudley, get me one of those long, fat logs so I can climb up to the window."

Looking in, Rebecca saw a disheveled, unkempt shadow of the once lovely Mary. She was sitting on the floor before the hearth, in a night shift. She hugged her knees, staring into the coals, rocking back and forth.

"Mary!"

The woman looked up, afraid, then recognised her friend.

"'Becca?"

"Yes! Open this window, and I'll climb in."

"It's been nailed shut, I think. The one over there is jammed…maybe we can get it open."

"Dudley! Come here and try the other window!"

Within minutes, Rebecca had hauled herself through the narrow aperture. "Good thing I'm not any farther along with this baby!" she thought. "I never would have fit!"

"Dudley! Go down to Otes until you can see the driveway. If anyone starts in this direction, let me know, instantly!"

"Yes, Mistress Throckmorton."

"Mary, my darling, tell me why you are in this place!"

"I live here now, with my, my husband."

Her voice was that of a young child, devoid of shades of meaning or comprehension.

Rebecca, stunned, asked, "And who is your husband?"

"R-roger. He takes care of me..."

Rebecca slid an arm around Mary's shoulders, but her friend cringed, uttering a moan of pain. Rebecca pulled out the neck facing of Mary's gown, looked down her back.

"God's blood! He's beaten you!"

"Oh, no. I, I did that. I'm very sinful, you know. Just full of sins."

"The only sin you have committed is letting that monster wreck your life. Why did you agree to marry him? Why?"

Mary uttered a sigh, then seemed to pull herself back to reality.

"He forced me. I was at the mill, looking into the water, wishing I could join with it forever, when he grabbed my arm. He said that wanting to die is a sin. he says that everything I do is sinful, so I try not to do anything...Anyway, Roger said that I let Satan call me to the mill stream in order to tempt him to fornication. And so that I would learn the error of my ways, to, to take my sin on himself, Roger forced me. He hurt me terribly, and left me to wander back to Otes, ruined.

The next day, he sent one of the village boys to call me out to the wheatfield near the greathouse. The boy said if I came out, I could be forgiven of all my sins. When I got there, Roger sent the boy away. Then he forced me again. He said he would find a way to get to me every day until I agreed to marry him. If we married, his soul and mine could be at peace, forgiven."

"My God in Heaven. Mary, how can you stand this? This is unholy!"

"Don't, don't say I'm sinful, 'Becca. Truly, I have repented of wanting to die. And now, the fornication is not sinful, because I am married...it's just the little things I do, everything I do, that is so bad..."

"No, Mary. Your sins are all forgiven! God loves you, and I love you. I'm going away, now, but I'll be back."

She thought for a moment.

"Do not make Roger angry by telling him I was here. Remember that it is bad for you to make him angry—so *don't* tell him."

"All right, 'Becca."

It was the child's voice again. Rebecca kissed her cheek. Then, feeling more helpless than ever before in her life, she wriggled out the window. Pulling it shut, she rolled the heavy log to the woodpile, then smoothed the traces of its passage through the yard.

"I hope to God Roger doesn't notice."

Walking on toward Otes, Rebecca found Dudley and sent him up to the greathouse to fetch Lady Joan. At this point, Her Ladyship decided that her soul was predestined for Heaven, and in no danger. She and Dudley came flying down the road in the light trap, collected Rebecca, and were soon at Hatfield Broad Oak again.

Before dismissing Dudley, Lady Joan gave him a gold coin and said, "Unless I bid thee otherwise, today thou didst nothing, hardest nothing, sawest nothing. I have trusted thee all thy life, and I trust thee now."

Dudley gave the coin back.

"Yore Ladyship, if what I did today will help Mistress Mary, then I want no other payment, and my lips is sealed."

Lady Joan laid a gloved hand on his powerful shoulder and squeezed. Then she led Rebecca to her chambers.

As they passed Bridge, she ordered, "See that Dudley receives twice as much pay from now on as he did in the past!"

"Very good, My Lady!"

Within the chamber, door closed, Rebecca told Her Ladyship everything. They both wept. Then they became angry.

Finally, Lady Joan said, "I have a plan."

On the morrow, Lady Joan and Rebecca, heavily veiled, met Dudley well before dawn. The three walked quietly past the Williams cottage to a bend in the narrow footpath to Otes. The light increased as dawn approached. Hiding in the thick brush, they had only a short wait before the chaplain came walking toward the greathouse for morning prayers, reciting scripture aloud to himself as he walked. He never saw any of them, or heard Dudley's soft tread behind him as the stable hand knocked him senseless with a heavy club. Effortlessly, Dudley threw the little man over his massive shoulder and carried him back to the cottage. Flinging Roger onto the ground before the door, Dudley rummaged in the parson's pockets, finding the key. He unlocked the door, but was unable to open it because of the bar on the other side. Rebecca called several times, with no response.

"I'll have to climb up to the window again."

Leaving Dudley to guard the unconscious Williams, Rebecca rolled her log back to the window, and set it upright. Finally, she got Mary's attention, and convinced her to unbar the door. Dudley carried Roger in, and carelessly dumped him on the unmade bed.

"Goodwoman Noakes should be here any minute," said Her Ladyship. "She'll set things right around here."

Rebecca was holding and rocking Mary. "Everything is all right now, my dear. Poor Roger was beset by robbers, but we have saved him and brought him home. Now Goody Noakes will stay with you until he is himself again."

"And," she added to herself, "poor Roger will continue to be damaged on a regular basis unless he learns to treat his wife with respect."

Goody Noakes was at the door. Fully six feet tall and heavily muscled, she tumbled Roger about as if he were an infant. She removed all his clothing, hid it, and tucked him into bed.

"Don't you worry about a thing, Mistress Williams," she clucked. "We'll have him right as rain in a jiffy. And I'll stay on as long as you need me."

The sun had come up, burning brightly.

"How would you like a little walk, Mary?" asked Rebecca. "Now that Goody Noakes is here, you can go out whenever you like!"

She and Lady Joan took Mary outside. As they walked, the women took turns telling Mary what a good person she was, and how much they loved her.

"Thou art going to teach Roger how to love thee," said Lady Joan. "Thou shalt teach him what a valuable part of him thou art. Thou wilt surround him with love."

"Yes," Mary said. "Yes."

They returned Mary to the cottage, and themselves to Hatfield Broad Oak with Dudley. At the main entrance, Rebecca thanked him sincerely.

"Mistress Throckmorton," he burbled, "that knock on the head was no more'n wot he deserved, if you take my meaning, and I'd be proud to repeat it any time you say!"

"Remember," Lady Joan cautioned, "thou didst nothing, sawest nothing, heardest nothing."

"Yes, Yore Ladyship."

Rebecca met John in the hallway, coming from morning prayers.

"Where the devil have you been these past two mornings?" he groused. "I suppose you were off with Dudley!"

"Actually, I was. And Lady Joan went with us. I think we have Mary's problems under control, and we may leave for home whenever you say. I miss the baby dreadfully."

"Let's go now. Packing won't take long, will it?"

"No. If you order the carriage, I shall pack. Then we'll say farewell, and be off."

"Fine."

So it went.

Colchester

One morning in late October, Rebecca looked out her window to see a large, warmly cloaked man dismounting a powerful horse. Recognising him, she ran downstairs to fling open the door.

"Father Throckmorton!"

He ran up the steps to the entry and surrounded her in a gentle hug, careful of her hugely distended abdomen.

"'Becca, my daughter! It is delight to see thee!"

"Come in, come in! Marie shall fetch some hot cider for you. Is all well in Norwich?"

"Aye, all is well. And when dost thou expect thy little one?"

"Soon now, very soon. I am in the Almighty's hand, once again."

"May he bless thee. Is little Joanie about?"

"Yes. Marie! Bid Annie to bring Joan to her grandfather."

Rebecca led him to the lodging parlour, seating him on a sturdy oak chair. After he had drunk his cider and kissed his granddaughter, Basingbourne turned to Rebecca.

"I just met with John, at the mercantile exchange. He says thou hast agreed to go to New England in December."

"Yes. I can't decide whether I am being saintly, or merely stupid. But John has convinced me that the New World will offer unlimited opportunities to us and to our children. Our group of 'planters' is partly sponsored by Sir Thomas Barrington, you know. He paid our ship's passage."

Basingbourne rumbled, somberly, "This is not the ideal time of year for an ocean crossing."

"So I'm told. The timing is economic, mostly. If we leave, as scheduled, December first, we have more cash to take along. John's income is largest and his assets most liquid right after harvest. The longer we live here on it, the less there will be to use in America, where we shall need it most."

"Thou art the bravest woman I ever met!"

"Oh, no, surely not. The deciding factor for me was that some of our acquaintances from Broad Oak will accompany us. You remember Mary Barnard, my maid of honour at the wedding."

"Yes. A beautiful girl."

"She and her husband are going, among others."

With tears in his eyes, Basingbourne stood, enfolding Rebecca in his arms.

"Dearest daughter, I knew I should lose thee to the future some time. But now that the day is nigh, I find it more than I can bear to let thee go."

Rebecca, reaching up, kissed his cheek and murmured, teasing gently, "John was so right about you."

"Meaning what?"

Some of his fierceness had returned.

"You are truly a warm and gentle soul. My main regret in leaving England is that your grandchildren will likely have no chance to know you."

"Aye. But thou wilt tell them of me, teach them my name?"

"You can depend upon it."

He stayed the night, but was off for Norwich with the dawn. They never saw him again.

Rebecca's baby, Mary, was born with little fuss on November first. Annie helped her learn to nurse the child, and also organised the sorting, packing, and sale of the Throckmorton's household goods.

Hatfield Broad Oak

On November fifteenth, the family left Colchester forever, heading for Hatfield Broad Oak in the coach. The next morning, after prayers with Lady Joan, they met in the great dining hall with the Williamses to finalise plans for the morrow.

Rebecca embraced Mary, showing her the children. Some of her friend's old energy had returned, and she was dressed nicely in clean, plain clothing. While Roger was talking at John, Rebecca took Mary aside to ask how she did.

"Much better, 'Becca. I know that you saved my life, and I am able to be grateful for that now, most of the time…I only wish that God would grant me children, because that would raise my value in Roger's eyes."

"Give it time, Mary. You are fortunate not to have the burden of little ones while taking this great journey."

"Perhaps you are right. It's just that I am so uncertain of what life in America will be. I think the routine of caring for a child would focus my mind, relieve some of my fears…"

"Just remember, we are in God's hands. As long as He permits, I will be near you. And there's something else…"

Putting her mouth close to Mary's ear, Rebecca whispered, "Lady Joan is sending Goody Noakes and Dudley with us on the ship. They'll be in America, too, whenever we need them."

Mary clapped a hand over her mouth. Running to Lady Joan, who was observing from her usual dining chair, Mary kissed Her Ladyship's hand, and was pulled to the older woman for a fond embrace.

The meeting was brief. They would take one coach and two saddle horses. Each family was permitted only one wooden trunk of possessions on the ship. This information set Roger off. He began to recite:

"'Come, now ye rich men, weep and howl for your miseries that shall come upon you. Your riches are corrupted and your garments are moth eaten. Your gold and silver are cankered, and the rust of them shall be a witness against you, and shall eat your flesh as it were fire.'"

John smoothly responded, "'Better is little with the fear of the Lord than great treasure and trouble therewith.'"

"Well said," thought Rebecca, "although the reverse is just as true."

She looked at John. Roger need not know that they were each wearing corselets lined with golden coins, hems stuffed with gems. They were taking next to nothing else, really. Their family Bible, in its own box, a few changes of clothing, several of John's books, and their personal grooming items had quickly filled the trunk.

Back in Colchester, she had told him, "Just leave the rest. God will provide for us in America."

John had taken her in his arms and replied, "He has already provided for me!"

That afternoon, Lady Joan had ordered a special farewell reception and supper for the Throckmortons. As the guests began to arrive, Rebecca's eyes filled with tears again and again.

All four of her sisters showed up, green with envy at Rebecca's wealthy connexions, but scornful of the idea of improving one's estate in America. It was a place for savages and ne'er do wells.

Thomas Cornell and the four Throckmorton brothers had ridden down from Norwich and Bungay. Rebecca marveled at the raw talent and good fortune God had settled on this handsome group. She felt humbled to be associated with them as they mingled with the Barrington family, suave and elegant.

Thomas spent the whole afternoon at his younger sister's side.

"I'll join you in New England when my training is complete," he promised. "You'll not be rid of me so easily!"

Each of John's brothers took Rebecca aside, wished her well, and thanked her for making their brother so happy.

"They know they'll never see us again," she thought.

Oliver Cromwell was there, bemoaning the fact that fine men such as John were compelled to leave England in order to better themselves.

"We shall need cool heads and stout hearts such as yours in the future," said he. "If America treats you not kindly, come back!"

Roger Williams had joined the party, uninvited, and was vehemently quoting scripture to an unfortunate whom he had buttonholed. Overhearing him, Cromwell slyly added,

"On the other hand, I'm sure there are some of whom England will be well rid. We are indebted to you for removing them!"

Rebecca pulled a face at him, and Oliver hugged her.

"Remember me and my good wishes for your new life!"

Rebecca hardly slept that night for excitement. Instead, wrapped in her cloak, she paced the ice cold halls of Hatfield Broad Oak for the last time, holding her baby warm against her skin. In the morning, she knelt next to Lady Joan for prayers, then walked to her waiting coach, Her Ladyship's hand clasped in her own. Both wept as they said their final goodbyes.

"I shall meet thee in Heaven," said Lady Joan. "And every day, whether here or there, I shall implore our Father to bless thee."

Rebecca responded, "You have been more than a mother to me. I shall ever hold Your Ladyship's memory dear. Farewell, My Lady."

Rebecca would have cried bitterly in the carriage with her children and Goody Noakes if not for an incident which set the tone for the years to come. She had intended that Mary Barnard Williams ride in her carriage, since the weather on the long trip to Bristol was likely to be nasty. In return, Mary could help with the children. But Roger had other plans.

"My wife will be riding the horse with me, not luxuriating in an ostentatious carriage."

"The coach is plain, undecorated. Surely you want to spare your wife the exposure to the elements…" began Rebecca.

"'The sluggard will not plow by reason of the cold, therefore shall he beg in harvest, and have nothing,'" he grated.

"Non sequitur," commented John, mildly. "Perhaps you'd do me the honour of riding with me, also, 'giving honour' to our wives as 'weaker vessels.' There is somewhat I would ask thee concerning a passage in the book of *Zephaniah*…Rememberest thou Chapter Two? I shall quote it for thee!"

Quickly bundling Mary into the coach with the other women and the children, Lady Joan whispered, "Between John and Dudley, perhaps he can be contained!"

"May God grant!" prayed Rebecca.

They departed, Dudley driving, beginning the long overland journey to Bristol. John, having connexions along the way, had arranged for them to lodge in private homes at every stop. He did not want his wife and children inconvenienced by the uncomfortable and unreliable accommodations of public inns. Williams had at first balked at the idea of staying with wealthy gentry, but soon saw the wisdom of not spending his limited means.

Loughton

At Loughton, they lodged with John's cousins, who happened also to be, on the wife's side, cousins of the Barringtons with whom Rebecca had stayed before. It was all they could do to keep Roger's constant "prophesying" from putting their hosts into a temper.

London

In London, they drove to Francis Barrington's. He understood all about Roger, and cooly refused to become ruffled by him. He did, however, crave time with Rebecca.

"If I'd known John would take you so far away, I never would have encouraged you two as I did," he teased. More seriously, he added, "My family owes you a great debt. We shall never forget you."

"On the contrary," returned Rebecca, "your family not only saved my life, but also shaped it. In my soul, I shall always be a Barrington."

Francis embraced her tenderly, and she kissed him.

There was a tap at the lodging parlour door, and Jackson entered.

"Mistress Chambers to see Master and Mistress Throckmorton."

"Jackson, will you call my husband? I believe he's in the study. Show Mistress Chambers in at once."

"Very good, Mistress."

Francis hurriedly went out.

Rebecca was shocked by the change in the bright soul who had dressed her so happily for the Lord Mayor's reception. The woman was robed in black, with white apron, cuffs, and falling bands, the image of a strict Puritan. The small portion of her hair visible under a white cap was gray, as colourless as her face. After embracing her, Rebecca was not sure what to say. Luckily, John came in, enfolding his old friend in strong arms.

"I just heard," he said. "Francis told me a little. Now you must tell me all of it, from the beginning."

The three sat, and Rebecca's stomach contracted in dread as Mistress Chambers began her tale:

"Richard always has been too outspoken; its his worst fault, God love him. A week ago, the king rode into London with his retinue. The Lord Mayor met him at Tempull Barre Gate, offering the Great Pearl Sword, as always. Richard and the other aldermen attended, of course. All might have been well, had not His Majesty chosen to address some ill advised remarks to the group, claiming that they owed their current prosperity to his beneficence. My Richard said,

'The merchants are in no part of the world so screwed and wrung as in England: In Turkey they have more encouragement.'

His Royal Highness looked startled, but did not respond. The next day three royal emissaries arrived to go over Richard's ledgers. They claim he's not paid his proper share of Tonnage and Poundage tax, and he's been locked in the Tower ever since. Oh, Master John, what shall become of us?"

Rebecca found her face flowing with tears for this good hearted woman. John was speaking to Mistress Chambers softly, comfortingly. He would stay in London tomorrow, make inquiries, visit Richard. Perhaps if he would retract his statement publicly, apologise...

Tearfully, the woman responded, "Oh, he's stubborn as an ox, is my Richard. He told me he'd die rather than take back a word. As for me, I'm joining the ranks of the Puritans, as you can see from my dress. Their speeches never meant much to me until this week. As Sir Robert Phelips says, 'To be an honest man is now to be a Puritan'! Well, enough of my troubles. I must return home."

John said, "I shall call on you late tomorrow afternoon, to advise of what I learn."

"Thank you, thank you."

Brokenly, she turned for the door. John escorted her to the coach. He and Francis returned to the lodging parlour, John inquiring as to the location of several offices he must visit at Whitehall the following day. They fell silent, and looked at Rebecca.

"'The liberty of conscience...'" she began.

"'...is a vision, a never ending ecstasy...'" continued John.

From the doorway came Roger's grating voice, "'...prerequisite to the Christian pilgrimage.'"

Mary, joining the group, finished for them all, "And that is our true quest in the Americas. May God grant us peace."

Tired as she was, Rebecca lay awake that night, her back pressed warmly to John's, baby Mary at her breast. She wondered for the first time about the degree of liberty possible in a new, unsettled continent. She was aware of Antinomianism; the idea of anarchy did not appeal to her at all. Did not the children of Israel come to grief in the years when "every man did that which was right in his own eyes"?

Yet there had to be a better way to maintain order than the public, savage punishments used too often by English courts. A traitor, for example, anyone who opposed the king, would first be half hanged, then disemboweled while still conscious, then beheaded. When such punishments were ordered arbitrarily by an unjust sovereign, they became even more intolerable.

Which was the more prudent course, to nurture the infant liberties of England, or to conceive new ones in a new world? Rebecca only had to conjure the vision of the supposed traitors' heads, mounted on pikes at London Bridge, to encourage her to follow John to America.

Then there were economic advantages...but somehow Rebecca doubted that additional wealth could bring more comfort than she was experiencing at this moment. Her belly was full, she was warm, safe...It was really for the children, John had explained. When they had sons, if they had sons, there would be unlimited opportunities for prosperity, and to carry on the ancient family name in a new world. Even the daughters would benefit, since wives were a scarce, valuable commodity in New England. They would be welcomed, cherished...and all of them would inherit that priceless treasure, freedom of conscience.

Finally, she fell asleep.

Next evening, the news were not good. John had been unable to do anything for Richard Chambers beyond making sure the merchant was well represented by counsel, and that his assets were transferred to sons in laws' names for protection.

John was nauseated after his visit to the prison, but nevertheless executed his courtesy call to Mistress Chambers with grace. When he returned to Francis' house, he ran upstairs to find Rebecca, who had just laid baby Mary down to sleep. Closing the chamber door, John seized his wife and held her for a long time.

Finally, he whispered, "I shall think a thousand years before I ever spew out words which will force us to be separated. God's death, what a fool Chambers is! He'll rot in the Tower, and what will it accomplish? Nothing."

Slowly, the couple walked downstairs for supper, glad for once to hear Roger Williams start one of his harangues. It was diverting.

Runnymede

Next morning, after bidding Francis goodbye, they proceeded upriver, west along the Thames Valley. At midmorning, near the Castle at Hampton Court, John ordered the coach to stop in a wide meadow.

Leaving the children with Goody Noakes and Dudley, John and Roger led Rebecca and Mary to the river bank. Signaling a passing fisherman, John paid him to row them across part of the river to an island. Advancing to a low hill, John dropped to his knees, beckoning the others to join him.

"Here we praise God for His gift of liberty to the English common man. On this site, some of my noble ancestors forced my royal ancestor, King John, to sign Magna Charta. Here lay the cradle of our freedom, here began our quest for liberty of conscience. Master Williams, would you consent to lead us in prayer?"

As they returned to shore aboard the small skiff, Rebecca marveled at the depth of feeling inspired by the simple act of worship, and at its ability to remove a little of the antipathy she still harboured against Roger Williams.

Windsor

They reached Windsor that night. The alderman of local merchants had reserved an unoccupied, staffed, furnished house for their use. The group was most grateful for the space and privacy this afforded. Rebecca had been especially anxious lest the children disturb the others, and this arrangement, with upstairs and downstairs rooms, allowed her to relax.

During their late supper, Roger began to talk, and Rebecca was shocked to find herself listening as if he were a normal human being.

"The whole time we were at London, so close to the palace of Archbishop Laud, I was in agony. For he hates me, hates my sermons, my thought; It is because of his powerful long arm that I must leave England. I cannot practice my faith in a land where he rules the church.

And late today, when we approached this town, I spied Stoke House, the home of my patron, Sir Edward Coke. He provided the means for my education, from preparatory school through my years taking a degree at Cambridge. It was bitter as death not to see him, to acquaint him with my flight to America."

Puzzled, Rebecca almost asked the obvious question, but he continued:

"Sir Edward is staunchly Anglican. He tolerated my Puritan beliefs, but we came to a final parting of the ways last summer. I told him how opposed I am to the ceremonies and false authority of the church. I told him that perhaps it is time to divorce religion from government. He flew into a rage, saying that he rues the day he put out his hand to help me. Yet I still honour him as one of the finest Attorneys General and M.P.s England has ever known.

It is a heavy burden to be hated by those I admire. I feel like Cain, a fugitive and a wanderer; I trust that John Winthrop and the true believers of the Massachusetts Bay Colony can tolerate me. if not, God must provide a place…"

John said, "'Let not your heart be troubled…I go to prepare a place for you, and if I go, I will come again and receive you unto myself, that where I am, there ye may be also.'"

Roger responded, "The question will remain, 'how shall we know the way?' Seeking the will of God may occupy the remainder of my life; I see no end to it."

John concluded the discussion: "We must compose ourselves for sleep. God grant that we see the morrow more clearly after we rest."

The next day, during the drive to Reading, the weather turned so nasty that Roger and John squeezed into the carriage with the women and children. At last they reached the junction of Thames and Kennet Rivers, and gratefully found their lodgings. The next day's travel took them to Newbury, the next, to Marlborough.

Marlborough

On the Lord's Day, Rebecca was grateful for the rest from travel, even though she had to listen to Master Williams expound on the benefits of poverty and hard work all afternoon. The family they stayed with were awed to be listening to such a learned man of God, although Rebecca doubted that they understood how flawed was his logic.

"If God bestows blessings, how could it be sinful to enjoy them, as long as one does so responsibly?" she wondered.

Rebecca had discovered that such questions only made Roger angry, so she restrained herself. Only John had the knack of cheerfully disagreeing with the hot headed parson, quoting scripture to support his position. Williams somehow never took offense, when the rebuttal came from John.

Bath

On the following morn, they rode through the Vale of Pewse, Wiltshire, to stay at Devises, and thence traveled to Bath, where they all partook of the famed hot mineral waters. Rebecca found her hot mineral bath to be, in its own way, rather more physically stimulating than anything she had yet experienced. She found herself purring and uttering strange sounds of bliss afterwards, and John found it necessary to walk the baby himself, since his wife seemed incapable of doing so.

Bristol

Their last day's land journey followed the River Avon to Bristol. Much excited, the men rode off as soon as the others were settled with their merchant host. Within an hour, John and Roger were back.

"We sail in three days! Everything is on schedule. The other passengers have been arriving, a few at a time," said Roger.

"How many people are sailing?" Rebecca wanted to know.

John answered, "Twenty passengers, including children, plus a crew of about thirty. The bulk of the space aboard will be taken up with supplies for the Bay Colony. They risk starvation and scurvy if the ship does not make haste."

"Oh, John!"

"This is their first winter, and they had no food reserves built up. It's one reason we did not accompany them in March; I foresaw this problem. Every first winter for a colony such as this is very difficult. By the way, the four of us have been invited to dine with our old friend, John Winthrop, Jr. tomorrow noon. He is here gathering supplies to send to his father."

They went in to supper, and passed a peaceful night.

On the morrow, Rebecca left the children at their lodgings with Goody Noakes, while Dudley drove the two couples across town to young Winthrop's house. John Winthrop, Jr. was by then qualified both as a lawyer and physician. He remained plump and cheerful, with a trim mustache and pageboy haircut. After greeting his guests and leading them into his lodging parlour, he began chatting about their ship, the *Lyon*. Since the parlour window overlooked Bristol Harbour, Rebecca asked,

"Which ship down there is ours?"

Winthrop responded, "It's not arrived yet. Captain Peirce should be here with it, today or tomorrow. He has been obliged to sail up and down the coast, collecting supplies, because the famine caused a shortage of the grains needed."

During the meal, Winthrop explained that he was waiting in England with his mother Margaret, his brother Samuel, and sister Mary until his infant sister, Anne, should be strong enough to stand the journey to New England.

"My family has been much bereaved this year," he confided. "We just lost my brother, Forth, whom you may have met. He was a minister at Groton, Essex. My brothers Stephen and Adam are with my father at Massachusetts Bay, but my brother Henry died there in July. He drowned while swimming a river, trying to fetch a canoe. Because my parents lost two other daughters called Anne to death, they want to be especially careful of the latest baby. We may not be able to cross the Atlantic for many months, yet. And my brother, Deane, will remain here to complete his education."

John spoke up, cutting off what promised to be a lengthy discourse on the topic of death from Roger: "Your family must be overwhelmed by grief. Henry was ever the adventurous type, I understand, and Forth was a fine man of God."

"Yes," responded Winthrop sadly. "Henry left a widow and unborn child at Groton."

"I am sorry to hear it. Your father is a man of great courage and dedication, to risk his sons in a new land."

"No more so than those who follow him," replied Winthrop. "If he deserves praise, it is because his vision has ever been to establish a community governed by the law of God. The corruption rampant throughout the English judiciary sickens him, as it does me. This colony is his attempt to bring God's kingdom to earth.

Would you do me the favour of delivering this packet of letters to him? They bear the sad news concerning Forth's death, and should be given to him at an appropriate moment, if such a thing exists."

John replied in the affirmative, then asked, "By the bye, have our accommodations on board ship and in Massachusetts been confirmed?"

Winthrop responded, "Each of the four married couples among the gentry has a private cabin, very small, you understand, reserved aboard. The few other passengers, all servants, will travel in the main quarters. The rest of the ship, except for the crew's lodgings and the galley, or kitchen, is taken up by the two hundred tons of supplies. Once you are in Massachusetts Bay, my father will arrange for shelter. His own house is not yet standing, but will be built next spring. He currently occupies a large cottage next the meeting hall."

John frowned, "It all sounds very tenuous. I prefer to have four walls around me when I sleep!"

Roger spoke up, "Where's your sense of adventure, John?"

John smiled ruefully, and said, "It wouldn't fit in the trunk. I must have left it behind. At any rate, are there buildings enough standing in the Bay Colony for our women and children?"

Winthrop reassured them. "My father will arrange everything. He knows you are coming, and he is particularly eager for the women to be comfortable there. The colony will never survive without them!"

Roger intoned, "'In my father's house are many mansions. If it were not so, I would have told you.'"

Nervously, Winthrop shot a glance at Roger, then said, "Exactly! Let us finish our meal with a glass of western metheglin. Have you tasted it before? It is a tradition in Wales, I understand, like spiced meade, distilled from fermented honey. Quite refreshing!"

The Williamses and Throckmortons partook, agreeing that the drink was delightful. Then they returned to their lodgings. That afternoon, the *Lyon* hove into port, and they all were very excited to see it.

On their last day ashore, the entire group of passengers assembled for a day of fasting and prayer for journeying mercies. The other couples, the Ongs and Perkins, who had never heard Roger lecture, seemed awed by him. Rebecca did not know whether to be grateful that someone distracted his attention from correcting Mary, or disappointed that his obnoxious behavior was being encouraged. At any rate, Roger's conviction that God spoke directly to and through him seemed to be accepted by the other passengers without question.

The Throckmortons were not accustomed to fasting. By the end of that day, Rebecca felt quite weak and sick. She got Goody Noakes to sneak a pint of ale into her bedchamber, for the baby's sake. When John came in, later in the evening, he seemed more cast down than his wife had ever seen him. He sat on the bed, head in hands.

Rebecca, who had been pacing the floor, nursing baby Mary, laid a hand on his shoulder.

"It's just so hard for me," he said. "I'm used to being in control, making the plans. Now I am giving my life, and the lives of my dear ones…"

He straightened and slid his arms around Rebecca, drawing her near.

"…into the control of sailors whom I've never met. If that weren't bad enough, they, no matter how skilled they are, have no control over the sea. It could swallow us up at any time in the next two months, without leaving a trace."

"You are merely experiencing the feeling of helplessness which surrounds us women during our whole lives. We pass from the control of our older male relatives to that of our husbands. We give up control of our bodies, our souls, trusting that the future will treat us kindly. Do you desire to return to Colchester? We would be welcome there, but no safer. There are plague, famine, fire, accident, old age, all waiting to end our lives somehow, sometime. What is your desire?"

John raised his head to look at her.

"'No man, having put his hand to the plough, and looking back, is fit for the kingdom of God,'" he quoted. "But my desire is all for you!"

Laying her sleeping babe aside, Rebecca, full of faith and love, yielded herself to him.

The *Lyon*

In the morning, all the passengers felt quite excited and eager to board the ship. To Rebecca, everything seemed to take too long, from packing, to feeding the children, to waiting for the last ride in her carriage (would she ever own another?) down to the wharf. The tide came in high and strong, so the passengers were able to board directly by means of a sturdy gang plank with handrails. Rebecca felt completely safe and relaxed, until she encountered the crew members as she stepped on deck.

John was yet on the dock, seeing that Dudley removed all the luggage, and that the correct person, the new owner's servant, took away the coach. Rebecca, having been assured by John Winthrop, Jr. that Captain Peirce was a gentleman, was shocked to notice a suggestive leer in his eyes. He, and every member of his crew were shamelessly ogling the eight women as they stepped aboard. Rebecca, used to being sheltered and protected from this sort of thing, had never felt so naked, or so humiliated.

Seizing Mary's arm, she pulled her to stand behind Roger. He, excited at the prospect of a new audience for his views, immediately began expounding on the judgments of Almighty God to vile sinners such as these. The sailors turned away, having heard enough.

Before long, John strode briskly up the gangplank and greeted the captain cordially, with his customary warmth and good humour, which put everyone at ease. The passengers were escorted by a cabin boy from the upper deck down into the main quarters. Here they would eat and meet together. There were bunks for the servants along the walls.

Next, they were led up the short flight of steep stairs to their cabins; the Throckmortons' was the first. Rebecca looked in. Half the cubicle was taken up by their trunk, the other half by a bunk which seemed scarcely wide enough for one person. John and Rebecca, carrying their children, squeezed into the room.

"First, so we can move about…"

John unhooked the bed frame from chains by which one edge was suspended. Its hinges folded, the bed frame hung fairly flat against the wall, though the straw filled mattress sagged uncooperatively. John showed Rebecca the hooks and drawers for their clothing, and unlocked the trunk.

"…if we unload this beast, they will store it below for us."

Together, they juggled the children and hung up their clothes. Rebecca found some partly enclosed shelves for John's papers and books, arranging them neatly. The two down comforters lay folded in a corner. John pushed the heavy trunk out into the passageway, then set up their bunk again. Rebecca spread the comforters on the bed, setting the girls comfortably on top. Soon, a swearing sailor hauled their trunk away. Rebecca looked at John.

"What did he say?"

John shut the door.

"Sounded like, 'god-rotting puke-stockings' to me. That would be us, of course. I think we must adjust either our ears not to hear, or our hearts not to misunderstand the sailors' talk. They express with every sentence a cheerful acceptance of their unspeakably rough lives. We would be wrong to judge them harshly."

"Does this forgiving attitude extend to rude stares from them, too? I was most chagrined to feel myself being stripped and ravished in their imaginations as I walked aboard."

John laughed as he pulled her close, saying, "Have a heart, Fair Lady! These 'jack-tars' only get to look at you. I used to do some rude staring, myself, before you let me do more…"

His hands were beginning to caress her when there was a tap at the door.

"Preparing to cast off, Good Master!"

"Oh, John, we must go on deck and bid farewell to England!"

He sighed, picked up Joanie, and led the way out.

"Watch your step, my dear!"

They descended into the main quarters, then climbed through the open hatchway, back onto the upper deck. A cacophony of sound surrounded them. There were shouted farewells of those standing on the dock, ships' bells, the boatswain's call,

"A-all ha-aa-nds! Up anchor, a-ho-oy!"

Then came the chants of the sailors, turning the windlass to raise the anchor, hauling on ropes.

Rebecca spied John Winthrop, Jr. in the crowd ashore, and waved. He blew kisses, and she laughed, the stiff, cold wind feeling fine on her face. John, delighted to see her look so happy, slid his free arm round her waist. Within minutes, she was glad of his support, because, entering the river channel, the ship began to rock earnestly.

If every day of their voyage could have been as pleasant as that first one, floating smoothly on the out bound tide, Rebecca would have harboured a great love of sailing ships forever. As it happened, that day provided both the most pleasant weather of the trip, and the smoothest sailing. That evening, as they reached the mouth of the bay, Rebecca remained on deck, admiring the change of colours in the sunset and the advent of stars. She had not seen these beloved sights so clearly since her childhood years in Bradwell.

Later, as John held her in their cabin, she tried to express the strong emotions stirred by the sights and smells of the seashore.

"It is part of me that has lain asleep for too long. John, will we be located near the shore in New England?"

"That is my understanding."

"Then I know I shall be happy there!"

Rebecca awoke early, as usual, when baby Marry stirred in her arms. Sleepily, she fed the little one, allowing herself the luxury of wakening slowly. Then the entire room turned sidewise, the wall nearly becoming the ceiling, but not quite, then falling back, past and under where it had been. Alarmed that she might crush the baby, Rebecca braced herself against the bunk frame with two legs and one arm. With the other arm, she clutched the baby, who continued to nurse as if nothing had happened. John, his back against hers, was likewise bracing himself, while holding onto Joanie.

"Papa!" the child exclaimed in delight. "Ride!"

The ship continued to roll violently.

"John...can you reach my bucket? I put it under the bunk, just in case..."

As the ship almost righted itself, John placed Joanie next to her mother.

"Hang on to Joan, and I'll find it."

She heard him rolling on the floor, crashing into the wall. Then he was back with her bucket. Just in time. John tenderly rubbed her back as she vomited, then used the container, himself.

She coughed, retched, then told him, "Now you know what it's like to have morning sickness."

When he was able to talk, he said, "Between learning to yield myself to this ship, as we discussed the other night, and puking in the morning, I am become more like a woman every day. Me thinks I like this not at all!"

"If you want," Rebecca offered, "you may conceive, carry, and deliver our next child yourself."

"I don't think so."

"Give me the bucket again."

The couple passed an uncomfortable morning, and from the look of the other passengers when they finally were able to reunite in the main quarters, they were not alone in their misery.

The first mate stuck his head down through the hatchway, cheerfully asking, "All passengers ready for dinner?"

They moaned.

"Perhaps just some hardtack with a little ale. Doc will send it round right smartly."

Rebecca climbed halfway up the ladder to the deck, looking through the hatch at the sky. It was a uniform charcoal gray, with fast moving clouds passing them like coal smoke.

Catching the mate's eye, she asked, "Is it always like this?"

Smiling at the stupidity of landlubbers, albeit lovely ones, he answered, "The sea always changes; there are no guarantees. She's like a woman!"

"How can I get a bucket of seawater? There is washing I must do."

"Way!" he roared at a passing sailor. "Fetch this gentlewoman a bucket of seawater!"

"It'll only be a half bucket by the time you get it, Mistress. The chop is still too rough."

"Then I'll need two buckets!"

While the sea remained relatively calm, Rebecca and Goody Noakes washed out the children's diapers and the adult's linen, hanging them at the unoccupied end of the main quarters to dry. Seeing their industry, others of the group began, likewise, to attempt improving their appearance and comfort.

Rebecca had just finished some hardtack and ale, and gone back to the cabin to rest, when the ship hit another squall, more violent than the previous one. And this became the pattern. Day after day, the passengers endured storms, then cleaned up after. They ate a monotonous diet of "salt beef, salt pork, salt fish, cheese, pease, pottage, water grewell, good biskits, and six shilling beer." When they had the strength, they prayed and sang together.

On the Lord's Days, as well as in between, Roger Williams attempted to lecture, and it amused Rebecca to imagine that God planned the strategic moments for interruption when the ship seemed about to roll over completely, either side to side, or end to end. Roger would first blanch, swallow hard, then turn green. Sometimes he would vomit before continuing, sometimes after. Hardly ever would he accept defeat; he was a man of great determination.

One relatively mild but windy day in mid January, Rebecca was at her usual place on the ship's puke rail, upper deck, when wind gusts began tearing at the sails. Several sailors were aloft, working at the rigging. Suddenly, she heard a long, anguished scream from the spit sail yard, then a splash, then the frantic cry, "Man overboard!"

Immediately, sailors began casting out lines in the hope that the unfortunate one could grab hold, but in vain. The man was stunned first by the fall, and then by the numbing cold of the water. He was able neither to swim, nor to grasp the ropes, though he did float for some fifteen minutes.

As the man's head slid below the surface, Rebecca turned away in horror, looking toward the quarter deck, where the ship's officers gathered. An agonised cry emanated from Captain Peirce.

"Way, my son, my son!" he exclaimed over and over, hands clawing at his own face.

The other sailors seemed not to know what to do, but stood, staring at their captain in his grief. Quickly, Rebecca mounted the stairs to the quarter deck and guided the captain toward his cabin.

As they passed the first mate, she told him, "Keep Master Williams away from here; I have never known him to utter a comforting word to anyone. And bring a double tot of rum for the Captain!"

The mate, not knowing what else to do, said, "Yes, Mistress!" and obeyed her.

Rebecca seated the captain in a chair, placed a small hand on his shoulder, and began talking softly.

"Your son was a fine man. You must always remember him as he was this morning, strong, the wind in his hair, in love with the sea."

Captain Peirce moaned, "My missus. He was her only son. She'll never forgive me for losing him…"

"She'll understand. It was no one's fault. The Almighty simply called him home."

"But why? Why my son? Would God I had died instead!"

"More than one man has gone mad asking 'why.' That question has no answer. What is, is. the sooner we accept reality as God's will, the sooner we can go on with life."

Softly, Rebecca sang to him the *Twenty-third Psalm*, set to a lovely tune she had learned in Essex.

When she was done, the captain kissed her hands and murmured, "Thank you, Mistress. If I call for you later, will you come back, escorted, of course, to pray with me?"

"Yes, Captain!"

Rebecca turned to the open cabin door, and saw that John was waiting for her. He must have been standing there for a while, because, as he helped her back down the steps toward their deck, he breathed in her ear,

"You little heretic!"

"I beg your pardon!"

"Comfort is where you find it, I guess, but don't ever try to use what you said to him on Roger, or on anyone in Massachusetts! They'll have you in the stocks for heresy in a heartbeat."

"What happened to the liberty of conscience?"

"From what Winthrop, Jr. was saying, they haven't exactly achieved that yet. The liberty at Massachusetts Bay is only for those who adhere to Puritan thought."

"Now wait just a minute. You have brought me across half an ocean under false pretenses!"

"From talking to Winthrop at the Sempringham Conference, I deduced that he is a much more kind, reasonable, and intelligent man than either King Charles or Archbishop Laud. The small size of the community allows it to be governed for the benefit of most inhabitants. Considering the recent tortures and mutilations of ministers in England by the governments, I think that Massachusetts will prove a more fertile ground for true freedom to develop. And I understand that new settlements are formed there all the time. We'll simply locate the one which suits us best, or start our own."

The Throckmortons continued to pray with the grieving captain every day until the voyage ended.

On February fifth, Rebecca heard the cry for which she had been waiting.

"Land ho!"

She raced to the upper deck, looked in the direction indicated by the sailors, expecting to see a harbour, or dock, or at least a beach. She saw nothing. There were a few seabirds, which had been sighted off and on for several days.

Captain Peirce, who had become a friend, called, "Mistress Throckmorton! Would you care to look through the glass?"

"Yes!"

She gathered her skirts, demurely, to the side, and gracefully ran up the steep steps to the quarterdeck, then to the poop deck. The captain indicated a spot on the western horizon, and handed her his telescope.

"Close one eye," he directed. "Brace the glass here, and watch that spot until the sea lifts us up...so!"

"I see it! Something brown and black instead of gray! Praise God! How much longer do we have aboard?"

He answered, "It will seem a long wait to you. Depending on conditions ashore, your feet will tread dry land within a few days."

All morning, Rebecca watched the shore grow nearer, but could spend no more than a few seconds at a time on deck in the icy wind.

Later, she heard the leadsman begin to call off the depths as the water shoaled. They had thirty fathoms when the land was still half a mile distant, and Captain Peirce ordered the sails trimmed so that the ship might steer northwest along the coast. The sea was calm. Before an hour had passed, the sails were clewed up, and the *Lyon* dropped anchor in twenty fathoms, off a cove where a few wildly gesticulating figures, women from their dress, stood.

The small boat, or shallop, was soon over the side, with the first mate and four sailors as rowers. A large barrel of biscuit and a small keg of lemon juice were lowered, and the landing party set off.

While waiting, Captain Peirce explained to Rebecca that this was Nantasket, an outlying cape of the large Massachusetts Bay. The people on shore would give news of the colony, saving time in case there were changes in the supply delivery site. In an hour, the shallop returned, with instructions for the *Lyon* to unload more food and lemon juice, since the Great Cove before Shawmut, or Boston, was ice bound.

At dawn on February ninth, Rebecca heard the sailors hauling up the anchor, and felt the ship begin to move. She climbed onto the deck.

"They've put in a dock opposite the mouth of Mill Creek," said the mate. "We'll unload there."

Shawmut—Boston

By afternoon they approached the dock through the ice chunks floating in Great Cove, where a crowd of at least fifty people stood. Rebecca noticed a particular intensity in their eyes as more food stores were unloaded. Some tore into the barrels and bags immediately, while others rolled or carried containers away.

"They look as starved as the Barringtons did after Marshalsea," she thought. "And I'm sure that some of them have scurvy. Yech!"

By the time the passengers disembarked, only a few men remained to receive them.

A hearty, ebullient man, Governor Winthrop, came aboard to escort them ashore.

"Captain Peirce tells me you have had a rough voyage. If you'll just follow me, we'll get everyone in out of this wind."

The group proceeded up a dirt street toward the wood framed, thatched meetinghouse. First he showed the Ong and Perkins families, with their servants, into a double wide cottage.

"This is your temporary home. I have ordered some of the supplies brought off the ship for your use. Goodman Phelps, here, and his wife will see to it that your needs are met. Now, if you'll excuse us!"

Next to the meetinghouse was the parsonage, where they at last stepped in out of the cold. Winthrop quickly introduced the pastor, John Wilson, whose wife had not yet crossed the Atlantic. The Williamses would be housed with him. Quickly leaving, and passing the meetinghouse, the Throckmortons, Dudley, and Goody Noakes entered a rather larger cottage belonging to the Governor. Passing the lodging parlor, they caught sight of Winthrop's two young sons, Adam and Stephen, who, at eleven and twelve years, were avidly quizzing Captain Peirce about the voyage.

Rebecca nearly cried at the sight of the cozy guest chamber which they were to occupy. It was well warmed by its own fireplace, and a wooden bathtub stood ready for their use. Goody and Dudley went off to the servants' quarters, and Rebecca spent a glorious hour getting her family really clean for the first time in over two months.

When John was ready to go out, Rebecca, who had been staring into the flames, asked, "When are you going to give those to him?"

He slipped the packet of letters from John Winthrop, Jr. inside his doublet, and sighed.

"After supper. Peirce knows not to say anything about it until then. The two will suddenly find much in common, each having lost a son. It is painful to carry ill tidings. How is baby Mary?"

"She is well. She seems to have taken my strength, for I feel…"

Rebecca sank to the floor. Alarmed, John lifted his wife, laying her on the bed. He took her hands, then patted her cheeks. Weakly, she sat up.

"I'm sorry, John. I'm not used to the heat, or to the floor being still…I don't remember eating today, I was so excited."

He said, "Don't be sorry, just rest. Goody Noakes will bring you something to eat. I'll take Joanie out with me."

John left, and in a few moments Goody came in the door.

"Poor lamb," she clucked. "All this way you've held up, nursing the wee one, wasting away to a stick…We must build up your strength! Now here's some porridge, sweetened with tree sap, maple they calls it. And some ale!"

Gratefully, Rebecca let the older woman feed her, then sat up to drink.

"These people have happy hearts tonight," continued Goody. "They's drunk nought but water, and et the poor leaving's of the natural world for six months. How's we to live here if all the food be in England?"

"I, I don't know, Goody. The Lord will provide, surely!"

"Well, he ain't provided much for these poor fools over the winter!"

She went off, muttering.

Slowly, Rebecca lay back down, turned on her side to nurse Mary. Next winter was a long way off. It did not cheer her to consider it now.

John came in later, saying, "If you are able, the Governor desires your presence at table. They have never had a gentlewoman to grace the meals of this house, except those who visit."

"Of course, John. See if Goody can watch Mary and Joan while we sup."

Rebecca walked into the lodging parlor on John's arm. Captain Peirce, Governor Winthrop, and his sons all rose to their feet.

Introducing the boys, Winthrop explained, "You see that I am trying to teach them gentle courtesies in their mother's absence. I earnestly long for the day when she joins us!"

Rebecca responded, "Your sons do you credit. One of the last, most pleasant events our group experienced in England was our dinner with your son, John."

Winthrop said, "Then let tonight be the first of many, many pleasant events in your new world! May I escort you in to supper?"

Rebecca took his arm, needing the support more than she had realized. She shook her head slightly to clear it, and gratefully sank onto a bench at his right hand.

The governor said, "Today has been one of prayer and rejoicing, for the arrival of the good ship *Lyon* guarantees the survival of our colony. Praise God!"

As they began the meal, Rebecca recognized many of the foods to which she had become used aboard ship. There were exceptions. A strange kind of poultry, called turkey, some mussels similar to those available in Colchester, and dried berries cooked into a pudding made from flour brought on the *Lyon* graced the table. The governor and Captain Peirce drank a great quantity of ale.

At the end of the meal, the governor said, "This has been a happy day for me, but I think it is about to become a sad one. Am I correct?"

John and the captain nodded.

"Are there letters I must read now?"

John presented the packet, asking, "Would you prefer that we withdraw?"

"No. I shall want you to pray with me in my sorrow."

A few minutes later the warm and gentle Winthrop and his sons were mourning for their son and brother, Forth. Mindful of what John had told her about heresy, Rebecca did not offer any of the comforting words she had bestowed on Captain Peirce, who looked at her questioningly. Feeling safe with the *Twenty-third Psalm*, however, she sang it softly before the men began to pray. Then, suddenly feeling rather faint, she withdrew, knowing that the prayers would continue for a long time.

When at last John came to bed, she turned to him questioningly, "Is it all you had hoped, my darling?"

"I won't know until I have seen more of the colony for myself. I think you noted Winthrop's temperament; he remains reasonable even in the grip of strong emotion. I must survey the area quickly in order to write and send back my impressions and recommendations to Sir Thomas. He wants to send more planters if I think it advisable. But you, my dear, you seem so weak. How can I help to build your strength?"

"Don't fret about me, John. I have ever been healthy as a horse. I think that blessed warmth, food, rest, and relief from the constant motion sickness are all the physic I shall require. And your love."

He clasped her warmly, and they drifted into sleep.

Next day, John rose early, beginning his exploration of the seven hundred acre neck of land chosen by Winthrop for his settlement.

In the afternoon, Mary Williams came over to visit. Her eyes glowed, and she seemed livelier than she had for a long time.

"Roger has been asked to lecture to the Boston Church this week! There is a position open as Teacher to the Congregation, and he is the best qualified man here. Oh, 'Becca! If only they like his preaching!"

Rebecca smiled at her friend, and said, "We must pray that God's will be accomplished in this matter."

At supper, Rebecca listened while John and Governor Winthrop discussed the relative merits of the settlement's location.

"You are well positioned for defense," offered John. "The narrow neck limits access to attackers from the mainland. And your hills give a good view round-about, to warn your defenders in advance. The harbor is superb."

"But?" prodded Winthrop.

"You already know the problems. If each household uses three-fifths acre of trees per year, there is not enough timber on the neck to fuel a sizeable colony. The marshy areas breed disease, and must be drained and filled; the higher ground is too rocky and infertile. Boston will make a great port, but its wealth will always come from elsewhere."

Winthrop sighed, and said, "Then we must plan accordingly. We shall claim additional land to the west and south, and our people will gradually move inland."

"And how will you defend them?"

"We shall build palisaded log forts, as the natives do."

"I beg your pardon," interrupted Rebecca. "What natives?"

The men exchanged glances.

"Surely you've heard stories about the Indians who are native to the Americas," began John.

"Yes, but the Americas are very large. Exactly where are the closest tribes located?" she enquired.

Winthrop took her hand, and answered, "There are many Wampanoag, Narragansett, Pequot, Mohegan, and other Indian villages within a few days' journey of Boston, Mistress, but I assure you there is no reason to become anxious. We maintain good relations with them by trading. Also, they seem afraid to mingle with us, since our diseases have an especially virulent effect on them. Sometimes entire villages are wiped out within days by such ailments as measles."

"Then why are you so concerned about defense?"

John answered, smoothly seeking to change the subject: "We just want to avoid returning to moated castles as living quarters. Remember our week at Sempringham Castle, Governor? I've never slept so uncomfortably as in those dank, chill chambers."

"Nor have I," agreed Winthrop. Not picking up John's cue, he continued, "But surely, Mistress, you can see that any new town must consider its location in terms of defense."

"It's just that I heard some stories, once, about Jamestown…I never thought about being in the same situation as those poor people."

"You're not, I assure you. We have learned much about dealing with the natives since those primitive times. As long as we treat them fairly, we need have no fear."

Thereupon the Throckmortons joined the Winthrop family for vespers.

On the following morning, John left with Captain Peirce on the *Lyon* to deliver supplies to Salem, a settlement some twenty miles to the north, governed by John Endecott. When he returned, he confided privately to Rebecca,

"Salem is by far the better site—of course it was settled four years ago, and has been improved. They have a fayre harbor, and much closer access to woods and fertile land, fewer swampy areas. I am worried by their isolationist attitudes, though. They refused communion to Winthrop and the Boston settlers, as well as to baptize William Coddington's infant last year."

"Refused!"

"Yes. Their minister, John Skelton, has been requiring covenanted membership before he will extend the church sacraments to anyone. We delivered a letter to him yesterday from John Cotton, in England, reproving the church for this policy."

"Extraordinary. So how will you advise Sir Thomas?"

"Well, this is confidential, you understand. It is my opinion that he will realize a higher, quicker return on money spent at Salem than at Boston. But Boston, because of Winthrop's wise, patient guidance and groundwork, may pay better returns over the long term."

"So what will you do?"

"I should like to set up a mercantile exchange route along the coast. Any settlement with a decent harbor could serve as a base for this. I shall soon determine which seems the most pleasant location for you and the children."

"John."

"Yes?"

"Are there Indians at Salem?"

"They're not as close to Salem as to Boston."

"Good. I must confess to being a little afraid of Indians."

"My impression is that they are easier to deal with than Roger Williams."

"That is possible. I am a little afraid of him, too. Do you think he will be called as Teacher to the Boston Church?"

"Winthrop has recommended him, which makes it almost certain. It will ease my mind to see the Williamses comfortably settled."

"Roger will never be comfortably settled."

"Perhaps you are right, my prescient little wife."

The Throckmortons had ample opportunity to gauge the reaction of the Boston Congregation to Roger's preaching during the following weeks. The man's thorough knowledge of scripture, including mastery of the original Greek and Hebrew, combined with his fiery, impassioned speaking style, attracted a strong following.

February passed, and most of March, during which the prospects of the Throckmortons and Williamses seemed bright. Roger continued to prophesy in Boston several times each week. John, having evaluated the relative merits of owning property in Boston and Salem, purchased a lot containing a fresh water spring in the latter, more established town. He hired carpenters to begin building a cottage very similar to the one he and Rebecca had occupied at Hatfield Broad Oak. The main problem was in furnishing it, since everything had to be either handmade, of new world materials, or imported from England.

"Don't worry," John told his wife, "we'll get by as the others do. Before long, another ship will come with all we need."

He transported Dudley to Salem, giving him instructions to begin digging a garden, planting it with seeds and fruit trees brought on the *Lyon*, as well as corn, bean, and squash seeds obtained locally.

Privately, he advised Rebecca of the relationship between the magistrates of the two towns:

"Legally, because of the royal patent, Winthrop and his Council of Assistants have power over all other settlements in the Bay. This does not include Plymouth, of course. They have their own patent. Practically, though, the governor of each town is in control of his own area. There is a great deal of rivalry among the governors, and an amazing amount of ill feeling. Endecott, at Salem, having arrived here first, in particular is resentful of being ordered about by Boston, and tends to act rashly in response. I should not have settled on Salem as our home, except for two considerations."

"And what are they?"

"Endecott has offered me first claim to a truly advantageous site, to be named 'Throckmorton Cove,' as a home for my merchant fleet."

"And what else?"

"Winthrop begged me to go to Salem. He is concerned that some of Endecott's wilder views may lead to actions endangering the royal patent. The colony will fail if we lose support from England."

"Sounds exciting. So you are to function as a diplomat and drag on Endecott, to control him."

"Something like that. At any rate, I am in a natural position to keep Winthrop informed of developments in Salem. He trusts me, which is an honor."

"Indeed. So when am I moving?"

"How quickly can you pack?"

"Oh, John! Very quickly!"

"Then you shall be in your new home by April first."

Salem

And she was. Goody Noakes, Joanie and baby Mary all joined Rebecca aboard the *Lyon* near the end of March, after fondly bidding farewell to Boston.

Mary Williams had come by, looking happier than Rebecca had ever seen her.

"John Wilson is returning to England on the *Lyon* in a few days to fetch his wife. He is recommending Roger as his replacement Teacher to the Boston Church, and the Council of Assistants will vote on it soon. I shall miss you, but I am so excited for Roger!"

Governor Winthrop bade her a grave farewell.

"Your presence here has made me realize even more how much I long for my wife to join us in this place. John is fortunate to have such a lovely, brave spouse as you. If ever I can assist you in any way, you have only to ask!"

Rebecca was thrilled with her new house. John had taken care to copy the details of their Hatfield Broad Oak Cottage, although the windows were much smaller, especially to make her feel at home. Captain Peirce accompanied the family for her first sight of it, and promised to visit whenever he was in port.

In mid afternoon, she was alone in the lodging parlor, arranging some driftwood and shells on the mantelpiece, when she heard a soft tap at the door to the room. A silky, yet deep male voice addressed her:

"Mistress Throckmorton?"

She started, then turned to behold an exceptionally handsome man in embroidered velvet costume. He wore a narrow goatee and carefully trimmed mustache. The sword at his waist, combined with his military bearing made her assume he was someone in authority.

Taking a wild guess, she asked, "Governor Endecott?"

He stalked toward her with the meerest suggestion of a swagger, and took both her hands. She noted a golden ring in the shape of a skull on his left hand.

"The front door was open. I'm sorry if I startled you." He looked deeply into her eyes and went on, "I trust that we shall become close friends. It is difficult to govern well without knowing one's constituency. I came to enquire how I may serve you."

Stepping to the side to avoid his arm, which was encircling her, Rebecca said, "I should like someone to show me around town. John has been too busy attending to construction of his building at the wharf to do so; I have only seen the area between here and there."

"It would be my honor. Would you care to begin immediately?"

"Would you stay to sup with us afterward? My cook is excellent."

His face lit up, unexpectedly boyish.

"Oh, yes!"

"Let me fetch my shawl."

In a hurried consultation with Goody, Rebecca ordered a special supper, and received the information that this man was a rake, with an illegitimate son in Europe.

"We just arrived here, Goody! How did you pick that up already?"

"From Winthrop's cook, before we left Boston."

"Don't worry. I think I can manage him. We especially need his favor, for John's business."

Taking Endecott's arm, Rebecca toured the bustling town of Salem. As they strolled, he explained that Salem was situated on a sandy spit of land between two rivers, the Bass and the South. Broad Street connected the rivers where they came closest to each other. She was shown Endecott's own "fayre house," the temporary meeting hall, the jail, the stocks, the whipping post.

"All the most fertile land is located across the rivers, so each lot in town is sold with a separate farm. You'll need a canoe in order to see the rest of your acreage."

"Where does the minister live?"

"The parsonage is down by South River, at the end of Broad Street. I would introduce you to Master Skelton, the minister, but he has been quite ill lately, some sort of lung trouble. It is hoped that he does not develop tuberculosis, as did his late assistant, Master Higginson."

Rebecca spent the afternoon tactfully avoiding Endecott's passes. His lips had brushed her cheek twice, and, back in her own parlor, he was doing his best to manage a real kiss, when Rebecca heard the front door open.

"That must be John!"

She sprang up from the bench to fling open the parlor door.

"I'm sure you men have much to discuss, so I'll check on our supper."

Thanks to Goody's skill, the meal went smoothly; the Governor left before vespers.

Later, at bedtime, Rebecca said, "Don't make any arrangements or plans for me that require me to be alone with tonight's guest."

John smirked, asking, "Was he living up to his reputation?"

She threw a pillow at him.

"You could have warned me! It's a wonder I wasn't ravished in the parlor this afternoon."

John embraced her.

"I think you were in no danger. Chasing women has been something of a hobby for our Governor, even before his wife died. I am always complimented to discover that other men concur with my taste in women."

"You haven't a jealous bone in your body, have you?"

"Oh, I believe I have one or two. Are you content in your new house?"

"Very content, John. Just don't invite Endecott to move in."

Little Joan, now nearly two, had some trouble adjusting to the new quarters, as she had not aboard ship or at Winthrops. Rebecca was at a loss what to do about her, since she cried at meal and bed times as if rejecting her new situation. Goody soothed Rebecca, giving her opinion that the child was "just at that contrary age." Unfortunately, that age lasted for months, trying the family's patience.

Daily life was settling into a routine, but was disrupted one cold, rainy evening early in April. Supper was nearly ready when there came a loud knock at the door. Dudley answered, and came into the lodging parlor, a quizzical look on his face. Closing the door behind him, he said softly,

"It's Master and Mistress Williams, and they's all wet and bedraggled, like!"

John rose, striding swiftly to the entry.

"Set two more places for supper," Rebecca called to Goody.

As Mary entered the parlor, Rebecca took one look at her woeful face and embraced her friend.

"Come with me. We must get you out of these wet things."

Mary indicated a roll of her own clothing: "My own are all wet, I'm afraid."

"I have a gown to fit you."

Closing her bedchamber door, and searching for clothes for Mary, Rebecca whispered, "What is amiss?"

"Roger has refused the Teachership at Boston."

"What?"

"He has his reasons, but they make little sense to me. The Council at Boston is very insulted by the way he rejected their offer. I am so worried! How will we survive without that job? He says he will dig a garden and plant food, but he doesn't even know how to do that, owns no land…"

Rebecca was more than a little worried, also, but tried to soothe her friend.

"We must have faith. God will provide for us all. The two of you may stay with us until things come right."

The two women returned to the lodging parlor, where Roger glared somberly into the fire. Rebecca gently took Roger's arm in both her hands.

"Master Williams, you must guard your health. I have laid out dry clothes for you in the other room."

She steered him toward the bedchamber, and closed the door after.

"Dudley, will you collect all the wet clothes and take them to Goody? She may hang them in the storage chamber to dry."

Rebecca swept back into the lodging parlor, to find John embracing Mary, who was weeping. His face was wrent with pity for their friend. Rebecca helped Mary to a bench, and began repeating her assurances.

"It will all come right, you'll see!"

When Roger rejoined them, Rebecca rose.

"Master Williams, will you join us for supper?"

She took his arm and led him to a bench in the dining parlor, seating him to her right. John followed with Mary, who sat across from Roger. John then sat on the only chair, at the head of the table. Taking their guests' hands, as did Rebecca, he led a short grace. The four ate in silence for a time.

Finally, John said, "I apologize if I am disturbing your thought, Master Williams. I think you would not have repaired hither if you did not trust us somewhat. If you tell us what has brought you so precipitately, no pun intended, perhaps we can serve you better."

Roger glared at them all.

"I had no choice. I durst not officiate to an unseparated people."

John touched the man's arm, seeking his gaze.

"They offered you the Teachership?"

"Yes."

"And you rejected it?"

"I did. They have not cut loose from the Church of England, with all her corruption. Let them repent, and become a pure church!"

John inhaled sharply.

"And how did they respond?"

"They bid me move out of the parsonage immediately, which I would have done soon anyway. Perhaps it was because they became angry about the other things I revealed to them."

"Such as…?"

"I informed them that they have no authority from God to enforce the first four commandments, and I refused to join in communion with them."

Rebecca said, "But Master Williams, surely you realize that everyone here regards the decisions of the Boston magistrates as the will of God."

Roger snarled at her scornfully, "It has been obvious to me since the Sempringham Conference that God may speak *to* John Winthrop, but not *through* him. Preaching God's will is my calling. Obeying it should be his. In this new world, King Charles and Archbishop Laud have no authority over us. Of this I am very sure."

John, controlling himself with an effort, said, "This is my household, and, being under my roof, you shall at least listen to what I say. You did not visit the Tower with me in December, where Richard Chambers was incarcerated for speaking before he thought. The worst pity of the entire episode was the anguish experienced by that fool's family. You are quite close to putting your precious wife through the same sort of experience, or worse. The magistrates of Boston are living the book of *Romans*, Chapter 13. They believe their power to be ordained of God. If you continue to insult them, make no mistake, they will break you."

"You think me a fool."

"I think you are less than cautious. We are strangers in a strange land, and must tread lightly here for a time. I have no doubt that God is guiding your thought as well as your speech, but I question your timing."

Roger said, "You are the only friend I can trust to tell me truth as you see it. I thank you. If you will shelter us for a short time, I shall, more tactfully, seek another position serving the Lord."

"My view is that by sheltering you, I likewise serve Him. You may stay as long as you preserve the peace of my household."

The two couples ended the evening with prayer, but no one rested well that night.

Rebecca had never led such a holy life as she did during the following months. Living with Roger Williams meant that every activity, every word was examined for vestiges of sin. Luckily, needing breathing space, she hit upon an idea. Roger for some reason longed to till the soil as a yeoman would. Being of the gentry, he had never had the opportunity to do so. Rebecca turned Roger over to Dudley, who nearly worked the man to death. The pair of them broke new ground, planted, cultivated, and harvested the Throckmorton's crops that year. In addition, they hunted in the woods, fished, gathered berries and other wild foods, and tended the Throckmorton's growing collection of livestock. When the weather was inclement, Rebecca presented Roger with paper and ink she had purchased, and shut him into John's study. In this way, she attempted to keep him out of trouble.

Watching the Williamses together, Rebecca realized that Mary did not see in Roger the child who so frequently needed firm guidance. Mary therefore could not provide that guidance, but only suffer from its lack.

On April twelfth, John came home for dinner at noon with a very cheerful countenance.

"Wherefore are you so happy?" asked Rebecca.

"Just wait!"

Near the end of their meal, John said, "I had an interesting conversation with Governor Endecott this morning."

Receiving little response, he went on, "It seems that Salem Church earnestly desires a qualified Teacher to replace the late Master Higginson."

"Oh, Roger!" breathed Mary.

John continued, "But they are backward about making an official call, being fearful of rejection. With good reason, I might add."

"Master Williams, do you know anyone who might be inclined to officiate as Assistant to Master John Skelton, to the unseparated people of Salem? Perhaps such a person would be able to influence them toward separation at a future date."

Roger said, "I have prayed long and earnestly about this matter. I cannot justify wasting my training and strength prophesying only to your crops and barnyard. I would be willing to accept the Salem call on a temporary basis, until God shows me what to do next."

John said to Rebecca, "Prepare extra for supper. There will likely be five additional guests."

An hour before supper, the oily Governor Endecott and four of his assistants filed into the lodging parlor, followed by John. Roger, dressed in his best black woolens, knelt before them as the Salem council placed their hands on his head. Solemnly, they prayed, marking his official call as Teacher to the Congregation. Mary wept with joy as Rebecca hugged her.

Soon they all adjourned to the dining parlor for a fine meal of Goody's best efforts. This was followed by a season of hymn singing, scripture recitation, and prayer, during which the governor kept playing kneesies with Rebecca under the table. She even saw Mary squirm away from him as the incorrigible rascal tried holding hands beneath the tablecloth. Rebecca held her breath lest Roger should notice and begin a harangue against the sins of the flesh.

The Williamses continued to live with the Throckmortons because Roger viewed the position as temporary. He longed for a Separatist pulpit. Understanding, John did not press him to live elsewhere, especially since the man and his wife more than earned their keep by working about the house. This, he saw, helped Rebecca so that she was able to spend precious time with their daughters.

Besides, God was blessing John financially, as he managed the entire colony's supplies. His family enjoyed good health. Everything was wonderful except for one thing: he had no son. He never spoke of this to Rebecca, but he could see her disappointment grow as, month by month, there was no sign of another pregnancy. At length, John wisely consigned this burden to the Lord, concentrating his energies on the building of the colony's mercantile exchange.

On May 18, 1631, both John and Roger signed the Freeman's Oath, and were admitted as freemen of Massachusetts Bay Colony.

After harvest, Roger came to John privately to voice his continued discontent with the Salem church.

"Can you get me transport to Plymouth?" he wanted to know. "I believe they share more of my opinions than the people of Massachusetts Bay."

John arranged for Roger to be shipped to Plymouth, and soon the man was back, eyes aglow.

"God be praised!" said he. "Mary and I are welcome to join their fellowship."

Once again, Rebecca tearfully bid her friend goodbye. Rebecca had heard, but refrained from telling Mary, that there definitely were Indians living at Plymouth. It was one place Rebecca had no desire to visit.

A year and a half passed, bringing change to the colony. John, his successful mercantile exchange backed financially by Sir Thomas Barrington, ordered a small pinnace built. After hiring a captain and crew, he used it to transport supplies and passengers between settlements. The colony's population was growing rapidly; famine in England made the reports of easily grown crops of New England enticing to potential settlers, who came in droves. Supply ships from England were increased, and John organized the collection of goods for export. Tobacco, furs, and wood products such as shingles were sent back in increased amounts.

"Empty ships returning to England destroy the profitability of the colony," he preached to anyone who would listen. "Proving our value to the Crown is essential to our survival."

One afternoon in August, 1633, John came in the door for supper.

"'Becca! I have a surprise!"

In the entry, Rebecca was overjoyed to be embraced by Mary Williams, who was quite obviously with child.

"Mary! What a blessing to see you!"

Mary smiled shyly, saying, "I have missed you terribly."

"Come in to supper; it's ready."

At table, Mary filled them in on Roger's latest activities.

"He's been Assistant Minister to the Plymouth Congregation. And he has a new ministry, to the Indians! He has learned their languages, and written a *Key* to them. Someone," she looked at John, "must have arranged a line of credit for us, because Roger was able to obtain an inventory of trade goods for the Indians of the Cape. By selling the furs they bring, and by tilling our acre of land, we have been able to more than survive, even to save money."

Rebecca, eyes wide, asked, "Mary, have you seen Indians?"

"I have. Several times Roger has brought them home, to return hospitality he received from them, and also to succor their sick. He has made a friend of the great Narragansett chieftain, Canonicus."

John took Mary's hand.

"When do you expect your little one?"

"Any day, I'm afraid…We thought it best for me to have the baby here, because, well, we're moving back to Salem."

"When is Roger coming?" asked Rebecca.

"Not until after harvest. He would lose the income from his labor, otherwise."

John said, "You must tell us. Has Roger quarreled with Governor Bradford and Elder Brewster?"

Mary answered, "He's written a *Treatise* condemning the methods Englishmen have used to claim Indian lands…he says King James told 'a solemn public lie' in claiming to be the 'first Christian prince' who had discovered this area, and that the king is guilty of blasphemy 'in calling Europe Christendom or the Christian World.' In addition, Roger used the book of *Revelation* to show that King Charles is on the side of Antichrist, and that he has 'drunk of the whore's cup.' Needless to say, Brewster and Bradford are not pleased. They consider the land at Plymouth to be their gift from God."

John squeezed her hand, dropped it, and looked at his plate.

Mary, tears in her eyes, asked, "How many times must he invite the anger of those in authority before he learns restraint?"

John looked up.

"Roger has a curse which I share. He sees alternative sides to every issue. Unfortunately, unlike myself, he feels obligated to throw his opinions violently in the faces of those who are most likely to be offended. You notice, he's not at my door, berating me for evilly accumulating riches. I would forgive him, and delight his heart by quoting scripture in rebuttal. But the beleaguered magistrates of these tenuous colonies feel threatened by Roger's attacks. Mark my words, sooner or later they will deal with him harshly."

Seeing that Mary was seriously frightened by his words, Rebecca looked at John and shook her head slightly. John was silent.

Mary whispered, "What can we, what can I do?"

Rebecca and John took her hands.

"We can pray for him," began Rebecca. "We can look for ways to influence and guide him through his folly."

John added, "It's more than folly. Roger is carrying some very important concepts, including that of liberty of conscience, to their extremes, testing whether those concepts are tenable for society. As Sir William Masham used to say, Roger has a divine madness, or genius about him."

Rebecca concluded, "What the three of us must do is to surround him, like a wayward child, with love. Our love may be his only refuge on this earth."

Rebecca was awakened, at about midnight, by soft knocking at her bedchamber door. Slipping out of bed carefully, trying not to awaken John, she opened the door to find Mary slumped against the wall in the passageway.

"Do you know of a midwife?" she gasped.

"Oh, Mary! Let's get you back to bed. Goody Wilson, just around the corner, is supposed to be the best midwife in Salem. I'll fetch her!"

"Don't, don't leave me."

"I must, for a minute. I'll get Goody Noakes to fetch the midwife."

She left the room to find John standing outside.

"I'll fetch Goody Wilson," he said. "Too bad Roger isn't here. He deserves comeuppance in the style which Lady Barrington used on me."

"Perhaps you can give it to him later," said Rebecca. "But make sure you back it with scripture!"

It seemed forever until the midwife arrived, and another forever until the baby was born. The child was strong, but Mary, with her small bone structure, had a difficult, exhausting delivery. For three days, Rebecca and Goody Noakes tended her, fearful that she would not live. By then, they had secured a wet nurse for the child. But because Mary implored them, they allowed the baby to nurse from her for a short time each day. Thus, they were able to bring in Mary's milk, so that she could feed the babe herself as she became stronger.

John had taken the pinnace to Plymouth. When he returned with Roger, it was obvious that he had gone to some trouble to put the fear of God into the man. Roger flung himself on the bed at Mary's side, weeping, and Rebecca withdrew.

Later, he appeared at her open sitting room doorway.

"Master Williams. Do come in!"

He looked at her, his face a mask of guilt.

"I know you hate me, just as the others do," he began. "It is hard for me to be so indebted to those by whom I am despised."

Rebecca stood up.

"My feelings for you are directly connected to the way you treat my best friend. Mary is a gentle soul, made to be loved."

Roger confessed, "Her love is the only dear thing on earth for me. But for that, I should seek to abandon this life."

"I seem to recall that you view such an attitude as sinful."

His eyes widened, and his voice quavered as he said, "As you must know, I am very sinful."

She replied, "God forgives us our sins. Even I am capable of forgiving much. But that will do no good if you fail to forgive yourself."

"Forgive myself?"

"Yes, one of my heretical ideas. But try it; it may make you feel better. And in the mean time, think long and hard about how your words and actions affect Mary and your little one. By the way, did you name the baby?"

"Yes. We'll call her Mary."

Rebecca stepped close, and grasped Roger's arm gently. Then she kissed his cheek.

"God bless you, and your family, Master Williams!"

He turned to leave, then back to face Rebecca again, rubbing his head thoughtfully.

"Mistress Throckmorton, do you ever employ clubs to help sinners see the error of their ways?"

"Why, Master Williams, I hardly know what you mean by that!"

He left.

At the end of harvest season, Roger returned from Plymouth with the proceeds of his year's labor. From Master Higginson's widow, he purchased the late Teacher's house on Broad Street, which included an acre of land, and moved his family there.

During his time at Salem, Roger Williams made an earnest effort to become a more loving husband and father. One could say he even enjoyed the baby, playing with and fussing over her. But he was also apt to forget his family at times, going into episodes of prayer, study, and writing during which he spoke to no one. At such times, Mary and her child left him alone, coming to visit Rebecca.

Medford

In November of 1633, John invited Rebecca to accompany him and Governor Endecott on a trip to Medford, not specifying why. As they disembarked, Rebecca heard a friendly voice addressing her.

"Mistress Throckmorton! You are in for a splendid surprise today!"

It was John Winthrop, Junior, who had been living to the north, at a new settlement he had founded, called Agawam, later Ipswich, Massachusetts, since March of that year.

"I am?"

"Yes! If you will just follow me…"

"I'll be happy to follow if you protect me from Endecott."

He laughed.

As they approached the nearby shipyard, Rebecca saw a group of dignitaries waiting, headed by Governor Winthrop. A new, sixty ton pinnace rested on a ramp, ready for launching. Glancing at the hull, Rebecca was mystified to read her own name painted there.

The governor said, "In gratitude to John Throckmorton, who has done so much to advance maritime merchandising in these waters, I christen this good ship after John's wife, Rebecca!"

He poured a mug of ale onto the ship's bow as it slid into the water. When the pinnace righted herself and floated, everyone cheered. Rebecca found herself being kissed by several of the more exuberant Puritans, among them the two John Winthrops.

In a teasing aside, John, Jr. told her, "We just couldn't bear to call it the 'John,' and the painter couldn't spell 'Throckmorton.' Besides, ships should be given female names."

"And why is that?"

"Because they're so unpredictable."

"No, no, son," interrupted Governor Winthrop. "It's because they're so lovely and alluring." Taking Rebecca's hand, he added, "I don't know where my son learned how to talk to women. Perhaps I should send him back to university."

Diplomatically, Rebecca took both their arms as they walked back to the wharf. On the way, Governor Winthrop explained that the *Rebecca* would carry the trader, John Oldham on an expedition to the Connecticut River on behalf of the Bay Colony.

"This has been a lovely surprise. I am so glad to know everyone appreciates John's efforts," she said as they kissed her goodbye.

Salem

Fall of 1633 passed, then winter. John was often absent, sailing up and down the coast, furthering his business interests. He was able to employ Roger Williams, since Roger spoke the various Indian languages fluently, as part of his trading operation. Roger also had continued to till the soil, on his own property across South River. Apparently, he derived deep satisfaction from this manual labor, despite the hernia he had developed while carrying away rocks from the new ground he was breaking. Roger once commented to Rebecca that the heavy work left his mind at peace, open to new ideas.

"That's a scary thought," she told him, but he did not find her reply amusing.

John Skelton, the tubercular Minister of Salem church, invited Roger to fill the pulpit more and more often.

One evening in February, 1634, John returned from Boston by boat. Rebecca, seeing his grim face, quickly helped him out of his boots and into warm slippers. There was a knock at the door, and Dudley admitted Roger Williams.

"I got your message," he said. "Is something amiss, John?"

John said, "You tell me. Why would a band of West Niantic Indians murder the captain and crew of a Virginia trading vessel?"

"Where?"

"On the lower Connecticut River."

"It almost certainly has to do with the Dutch fort on the Connecticut. They are habitually cruel and careless of relations with the Indians. The West Niantics are close allies of the Pequots, with whom the Dutch have made trouble. Who was killed?"

"Captain John Stone."

Roger turned to the fireplace, gazing into the flames in silence.

Finally he said, "I pled with him to turn from his drunkenness and fornication...I fear he died in his sin."

"He was drunk when killed, according to the report."

"I must ask my Indian contacts about it. When did this take place?"

"In November, after the Court of Assistants banished Stone from the Bay because of his undisciplined behavior. The report just reached Boston...But that's not why I called you tonight, Roger. Winthrop and the magistrates have read and made a ruling concerning your TREATISE against the Patent.

"And?"

"They will consider it a private document, and therefore not dangerous, if you will take an oath of loyalty to the king."

"To that unregenerate pile of corruption?"

"The same."

"I'll have to think about it."

"Think well. Do you recall the penalty for treason?"

"They wouldn't dare lay hands on me!"

"They could ship you back to England."

"Oh, no. Anything but that. I'll not go back while Charles and Laud, in league with Satan, rule the country."

"Roger, I beg you to remember that your family is dependent on your restraint. Yet I know you must do as God directs."

"I will leave you now."

"Good night, Roger."

John and Rebecca ate silently that night. Even the antics of little Joan, at four and one-half years, and of Mary, at three, failed to lift their hearts.

At bedtime, Rebecca said, "That's where you want to go, isn't it, to the Connecticut?"

"'Becca, I have been to the Connecticut."

She turned very pale.

"When? Why?"

"Remember when I was gone for three weeks last fall? I went by boat, scouting the region for Winthrop. Subsequently, we decided against trade there, just yet, because of the trouble between Dutch and Pequots. Stone just wouldn't listen."

Rebecca turned her back on him.

"How could you go there, putting yourself in danger that way?"

Her voice was cold.

John said, "For one thing, the Indians were not murdering whites at that time. For another, we never went ashore, never got drunk or fell asleep with Indians aboard, as did Stone. Do you think me a complete fool?"

"No. No, I don't know what to think."

"'Becca, come here."

She didn't move. Then she felt his arms around her, his lips on the back of her neck.

"'Becca, Heart's Lady," he murmured. "I returned from the Connecticut to you. Turn from your anger, to me."

She turned, hiding her face over his heart.

"Just hold me, John."

"You know," he commented, "that's something I never have been able to do."

The following Lord's Day, Rebecca attended church as required by law. She had carefully chosen her costume for dull colors and poor quality cloth. As one of the wealthiest women of the town, she had to be extra careful of her dress in order not to be suspected of pride and ostentation. She entered the building, as always, head down, through the separate women's entrance, and sat with Mary Williams near the back. After the singing from Ainsworth's Psalter, which she always enjoyed, and prayers from several elders, which she did not enjoy, Rebecca prepared to daydream through another of Roger's sermons. She briefly wondered what his topic would be, then groaned inwardly as he announced the text, *I Corinthians*, Chapter 11.

"He's after us women again," she thought, keeping her eyes lowered. She let her mind drift away to Bradwell, to Hatfield Broad Oak, to London…Suddenly, her head came up with a nearly audible snap.

"'…for her hair is given her for a veil.'"

Roger was quoting verse fifteen.

"And notice, in verse five, Paul says, 'every woman that prayeth or prophesieth with her head uncovered dishonoreth her head,' then in verse three he says, 'the head of the woman is the man' and 'the head of every man is Christ.' Therefore, I submit to you today that women who pray, or attend church without their entire heads and faces being covered by a veil, willfully dishonor Christ. They thus cannot be regenerate, and we, the men of Salem church, will not commune with them."

He stopped. A shocked silence filled the meeting house. Roger had just consigned every woman there to Hell.

Rebecca sat through the rest of the service as though chained to her bench. She thought of Lady Joan, so far away, and of Mistress Chambers, of the other strong women she had known.

After church, walking home with John, she said, "You're taking me to Boston tomorrow."

"I am?"

"You are."

Boston

They sailed across the bay early next morning, and Rebecca said, "I shall return to the pinnace by noon."

"Where are you going?"

"I am visiting the Pastor, John Cotton."

"You can't do that. He studies scripture and prays twelve hours each day, sees no one except at church."

"He'll see me."

Briskly, she walked through the town up the street toward the meeting house. She stopped for a moment outside the parsonage, donning a thick veil, then rapped loudly at the door. A servant answered, then started, taken aback by the veil.

"I must see Master Cotton, at once!"

"Does he expect you?"

"Do you expect to see tomorrow?"

The man vanished inside. When he returned, he said, "If you will follow me…"

Rebecca entered the lodging parlor, sat on a hard, wooden bench. A few moments later, a woman entered the room.

"I'm Sarah Cotton," she began. "Richards says you have asked for my husband. He actually sees no one…"

"I'm John Throckmorton's wife, Rebecca. I'm here on behalf of the women of Salem Church. In a sermon yesterday, Master Williams consigned to Hell every woman of his congregation who was not veiled as I am today. I thought your husband might have somewhat to say about it."

The woman stared at Rebecca thoughtfully, then said, "I'll see if he can spare a moment."

John Cotton entered the room as if waking from a deep sleep.

"Mistress Throckmorton, have you been born again?"

"Yes, Master Cotton."

"Then you need not hide behind a veil, here, or in church. I shall preach a sermon to that effect, this very week. Perhaps Thursday would be appropriate timing, when Endecott is in town. I shall travel to Salem, if necessary, to set Master Williams straight on this matter. In the mean time, the best course is for the women of Salem Church to act in concert. If all leave their veils off, Master Williams will have no power over you."

"Thank you, Master Cotton."
"Good day to you, Mistress."

Salem

Rebecca left, thoughtfully removing her veil as she stepped into the street. By mid afternoon, she was back in Salem, and paid a series of calls to women living in different areas of town. Each agreed to help spread Cotton's message. By nightfall, every woman in town had heard it. Not one of them, including Mary Williams, wore a veil to any of the five regular church services during the following week.

Roger continued to preach against them. He refused to serve communion to or pray with them, but they all acted as if stone deaf on this matter. Before long, Governor Endecott returned from Boston with word of Cotton's opposing view. Then John Cotton hit town, the wrath of God incarnate. He stalked to the meeting house, Bible under his arm, and began to prophesy. The women smiled. The men frowned. Roger remonstrated, but Cotton won. The issue became moot. No matter what the result of this great debate, Salem women were not going to be veiled in church.

Roger did not take defeat gracefully. He maintained his right not to pray with his "unregenerate" wife, so would not say grace or eat while she was in the room. Rebecca found out that Mary was taking meals alone in her kitchen, and spoke with her privately.

"Is this the way you want your life to continue?"

"No."

"What are you going to do about it?"

"Well…it has occurred to me that if Roger won't eat with an unregenerate, he probably should not sleep with one, either."

"Go on."

"'Becca, what would happen if I move out to the barn?"

"I'm not sure. How long are you prepared to stay there?"

"As long as it takes."

"Mary, if you do this, you risk much. Think it through."

"I shall."

Mary spent the remainder of that week in the barn with her baby. Luckily, the spring weather was mild. Rebecca, visiting the wives of church elders, saw to it that Roger was asked daily by several different influential men whether there were some personal problem with which they could assist him. On the night before the Lord's Day, Mary moved back into Roger's house and bed. Next morning, he made a brief statement to the congregation that God had spoken to him. The scripture concerning the covering of women's heads remained clear, he said, but as long as women wore their usual caps to church, God would consider that they were willing to adhere to His commands. The entire gathering breathed a sigh of relief.

The spring of 1634 melted into a memorably hot summer. The death of Salem's minister, John Skelton, from tuberculosis, seemed imminent. Roger was officially invited to replace him. Once in full control, after Skelton's death in August, Roger ceased trying to restrain himself. Every sermon seethed with his favorite radical themes, most of them dangerously controversial. He never lost opportunity to preach Separatism from the Anglican Church, claiming that the vestiges of papism retained in its rituals and symbols threatened all adherents with damnation. Rebecca never quite followed his logic in this, but as it made little difference to her daily life, she remained unconcerned.

"Have you seen this?" Mary asked Rebecca one day in September. "Roger says it's the new dress code passed by the Court of Assistants in Boston, but I cannot make out all the words."

Rebecca took the paper and read aloud,

> The Court taking into consideration the great, superfluous and unnecessary expenses occasioned by reason of some new and immodest fashions, as also the ordinary wearing of silver, gold, and silk laces, girdles, hatbands etc., has therefore ordered that no person, either man or woman, shall hereafter make or buy any apparel, either woolen, silk or linen, with any lace on it, silver, gold, silk or thread, under the penalty of forfeiture of such clothes.
>
> Also, that no person, either man or woman, shall make or buy any slashed clothes, other than one slash in each sleeve, and another in the back; also, all cutworks, embroidered or needlework caps, bands and rails, are forbidden hereafter to be made and worn, under the aforesaid penalty; also, all gold or silver girdles, hatbands, belts, rugs, beaver hats, are prohibited to be bought and worn hereafter, under the aforesaid penalty.
>
> Moreover, it is agreed, if any man shall judge the wearing of any of the forenamed particulars, new fashions, or long hair, or anything of the like nature, to be uncomely or prejudicial to the common good, and the party offending reform not upon notice given him, that then the next Assistant, being informed thereof, shall have power to bind the party so offending to answer it at the next court, if the case so requires; provided and it is the meaning of the Court that men and women shall have liberty to wear out such apparel as they are now provided of (except the immoderate great rails, long wings, etc.).

"Whew!" exclaimed Mary. "I'm in luck. Roger hasn't ever let me wear anything like that. But it's an excuse for you to put away some of your old things from England, and replace them with new, plainer attire."

"I suppose that's the bright side of it, all right," said Rebecca. "I still have one or two pieces from my trousseau...See! Here's that fabulous gold embroidery we did together. I may never wear these sleeves again, but I'll always treasure them."

"The young girls are sure to complain," said Mary. "So Roger is going to do another sermon on modesty of dress."

"How about Endecott?" snickered Rebecca. "He'll suffer from this worse than any girl!"

"He'll probably use the clause that allows him to wear out old clothes. I wonder if the thing was written with him in mind!"

"Mary, you have a suspicious nature!"

Roger spent some of his pulpit time on modesty of dress that fall. One Lord's Day in October, however, he apparently felt the need to bring his lofty Separatist ideals home to the Salem congregation. Deep in a discussion of the ravages of papism on the European continent, he paused, and Rebecca heard a gasp from the crowd. Looking up, she saw that Roger had pulled forth a crumpled English flag from inside his doublet.

"You think Satan's papism touches England not?" he cried. "Here is its symbol: The blood red cross of St. George, stamped upon our flag, the footprint of the Devil!"

With a roar, the excitable Governor Endecott rose to his feet, drawing a sword. He advanced toward Roger, who took a step backward. Snatching up one end of the banner, Endecott slashed at it with his weapon.

"We'll cut out the vile print of Satan!" he exclaimed.

The two men wrestled clumsily with cloth and sword for several minutes. When they were finished, Endecott brandished the mutilated fabric aloft.

"My troops shall march under this henceforth!" he announced.

"Praise God!" cried Roger.

"Praise God!" responded many of the congregation, most of them men.

Walking slowly home from church, still stunned by what they had witnessed, John asked, "Do you require anything from Boston, my dear? I believe I will be there tomorrow—business, you know."

"I shall write a greeting to Mistress Winthrop, John. Perhaps you could be good enough to deliver it to her."

"Yes."

"Master Winthrop has never been overly fond of the British flag, has he?"

"It's never been displayed at Boston, to my knowledge. They only use it for military exercises."

"Such as those recently scheduled."

John sighed, then spoke softly and urgently.

"The council has received word from London that our Patent will be revoked. A governor-general will be sent here to enforce the king and archbishop's will on the colony. If a British official arrives to find mutilated flags and congregations running amok, we could be in serious trouble."

"We?"

"Anyone who is or has been in authority."

"Oh. I think I'll speak to Mary Williams tomorrow, as well as the other women."

"Good idea. After the veil episode, I have new respect for their influence."

The next day, Rebecca called at the Williams home. When Mary opened the front door, a strong, sweet odor wafted into Rebecca's face.

"Mary, what on earth..." she began.

Her friend, finger on lips, led her past the sitting room to the kitchen.

Dropping onto a bench, eyes wide, Rebecca gasped, "Mary, there are Indians smoking pipes in your front room!"

"I know. They are Narragansetts; Canonicus is the sachem. Roger is negotiating with them for land."

"What land?"

"I'm not sure. It's located to the southwest of Plymouth, along the Seekonk River...Roger calls it our retirement home."

"He plans to live there?"

"As God wills. He no longer desires to live under the British flag."

"So I gathered. Do you realize how dangerous this all is? I once saw the gallows at Tyburn gate in London. The floor of it is slanted, so that the blood from the disembowlings flows away..."

Mary put her hands over her ears.

Rebecca shook her gently.

"Mary, do you want him to live?"

"How can you ask that?"

"Easily. Unless you find strength to speak sense to your husband, you could lose him like that."

Rebecca snapped her fingers.

"I'll do what I can. He seems driven to self destruction."

"Indeed. And what is that odor? It's not tobacco."

"Hemp, I think. They smoke the dried plant, and see visions..."

"I'm leaving."

Rebecca made the rounds of the most assertive women that day, making her point in no uncertain terms. They all promised to influence their men as much as possible.

The flag desecration controversy, however, was not as easily resolved as the veils issue. It dragged on for more than a year, since most ministers of the Bay Colony, including John Cotton, sided with Roger and Endecott. Luckily, the governor-general's ship, when launched in England, was defective, and he did not show up in Massachusetts.

Rebecca became pregnant in November of 1634. In February, she told John about it, and they celebrated privately.

By March of 1635, the Bay Colony magistrates were looking for ways to make themselves look patriotic to any observers who might report on colonial activities at London. They thought themselves especially clever to replace the Oath of Allegiance, required only of property owners, with the Residents' Oath. This would be required of any male over sixteen years of age living within their boundaries.

Opponents of the idea were swiftly squelched, until April, when Roger began to prophesy against it. He opposed requiring potentially unregenerate souls to swear in God's name. He called this taking the Lord's name in vain, a sin both for those swearing, and for those requiring them to swear.

At home, after Roger's first sermon on this topic, John just shook his head.

"They are losing patience with Roger. He is being summoned to Boston every other month to explain his position on this or that. He promises not to preach on a topic, then breaks his promise. I am at a loss to protect him...Winthrop has no power to do so, since he is not governor any more...we must leave it in God's hands."

Rebecca asked, "When the worst comes, have I your permission to shelter Mary and the babe?"

"By all means. She is not at fault in any of this."

"Did you realize she is with child again?"

"No. How did you both manage to get pregnant at once? No, wait, I don't want to know."

"It wasn't our idea, believe me."

The summer was not as horribly hot as the one of 1634, but there came one stifling morning in August when Rebecca, suffering in the stagnant, humid air, begged John, "Please take me out in the pinnace. At least on the water I can breathe."

"The weather looks bad, according to my captain. He advises hugging the shore."

"I can't stand this. John, if you want me to bear your children, you'll have to find me some fresh air to breathe."

"All right. Get your things, and we'll sail over to Boston. There are plenty of places to put in along the way, if necessary."

Rebecca saw the pilot frown as she stepped aboard.

"Come, now, Captain Sparks," she said. "Surely you won't begrudge me a few hours' respite from the heat!"

"Master Cotton named his child Seaborne when he took his pregnant wife to sea," he commented. "If we're not lucky, you may have to call yours Storm-borne, or Shipwrecked, or some such name."

Rebecca laughed. "The Almighty watches out for me. If He wills it, we'll make Boston safely. If not, at least I'll not suffocate ashore."

Rebecca was delightfully comfortable for the first hour. She stood easily at the rail, delighting in the fresh wind, John's steadying arm around her shoulders. Then the wind and waves became rough, the skies filled with lightning, and she began to feel ill.

Going below, she sat on the bunk in John's tiny cabin with a bucket. She didn't vomit, and was surprised, until she realized that what was making her ill was the onset of labor.

John looked in on her.

"Too much fresh air?" he asked, then grew concerned as he saw her hands tighten around the bunk rail.

"How long to Boston?" she gasped.

"Not long at all."

"Do you know of a midwife?"

"Yes, the merchant William Hutchinson's wife is supposed to be the best in the colony."

Boston

As soon as they docked, four of John's sailors carried Rebecca carefully, through the rain, on a litter. They walked for about fifteen minutes, to the corner of Sentry Lane and High Streets. John beat vigorously upon the door.

A child answered, followed by a tall, handsome woman who took one look at Rebecca and said, "Bring her this way," then, "Hold that litter beside the bed."

As the woman stretched forth muscular arms to slide her onto the bed, Rebecca looked into a pair of steel gray eyes which exuded strength. As the sailors left, the midwife looked at John.

"I presume you're the husband?"

"I am John Throckmorton, and this is my wife, Rebecca. We live at Salem."

"I prefer that you wait elsewhere while I tend your wife."

John replied, "I'll go across the way to Winthrops'." He approached the bed, took both Rebecca's hands, and smiled reassuringly as he said, "I shall pray for you. May it please Almighty God to give you safe deliverance, and to reunite us when this day is over."

Rebecca saw his tears begin as he turned away. Glancing at Mistress Hutchinson, she noticed a grim smile on the woman's face as she stared after John.

Remembering her patient, the midwife said, "You have a good husband. Let us work together to bring him a strong child. My name is Anne, and I am your friend."

Rebecca had never been tended so skillfully through a birth. From the draughts of herb tea to the application of warm and cold towels, Anne's every action was calculated to ease the mother's discomfort. Most valuable and strengthening of all were the things the woman said, all designed to boost Rebecca's confidence and desire to triumph in delivering this baby. Early that afternoon, a lusty son was born.

Wrapping and putting him to nurse from Rebecca immediately, Anne said, "Nursing him will help expel the afterbirth and slow your bleeding. Drink this tea of horehound. It will help, also."

Rebecca said, "With my first, all the physic I had was a tot of rum."

"If it were available, I would give it to you now. Strong drink is not easy to come by in the Bay Colony."

"If I'd insisted, John could have got me some, off one of the big ships. It's amazing what he can find, with his connections. I just have to be careful not to flaunt that fact before the other women."

"Why?"

"It would not do to make enemies here. The entire colony seethes with petty jealousies and intrigue. The favorite pastime is identifying and rooting out sins, whether one's own or others'."

"A pity. Seems like time wasted to me."

"I agree."

Rebecca remained at Hutchinson's until evening, then was able to walk slowly, during a break in the rain, to Winthrops' house across the street.

As they went out the door, an exuberant John asked Anne, "What is your usual fee?"

Mistress Hutchinson replied, "I just learned from my husband who it was that helped him obtain the lot and set up his store when we arrived here last year. You owe me nothing. Your son comes to you as freely, yet through as much suffering as your salvation. Treasure them both."

"Thank you, Mistress."

The Winthrops eagerly greeted them, Margaret taking the child from Rebecca.

"What is his name?" she asked.

Rebecca looked at John.

"We'll call him Freegift," he replied. "Never let it be said that the Throckmortons lack a sense of humor."

Margaret put Rebecca to bed with the baby, and fed her a nourishing meat stew. Hesitantly, knowing Rebecca would be tired, she asked, "How was she?"

"Who?"

"Mistress Hutchinson. As a midwife, I mean."

"The best I ever had. Very kind, and skillful."

"That's what I'd heard. It's too bad she's so, you know, outspoken."

"What do you mean?"

"She has offended and threatened many of the men in town by her forthright manner and unorthodox opinions."

"Sounds like our problem child of Salem."

"I beg your pardon?"

"Roger Williams."

"Well, perhaps. But the fact that Anne is a woman daring to oppose authority has made the men fear she communes with evil powers."

"Impossible. She seemed as regenerate as you or I, calling on the name of Jesus to help me today."

"She holds religious meetings at her house several times each week. She prophesies like any minister you ever heard, reports visions, reinterprets scripture to suit herself. Surely she is possessed at such times."

"Have you witnessed this?"

"Well, no. John will not permit me to attend."

"I should be careful of calling a person possessed of evil while her actions remain kind and good. Master Williams, for example, without going into gruesome detail, is no saint. I cannot envision him being one-tenth so kind to anyone as Anne was to me today."

"I must let you rest. I only wanted to hear what you thought. If Mistress Hutchinson continues on her current course, however, there will be trouble, mark my words."

"We, likewise, expect trouble with Master Williams. In fact, now he is encouraging adults not to pray with unregenerate spouses and children. His definition of unregenerate is so broad as to include many of the holiest saints."

"Remarkable. I guess we don't realize how lucky we are to have John Cotton and John Wilson ministering to us at Boston."

There was a tap at the door, and Margaret opened it. John came in, and she said, "I'll be across the hall if you need anything tonight. Otherwise, we'll talk tomorrow."

John approached the bed, gingerly lifting baby Freegift.

"Another healthy one, my love," he murmured to Rebecca. "And the potential that our name will continue after us in this new world."

"He is strong," said Rebecca, "and, curiously, I feel stronger this time than I did with the girls. Anne's care spared me much of the exertion I had before. I think the herb tea made the delivery go faster. At any rate, God has blessed us. We must thank Him."

"Indeed."

The thunderstorms had continued off and on all day. That night they worsened, the winds screaming across the bay and onto the land. Many trees were down, and the more flimsy buildings collapsed. Boats were beached, and a few people were drowned by huge waves while trying to secure their property near the docks. Captain Sparks, reporting to John that the pinnace still rode safe in the harbor, expressed his opinion that the storm was, in fact, a hurricane. For three days, violent storms continued to pound the Bay Colony, and the Throckmortons fretted about their daughters at Salem.

On the fourth day, the storms let up, and they presented Freegift at the Boston Church for baptism. John Winthrop and William Hutchinson stood as godfathers, Margaret Winthrop as godmother. John Cotton performed the ceremony, and they all rejoiced together afterwards.

On the fifth day, they sailed home, amazed at the storm damage, and delighted that it did not affect their own property.

Salem

After greeting her daughters, and introducing them to their new brother, Rebecca was ready to settle back into Salem life, until Mary Williams came to call. Holding baby Freegift, Mary turned to Rebecca and said,

"Roger has abandoned his pulpit."

"Why?"

"Endecott and the elders have stopped defending him to the Council at Boston."

"But I thought…"

The Magistrates refused to release for use by Salem some valuable land at Marblehead until the church softened its Separatist stand. Endecott is a practical man; Roger has him in deep trouble already over the flag desecration issue…Roger says those loyal to God may worship at our house…"

"Oh, Mary, I'm so sorry. If only we had been here the past few days…maybe John could have helped."

"Roger will just have to take his medicine this time, I'm afraid. He has been summoned to the October 8th Court in Boston. I am so worried that they'll do something terrible to him."

"Do you want John to go with him? He has some legal training, as well as friends on the court."

"Do you think he would?"

"I'll ask. The other side of it is, will Roger want John's help?"

"I don't know. Perhaps the best thing is for you two to come to supper, and we'll talk. Is tonight too soon?"

"No. We'll be there."

The upshot of the evening's conversation was that Roger really didn't care what the court decided. God had spoken to him, given him a mission among the Indians. He would leave civilization, live in the wilderness.

"What about your family?" John had asked.

Gazing at the ceiling, Roger answered, "My wife has often spoken to me of love. If she loves me, she will show it now by following me and supporting me in my dark hour. If not, then let her follow her own unregenerate way."

John remonstrated, "Roger, look at her. She's due to deliver your child in October. Have you no pity? She and your little ones cannot live in the wilderness through the winter, no matter how much she loves you."

Roger whined, "I am tired of debating everything all the time, everywhere, with everyone. I am tired of standing alone when God has forced me to speak out. You have spoken more than once about the liberty of conscience. Did you mean what you said?"

John replied, slowly, "I believe that a man has a duty to do no harm to others. Other than that, he should be able to think, say, and do anything he believes to be right."

Roger asserted, "You'll never be permitted to live that way in Massachusetts."

"Perhaps there is no place that free on earth."

"Yes, there is. I have been there!"

"Please explain."

"There is land in the Americas not covered by Satanic patents. I rented some of it, on the Seekonk River, for my lifetime from the Narragansett sachem, Canonicus."

"But that land is claimed by the Crown."

"Do you think King Charles is going to build a palace on it? It is still open to whomever settles it first. And as to being free, how do you think the trader Oldham and the settlers who joined him are behaving on the Connecticut River? The Council is furious, but it cannot touch them, because they are beyond Massachusetts boundaries. I shall repair to my land very soon, where I shall build a sanctuary. Those who seek true freedom from tyranny, including you, my beloved friends, may join me there."

On October 7th, John took Mary, then hugely pregnant, and Roger to Boston in the pinnace. He had convinced Roger that he would be honored to accompany him to his court appearance on the following day. The three would stay at Winthrop's. Rebecca remained at home with her children, as well as little Mary Williams, and spent most of three days in prayer for her friends.

John returned home on the evening of the ninth. Rebecca had been with the baby, and did not hear him enter the darkened lodging parlor. When she looked in, to bank the fire, he was kneeling in prayer, much as he had appeared that night long ago in the manor chapel. Touched, she approached and knelt at the bench beside him, setting down her candle. As he grasped her folded hands, she trembled.

"Mistress, I do not mean to frighten you."

"I am frightened, none the less. What is it that you must tell me which requires prayer beforehand?"

"You read me very well. I think I must always pray before I tell such a woman how much I love her."

He pulled Rebecca close, kissing her cheek, then her mouth. This time, she did not run away.

Later, as she lay in his arms, he said, "There is much to tell, 'Becca. Roger is banished from Massachusetts Bay in six weeks, and has an injunction of silence laid on him."

"It will kill him to refrain from prophesying."

"We shall see. He and Mary have a new daughter."

"Oh, John!"

"Mistress Hutchinson tended Mary. It was a very difficult delivery; there was some question of whether either she or the babe would survive. Roger was prostrate with anxiety."

"I can't imagine that."

"Nevertheless. After the birth was accomplished, and his sentence pronounced, he prayed for a season with Mistress Hutchinson. This seemed to restore his resolve, and he became quite defiant. He has named the new child Freeborne. He swears he will not return to England, but I think I convinced him of the necessity to keep that information quiet."

"When will the Williams family return to Salem?"

"In a few more days. Mary should be strong enough by then to travel in the pinnace."

"John, is this the end, or a new beginning for Roger?"

"Time will tell. But now I have a problem."

"What is that?"

"I have an overwhelming desire to accompany him, to the freedom of the wilderness."

"Have you gone mad?"

"Possibly. There is, of course, an economic advantage to being the first settlers in an area. The Seekonk is strategically located on a large bay between us and the Dutch...I have seen it. We could end up with the best of everything by following our divinely mad minister."

"Or we could end up with nothing."

"There is always risk. But I have met with Canonicus..."

"*What?*"

"...and he seems in control of the Seekonk area. Roger has his guarantee of safety. Winthrop is interested in the venture, wants Roger to secure land for him, also."

"Winthrop would leave the Bay?"

"Not as things now stand. But this would be an investment, a safety net if things turned against him more than they have been already."

Snuggling against him, she said, "Let's get some rest. It sounds as if you have a great deal of work ahead."

During the next month, Roger quietly mortgaged his Salem property. With the proceeds, he purchased a quantity of supplies and trade goods, storing them in John's warehouse.

As Rebecca had predicted, it was impossible for Roger to refrain from prophesying. He did so only in his own house, but people sought him there, to hear what he would say. Twenty of them, including John when he was in town, attended the services Roger held there. This group identified themselves as a Separatist congregation, in defiance of the law.

Regular services continued at Salem's meetinghouse without Roger. Before long, a minister was sent over from Boston, Hugh Peter, who had recently arrived from England. Plump, coarse, and red faced, Peter preached with fanatic zeal. He immediately began nudging the wayward congregation away from Separatism, back into the Anglican Puritan fold.

Because John and Roger wanted to protect Rebecca and Mary from charges of Sabbath breaking, the women were sent to Peter's services. Often, they bore the heavy burden of public castigation, as the rabid Peter preached against them and their husbands. Often, after these humiliating events, John Endecott would escort the women home, sympathy in his every word and gesture. He had been removed as governor for a year because of the flag desecration, and apparently identified with their position.

One morning in early January, 1636, Rebecca had been visiting Mary Williams, and was preparing to return home for dinner. Roger was in his study, upstairs. As Rebecca walked toward the front door, she heard a commotion in the yard, followed by vigorous pounding at the portal. Some instinct told her not to answer it, and she turned to see Roger descending the staircase. In his arms he carried two pillows and a down comfort.

He held up a hand to Rebecca: "Wait!"

Spreading the comfort and pillows on a couch in the parlor, he lay down and wrapped himself up.

"Now open the door!" he hissed.

Rebecca obeyed, seeing that Mary was too frightened to do so. A very large, red faced Puritan brushed past the women, strode into the parlor, and glared at Roger.

"Master Williams. I am Marshal Penn, officer of the Court of Assistants at Boston. By their command, I am to fetch ye thither."

Roger groaned, "'Truly as the Lord liveth, and as thy soul liveth, there is but a step between me and death.'"

"Ye shall come with me!" The man advanced toward Roger, clearly intending to remove him by force.

"Stop!" Rebecca had no idea what to say next, but she felt an inspiration coming. "In the name of the Lord Jehovah, I abjure thee that thou 'touch not His anointed, and do His prophet no harm'!" Raising her right hand high, palm outward, she covered her eyes with her left hand, and continued, "I see thy death, on a day not far hence. When thou standest before Almighty God, dost want Master William's lifeblood on thy hands?"

"Mistress, if ye affirm that removing Master Williams from his bed will endanger his life, I shall refrain from doing so."

Rebecca heard uncertainty in the man's tone, and lowered her hands.

Choosing her words carefully, she responded, "There is no doubt that removing Master Williams to Boston endangereth his life. 'Whoso sheddeth man's blood, by man shall his blood be shed.'"

When Penn had left, Rebecca turned to Mary, who had turned a ghastly white. Seating her friend in the parlor, Rebecca told her, "Breathe!" After a few deep breaths, Mary looked better, but still terrified.

Roger was sitting up, face buried in his hands. Standing, he embraced Rebecca.

"You have saved me," he said. "I never expected your support."

"I have not saved you. Only God can do that, for you are still wanted at Boston. Winthrop told John they intend to send you back to England by the next ship; it must have come in to port."

"That will never happen. Mary, where is my knapsack?" Moving toward the kitchen and storage areas, Roger called back over his shoulder, "I'm off for the Seekonk. Massasoit and Canonicus will shelter me."

Rebecca held Mary, who sobbed softly. When he was packed, Roger returned to the parlor, carrying his two daughters. Placing them on the couch, he drew Mary toward them by the hand. Taking her in his lap, and gathering the little ones, he began to recite, in a more loving and tender tone than Rebecca had ever heard him employ:

"'Let not your heart be troubled; ye believe in God, believe also in me…I go to prepare a place for you. And if I go and prepare a place for you, I will come again, and receive you unto myself, that where I am, there ye may be also."

Rebecca turned to go home, but Roger saw her and said, "Once again, Mistress, I leave my family in your care. Can I depend on you to protect them?"

"To my last breath," she replied, and went out the door.

Three days later, Rebecca heard the beat of a drum, and glanced out her window toward the street. An officer and ten soldiers were marching rapidly by.

"Captain John Underhill, of Boston," she thought. "Now there's a rascal! If half the tales be true, he seduces more than his share of maids...of Boston! Why are Boston soldiers marching up our street, toward...Mary's house?"

She began running, down the stairs, out the door, without her cloak, through the snow, running to the Williams home. As she drew near, she heard screams, and recognized Mary's voice. Her side aching, she ran still faster, to reach her friend, who lay huddled outside her door in the snow.

"My baby!" screamed Mary. "My little girls!"

Looking up, Rebecca saw Captain Underhill bringing the children out. She stood to receive them.

"Mary, let's go!"

From the sounds, she knew the soldiers were ransacking Mary's house and barn, searching for Roger. She wanted to get Mary out of sight of the destruction, and out of view before it occurred to Underhill to take Mary into custody. Rebecca staggered toward home, carrying the two children and supporting Mary. Nearly there, she heard running feet and looked back to see John. His face showed more anger than she had ever seen there. He lifted Mary, and they proceeded on to their dwelling.

John placed Mary on the couch in the parlor, and asked, "Are you injured?"

She looked at him in terror, as if she had never seen him before. When she spoke, it was with a child's voice:

"'Becca? 'Becca, help meeee..."

Rebecca, entering the chamber with the children, felt the hair rise on the back of her neck at the sound.

"Mary, I'm here. Here's Freeborne and little Mary. They're safe. Are you hurt?"

The child's voice came again, "My, my arm. The soldier grabbed me..."

John had turned, leaning against the wall and was listening, arm over his eyes.

"These are the ones who pay the price of liberty," he said, to no one in particular. "The innocent and weak."

He went out.

Goody and Rebecca tenderly cared for Mary for weeks, trying to restore her sense of security enough for her to return to reality. They were somewhat successful, but Mary flatly refused to return to her house, and in fact never so much as looked at it again. The neighbors straightened the place, bringing the clothing and other valuables to Throckmorton's. The mortgagor foreclosed, and the property passed into other ownership.

One night in late February, John sat at supper, silent, listlessly toying with his food. Later, he sat in the parlor, staring into the flames. At bedtime, Rebecca came to him, sitting on the floor and laying her head on his knee.

"When are you leaving?"

He stirred, too used to her insights to be surprised that she knew the reason for his melancholy.

"Tomorrow. I expect to be gone many months, something I swore I'd never do. I have to take Roger his supplies, and I expect to stay to help him build his 'sanctuary'. Then I'll return for you."

Withdrawing a heavy pouch from his doublet, John dropped it beside her.

"Here is the rest of our money. I will put it in the strongbox for you. The total is two thousand gold guineas. Winthrop, Jr. is prepared to handle sale of all my property, if necessary; that will yield at least another thousand.

My darling wife, if I never come back, you have enough to return to England or to remain here. In either location, this is a substantial widow's dower, enough to attract a fine gentleman..." His voice broke as he continued, "I can't bear to think of you being alone, with no one..."

"Worry not, just come back," she said, wishing to lighten his heart. "You know I expect my brother Thomas from England very soon. I always seem to be surrounded by loving care. Let us banish sorrow, and delight in each other one last time."

John carried her to bed, and was gone before she woke at dawn. Rebecca mourned his absence almost as if he had died.

On the following Lord's Day, Rebecca attended morning and afternoon services alone, as Mary was still exhibiting signs of mental instability. Rebecca sat in her usual place, at the back, her heart leaden in her chest. She moved her lips, but could not sing. She bowed her head, but was unable to pray. As the sermon began, she steeled her ears not to hear, in case it contained another diatribe against Roger and John. Eleven other men had followed Roger to the Seekonk, and were often included in the merciless public castigations. At the end of the last service, before the benediction, Hugh Peter paused.

"I have an announcement," he said, smiling maliciously. "The following men *and their wives* are hereby excommunicated from the Holy Anglican Church, for their disaffection and estrangement from the same."

He began reading names:

"Roger Williams. John Throckmorton. Thomas Angell. William Arnold. William Harris. Stukely Westcot. John Green. Richard Waterman. Thomas Joseph. Robert Cole. William Carpenter. Francis Weston. Ezekiel Holliman."

At the reading of her husband's name, Rebecca rose. She left the meeting house, never to return. The other wives whose husbands' names were called did likewise.

"I'm damned to Hell. I'm damned to Hell."

The words kept running through Rebecca's brain. She felt as if her skull would burst apart, and terror was making her heart pump as if she had run a long way. Her mind sought the usual avenues of comfort and found them all blocked. John…gone. Prayer…rendered useless by her new religious standing. God's Holy Word…just words now. How could she return home, resume her position as gentlewoman, mistress of household, mother, friend? Her world was unmade.

She wandered down to the river bank, where she turned east, toward the sea, toward England. The sound of footsteps followed her.

It was John Endecott.

"Pray do not be alarmed, Mistress. I mean you no harm."

"No one can harm me more than has already been done today."

"You have my sympathy."

Somewhere, in another part of her mind, Rebecca realized that Endecott's sympathy was a dangerous thing. But her present agony of spirit made her extend her hand.

"Walk with me," she begged. "I want the sight and sound of the sea to cleanse my soul."

They strolled down the river bank to the sea shore, where she gathered colored rocks and shells, played with horseshoe crabs. At dusk, when the wind became cold, Endecott folded Rebecca warmly inside his cloak, against his chest. His questing mouth caressed her face and neck, as his hands slowly massaged her back. She turned her face away from him; he brought a hand up to turn it back. Then she saw his skull ring.

Pulling away, Rebecca said, "Damned though I be, I am no adulteress."

"Of course not, Mistress. The situation has its charm; I was merely trying to comfort you."

"You have given me all the comfort that you may give. Now I would return to my children."

Gravely, he escorted her home.

"I'll not ruin your reputation by stepping inside," he said. "But when loneliness becomes too great a burden, come to me; we can find Paradise, together. And if you wind up in Hell, be assured I'll be there, too."

This made her smile, grimly, but she vowed to face the night by herself. Going into John's study, she looked beneath the papers in a drawer, and located his jug of rum. It was full, and she poured herself a large tot. When it wore off, at about midnight, the nightmares began. She woke herself, screaming, but no one else heard. Rebecca poured more rum, and drank until she passed out.

Late in the morning, she sat in the sunlit parlor, aching head in her hands. She heard Goody answer a knock at the door, followed by a familiar male voice asking for her.

John Winthrop, Jr. entered the room. He took one look at her face, and knelt beside her chair.

"'Becca, I came as soon as I heard. John would not want you to face this alone. We can find a way to fight this thing, to appeal it…"

Bitterly, she replied, "I'm not alone; Endecott offered to accompany me to Hell."

"'Becca, listen to me. Hugh Peter has no great standing in the Anglican Church. We can get someone to overturn this, this farce."

"I no longer believe in the Holy Anglican Church. The faith I misplaced there has betrayed and damned my soul. Therefore, I relinquish it."

"You're not making sense. You are understandably distraught, but you must avoid saying things like that."

"I think I know when I am making sense. And what I just said is what one would expect from an excommunicant. I'm sure you have noticed that nowhere in the Bible is included the word 'Anglican'. There is only 'the church.' There is even a 'church in the wilderness' mentioned. I think that soon I shall become one with that church, and abandon any other."

"You must promise me you will not speak like this to anyone else. You put yourself and the children in danger. I will get word of what has transpired to John. I think that's all I can do for you."

"Indeed. I have drunk gall, and have yet to find it sweet."

After he had gone, Goody sent the children in to the parlor, hoping to lift her mistress' heart. Joan, at six, was dark and handsome like her father.

"Mama! Let's play, 'I See An Indian,'" she demanded.

Mary, five, was fair, looking very much like her uncle, Job. Rebecca nearly cried whenever the child unconsciously adopted one of his mannerisms. Little Freegift, at seven months was crawling all over, and had to be restrained often. With them came little Mary Williams, two, with her father's ice blue eyes and her mother's sweet nature. A few minutes later, Mary herself came in, carrying baby Freeborne. Rebecca rose, took Mary's hand, and drew her into the center of the room. The women sat on the floor with their children, and were cheered by the mingling of joy and love.

By evening, Rebecca and Mary had settled on a course of action. They and the other excommunicated wives would meet together at each of the five weekly worship times until they removed to the Seekonk. This would unify them as well as give some protection against charges of Sabbath breaking. Together, they would read scripture, sing hymns, and pray fervently for the men.

A few weeks later, brother Thomas arrived from England, bearing greetings from all their friends and relatives. Rebecca was thrilled to see him, but immediately noticed a shadow of grief in his eyes.

After vespers on the night of his arrival, she said, "You must tell me about it, Tom."

He sighed, and asked, "Is it that obvious? I did not want to add to your burden of woe. I married last year, a lovely girl, called Helen. We have a child, Edward, named for Papa. But she died giving him life. The agony of losing her nearly destroyed me."

"Where is your baby?"

"I cannot bear to look at him. I left him with our sister Elspeth to raise; she's well off, has no boys. I gave her enough money to care for and educate him. But I don't know if I'll ever try love or marriage again—the risk of pain is too great."

"Nothing of value comes without risk."

"You are right. I'm just not strong enough for it now."

Dudley planted and harvested their crops for 1636, with the help of a boy Rebecca hired to assist him. Between the food he provided and the money John had left, the two families lived comfortably. They received several "All is well" messages from John, usually through John Winthrop, Sr. But by winter, it was as if the earth had swallowed him, and Rebecca fought melancholy on a daily basis. Only Thomas' steady faith in John's eventual return kept Rebecca from despair.

Then, one winter evening, daughter Joan came in the back door.

"I see an Indian!" she called.

Rebecca admonished her, "We have not time to play. Wash your hands for supper."

"But Mama, I really *do* see an Indian!"

Noting the child's serious tone, Rebecca asked, "Where?"

"Among the dead grape vines, in the arbor."

Mary Williams, hearing this exchange, opened the door and stepped out.

"Mary, wait!" called Rebecca, but the woman did not stop.

Rebecca looked after her, terrified. She saw the red man talking, gesturing, and then Mary clapping her hands in glee. In a few moments her friend was back, with news.

"Since the ice in the harbor has broken up early, John will bring the pinnace for us February first. We are to be packed and ready to go. He may come at night, so as to avoid questions from the authorities. We are to notify the other women; boats will be provided for them, also."

"Are you sure? How could you understand him?"

"I know a little Narragansett. He knows a little English. We managed."

"Praise God! I can't wait to leave this accursed town. I'd rather live among savages than here any longer."

On the last night of January, 1637, Mary, Rebecca, and Goody put the children to bed as if nothing unusual was afoot. Then they, with Thomas and Dudley, began to pack. All the clothing, bedding, and other precious textiles went first. Then cooking and eating implements were stacked. All was loaded with the lighter garden tools into a wagon Dudley had drawn up to the back door. Furniture would be left behind; Dudley had gradually sold off or slaughtered for table use all their livestock. Late into the evening they worked. When all was complete, Thomas, Mary and Rebecca sat, praying together at the dining table.

Before long, they heard soft footfalls in the passageway. The dining parlor door swung open. There stood John and Roger with fingers to their lips. Rebecca had never participated in such a quiet rejoicing. Before she could step toward John, he had taken one long stride and caught her into a tight embrace. He had lost a lot of weight, and his muscles, evidently from hard work, felt like iron. The thumb which caressed Rebecca's cheek was calloused. As John turned to greet Thomas, he swung Rebecca with him, not willing to let her go even for a second.

As they turned, Rebecca saw Roger on his knees before Mary, who stood, his face buried in her skirts. He was sobbing brokenly for her to forgive him for the trials he had brought on his family. Mary was stroking his hair, crooning softly to him as she would to one of the children.

After a minute of this, Roger stood up, wiped his eyes, and quoted:

"'Thus saith the Lord, Let my people go, that they may serve me. Thou shalt bring them in, and plant them in the mountain of Thine inheritance, in the place, O Lord, which Thou hast made for Thee to dwell in, in the sanctuary, O Lord, which Thy hands have established.'"

"What he's trying to say," quipped John dryly, "is that it's time to go. The other families are on their way. We have three pinnaces waiting at the wharf."

The group proceeded by torch light. Dudley and Thomas drove the little wagon. Rebecca carried the fat toddler, Freegift, in case he woke; John and Goody each carried one of the girls. Roger and Mary brought their daughters. At the gangplank, Roger stopped them.

"Shake off the dust of your feet," he said.

They obeyed him.

He quoted: "Whosoever shall not receive you, nor hear your words…Verily I say unto you, It shall be more tolerable for the land of Sodom and Gomorrah in the day of judgment, than for that city."

"All aboard, Roger," said John. "No need to waken the town."

They heard rapid footsteps, and a tall, cloaked figure approached out of the gloom.

"John? Roger!" It was Endecott.

He first addressed Roger: "You saved New England with your negotiations last summer; you have prevented an Indian alliance which could have pushed us all into the sea. My soldiers, with great effort and loss of life accomplished far less last year than you did alone, sitting quietly at Canonicus' fireside. Whether Winslow and Winthrop realize it or not, we owe you a great debt."

Turning to John, he asked, wistfully, "What's it like? What is it to be really free?"

"Come and see!" offered John.

"No, no. I'll be governor here again soon…my destiny has ever been Salem, peace, you know…but I'll always wonder."

He turned toward the women, kissed Mary, and embraced Rebecca rather more closely than she liked.

He breathed into her ear, "I trust, Mistress, that you will not be needing my companionship in Hell?"

"That remains to be seen," she replied. "Yours is the best offer I have received for sharing my damnation."

"May God Almighty have mercy on all of you!" he intoned, as he backed into the mist. "And have no fear; there will be no pursuit."

The Boat

Rebecca, her family and friends boarded the three small ships, and the sailors cast off more quietly than she thought possible. John guided the Williamses to one little cabin. Thomas, Goody and Dudley were each shown to bunks, and the three sleepy Throckmorton children ensconced in another. Then he led Rebecca, who was growing quite cold, to their cabin. He set their candle into the wall, and turned to his wife.

"There's only one way to get warm, my dear…"

She stepped into his arms, and let him set her on the bunk. They helped each other out of heavy boots and cloaks, and lay, shivering at first, under a thick down comfort.

"I'd forgotten how beautiful you are," whispered John. "Your eyes, your face, your wonderful, soft body…I've tried a thousand times to hold your image in my mind, but I never could get it right. Now I long to hear your voice. Do you recall how you used to hold me and tell me all that was in your heart?"

"You are all that is in my heart tonight, John. The past year has been an agony of longing for you. We must never separate for so long again. Please."

"Never again, my love, never again."

The next day, Rebecca managed to speak with Roger alone.

"Master Williams?"

"We call each other 'Neighbor' now," he responded gently. "But you may call me anything you like. I owe you much."

"My spirit is deeply troubled, and no one has been able to help me."

"Have you confessed and repented of all sin?"

"Yes."

"Then what could be amiss?"

"I tend to believe everything I am told by a minister in church."

"And you believe Hugh Peter?"

"Yes. That is, my mind does not believe him, but my spirit remains in terror. There are nightmares, sometimes, visions of Hell…How can I be free in our new home if my spirit lies chained in Salem?"

"I shall pray for you. My own thought at this time is that those whom God has predestined for salvation cannot be damned to Hell by anyone, however much that person might want to do so."

"Have not the ordained magistrates and ministers of Massachusetts Bay power from God over the souls of their constituents?"

"Perhaps. Notice, however, that you are no longer a constituent of theirs. My observation has been that the harder they try to enforce their idea of good on others, the more evil they produce. I have been in their position; I know how hopeless is their task, no matter how admirable their intent."

"How will things be any better in the sanctuary to which God has led you?" Roger embraced Rebecca, then released her.

"We shall live in love, one for another, as Christ intended. I do not pretend to know anything more. I have obeyed God in establishing this free haven for those persecuted for conscience' sake. Others will have to help organize and govern it. The result, I trust, will be a new manifestation of God's providence. For Providence is the name of our new home. It is founded on faith and love."

"Master, that is, Neighbor Williams, I feel as if layers of my spiritual identity have been stripped away. First my prayer book, then the ceremonies and symbols of faith, now my church itself have all been taken away. Will God still know my name after all the changes, in Providence?"

Roger looked at her with more tenderness than she would have thought possible even a year ago.

"I would know the proud, brave, and honest Rebecca anywhere, with or without her prayer book. Our Father in Heaven knows and loves you better than I ever could."

Rebecca turned her head away as the tears came.

"Thank you...I still covet your prayers."

Later that day, watching Mary Williams, Rebecca saw the beginning of her friend's transformation. Being treated with love and respect by Roger was causing the woman's spirit to blossom. This translated into new grace and confidence beautiful to see.

The three little ships sailed southeast all morning. At midday, two of them split off from that occupied by the Throckmortons and Williamses, heading east around Cape Cod. John explained to Rebecca that he and Roger had business with Governor Edward Winslow at Plymouth Plantation.

Plymouth

Ashore in Plymouth, they were guests of the governor at supper. John and Roger were urging him toward unity with the other English settlements against the aggressive Pequot Indian Nation.

"It's not our fight," Winslow replied. "We have ever lived in peace with the natives here. When we did have a problem, with the French north of Salem at Kenebeck, Winthrop refused to help us. And when we moved onto the Connecticut River, it was English of the Bay, not Indians, who drove us out. You, of all people, Roger, should be slow to help Winthrop. He's banished you."

Roger responded, "Winthrop never meant me any harm. He was only protecting his precious Patent, just as you have done. His actions surely were God's will, since they resulted in establishment of our fayre new home, Providence. You really must come for a visit..."

John put in, "More to the point, Governor, is that the Pequot aggressiveness threatens us all. Our colony is protected by the surrounding peaceful Narragansetts; yours by the Wampanoags. But if the Pequots rise in concert, they could conceivably wipe out the Bay Colony. Any display of strength on their part could draw the Mohegans and other tribes to their banner, perhaps even those now friendly to us. We could be driven into the sea."

Winslow responded complacently, "That will never happen. The native Americans are incapable of concerted action on a large scale. It will take more than vague threats to the Bay Colony to get us involved. When there is open war, there will be time enough to join forces."

John said, "There is yet the matter of trade. While under threat of war, it would be more prudent for my ships to deal only on the southern coast, with the Dutch and Connecticut settlements, rather than sail all the way up here...Perhaps you no longer need our supplies?"

Rebecca saw the shaft go home behind Winslow's eyes. Without changing his tone of voice, the governor replied:

"When it is no longer profitable for you to sail to Plymouth, John, I'm sure you'll not be here. However, for the sake of our continued mutually beneficial trade, let us agree that if Providence itself is ever threatened, Plymouth will come to her aid."

Later, lying in John's arms, Rebecca said, "You wanted me to hear that tonight, didn't you? You could have talked to Winslow on the way to Salem, or privately, but you're trying to let me know that there is danger..."

John answered, "I'd be less than honest to claim complete safety for us anywhere in New England. At this point, however, I believe Providence to be safer from attack by Indians than any of the other settlements, especially those of the Bay. Roger is truly gifted at dealing with the natives. He and they share an emotional bond which runs very deep. I saw him turn the Narragansetts around last fall...

When we arrived at their main camp, it was doubtful whether we would ever leave alive. They were so close to uniting with the murderous Pequots—you heard how they slaughtered John Oldham, as well as many others, I assume. By the time we left, the sachems would do anything Roger suggested—he never tries to command them—all in exchange for a gift of sugar and hours of his talk."

"When I first met Roger, I never dreamed I'd be entrusting the safety of my children to his ability to charm savages."

"Nor did I."

That night, Rebecca woke in a sweat, thrashing on the bed. She had clearly seen Satan, dressed as an Indian sachem, coming out Marshalsea gate, after her children. As she began to cry out, she realized that the arms about her were John's, and that she was safe, for the moment. He held her as she sobbed in relief, and he gentled her back toward sleep.

In the morning, before leaving the chamber, John faced Rebecca, grasping her shoulders.

"I'll take you back," he said. "To Salem, to Boston, to England if you want. We can forget the whole venture, and begin again, elsewhere."

"Don't worry about me, John. It will only require a short time for me to adjust, I'm sure. I was finally getting used to the idea of being damned to Hell; now I must get used to the means by which I may be dispatched to that place."

He looked at her closely.

"You really believe in the excommunication, don't you?"

"What else can I believe?"

"Belief in nothing at all would be preferable to believing the word of that whited sepulcher, Hugh Peter. It's obvious to me that he has never experienced the redeeming love of Christ. How could any true follower of our Lord be so full of hate?"

"I, I don't know."

"What is the fruit of the Spirit of God?"

"'Love, joy, peace, long suffering, gentleness, goodness...' I forget the others."

"'...faith, meekness, temperance,'" he finished for her. "Did you observe any of those characteristics in Hugh Peter?"

"No."

"Then dismiss him from your mind. He has no power over you."

Rebecca looked at him, wanting to believe his words.

"I'll try, John. It still may take time. Please be patient with me."

He embraced her.

"I made a serious error in leaving you at Salem so long. I am sorry, 'Becca. I wanted the house built, food supplies assured...I see now that providing for the safety of your spirit was as important, if not more so, than providing for your physical safety. It seems that I have asked more of you than I intended...forgive me, my dear."

Roger, John and Thomas conferred with the Plymouth Council all morning, discussing both trade and military alliances. At noon, they were done. After dinner, the travelers bid Winslow farewell, and embarked for their northeast voyage out of Cape Cod Bay.

The Boat

After three days of sailing, past countless bays, necks, capes, and mouths of rivers, John told Rebecca that their voyage was nearly over. It was dusk as they reached their destination.

"We have arranged a small surprise," John said, as Captain Sparks waved a lighted torch in the bow. "Bring the children on deck so they can see."

Soon they saw lights on the shore. Some seemed to be candles, in windows, while others were small bonfires. Before they gained the dock, the entire settlement of twenty buildings was marked out by lights.

"How lovely!" cried Mary Williams.

Holding up his daughters, John told them, "See the lights in the fourth house down from the bluff top? Those are the candles of your new home!"

Providence

They soon disembarked, and began walking up Towne Street along the ridge. John stopped at the house he had built for Rebecca, and bid the Williams family goodnight, as Roger and Mary proceeded uphill, to their own new home.

From the outside, Rebecca's new house looked much like the others they had passed. It was built of logs, with a massive stone fireplace at one end. Inside was a large all purpose room, and a half storey loft for sleeping and storage. John had added three cubicles at the back; one each for Goody and Dudley, and one for guests, which Thomas would occupy. He explained that one side and the back wall were temporary, and that more additions were planned.

"We thirteen men constructed more than twenty buildings in ten months, in addition to growing crops and setting up a supply system with the Dutch. We'll be at close quarters for a time, but we'll expand the household soon. The surrounding area is very beautiful—I think it's much better in every way than the Salem or Boston town locations."

A neighbor had started a fire in their hearth to warm the house before they arrived. Having supped earlier, aboard the pinnace, the family gathered around the cheery flames for vespers before retiring.

John led Rebecca up the open staircase, showing the way to two sections of the loft. Each one contained a "jack bed" of wooden posts fastened to ceiling and walls, with feather beds on top.

The daughters would share the warmer side, near the chimney, while the parents, with a trundle bed in their room for little Freegift, had the cooler side.

In the morning, Rebecca rose with the dawn and began peering out the tiny, diamond paned windows, full of curiosity about her new surroundings. Three houses stood, spaced evenly, up the hill to the east along the road. Rebecca knew that the nearest one was Roger and Mary's, and she felt good, knowing they were so close. Next up the hill from the Williams home was that of Joshua Verin; at the top lived Richard Scott, a shoemaker whose wife was Anne Hutchinson's sister, Katherine. Down the hill were more houses, and at the foot of it were public buildings and businesses. These included a small meetinghouse, John Smith's mill, and John's warehouse and store.

In back of Rebecca's house was a storage shed and a few cleared acres of land. The beginnings of an orchard were visible, as well as stone fencing constructed from rocks dug during the building of the house and planting of crops.

Across the road, on the edge of the bluff was a spring, surrounded by a rock wall. Intent on viewing the neighborhood, Rebecca did not hear John behind her. He took her shoulders in his roughened hands, and turned her to face him. Quiet pride rested in his face.

She said, "It's all so lovely, so aesthetically pleasing. The homes seem to grow out of the hillside naturally—it all fits, somehow."

"Chad Brown, Greg Dexter and I laid out the home lots—each has five acres stretching back in a narrow strip from the road. I have ordered more trees for our orchard, livestock for our future barn."

Gesturing toward the room, Rebecca asked, "Where did you get the furniture? I've never seen anything so exquisite!"

"At New Netherland. The things the men here were making looked crude by comparison. The Dutch things attracted my eye, so I took the chance that you'd approve. Of course, I can get rid of anything you really dislike..."

"Oh, no, I love it all! Imagine having a chair for each of us, and for guests as well, instead of only benches. And the cabinets will hold all our tableware, the chests and armoire our linens and clothing...everything is so nicely carved and decorated!"

John smiled.

"I'm pleased that you like it. Did you see the blue and white tiles around the hearth? I bought and set those in, myself."

"Yes; they're beautiful. You must have worked yourself nearly to death."

"We all helped each other, all shared our dreams for our families. I never expected to feel such closeness with any group, since leaving my brothers. Of course, we all fought, too, over everything, as brothers would. For example, Roger decided when we first arrived that we'd all be Anabaptists. Holliman baptized him, then Roger baptized the rest of us. We were a sight, dipping and praying in the icy water. Then, a few months later, Roger upset everyone by abandoning Anabaptism; now he claims to be a Seeker!"

"I think Roger has always been a Seeker."

"Well, it would have made life easier if he'd noticed that ten years ago!"

"Indeed."

"Anyway, the upheaval has left us without an official minister or church. Everyone worships whenever and with whomever he pleases."

"That would scare the authorities at Massachusetts Bay to death."

"Indeed."

As they came downstairs, they discovered that Goody had stoked the fire, and that Dudley had already made two trips to the wharf, bringing up their clothing and other belongings.

"There's a horse in the shed," John told him. "He'll pack the heavier things up the hill for you."

"Beggin' yore pardon, Master," Dudley said, eyes alight, "where be the land you set aside for me?"

Dudley's indenture would be complete the following year, and John had promised to provide the man with his own place.

John smiled broadly and laid a powerful arm across Dudley's shoulders, a familiarity he never would have attempted in England.

"I claimed a prize piece of bottom land for you along the Seekonk River—six acres of fertile ground next the common meadow. If you'd like, we'll walk over there right now."

"I don't want to trouble you, Master."

"It's no trouble at all—let me get my cloak, and I'll help you with that horse—he and I are acquainted. We can bring another load off the pinnace. Are you coming, Thomas?"

Rebecca shook her head, mystified. John had behaved perfectly normally during their voyage, but now was showing distinct Levelist tendencies. Imagine treating the servants as equals!

"It won't work," she thought. "He's got 'Master' in every gesture, every tone of his voice."

She and Goody began to unpack, and were nearly finished by the time the children woke. At midmorning, neighbor women, most of whom had only been here a few days, began to arrive with gifts of food, enough for several meals. All voiced their appreciation of John's thoughtful organization of the community's land.

Until late afternoon, Rebecca thoroughly enjoyed her new situation. She had started across the road for a bucket of spring water. Looking down at the river, she saw many canoes beached there, with many more arriving, loaded with Indians. Turning toward the Williams home, she saw that perhaps fifty of them were constructing temporary shelters of hides and poles in the yard. Fires were being lit, and fresh meat was being butchered for cooking, all by greasy looking red women. From somewhere behind the house came the beat of a drum and the sound of chanting. Strong odors wafted on the breeze. Deeply worried, Rebecca returned home.

When John came in, a few minutes later, he comforted his wife.

"The Narragansetts have come here for a special purpose. They are welcoming the family of their sachem's great friend. Roger and Mary asked that I bring you over to meet them at sunset."

"Are you sure it's safe, John?"

"Do not be afraid. I know these people."

At sunset, after making sure that Goody, Dudley, and the children were fed and comfortable, Rebecca stepped into the cloak John held for her. She followed him and Thomas out into the dying sunlight and cold wind. They walked uphill for fifty yards, entering a large Indian lodge in the Williams front yard.

At first, Rebecca could not see anything. A deep silence lay like a quilt over the room, and an odor like the barn in Salem filled her nostrils.

As her eyes adjusted to the firelight, Rebecca saw that perhaps fifty scantily clad Narragansett warriors were pressed together, sitting in a tight circle. Roger had joined them, and sat shoulder to shoulder with the sachems, or chiefs, of the tribe. A kind of ceremony was beginning, involving Mary. She stood in the circle, face aglow, each of her hands on an Indian's head.

"God bless you," she murmured. Mary sidestepped to the next pair of sagamores, repeating her blessing, and continued around the circle until she was through.

John breathed in Rebecca's ear, "They see her as an angel of God—she cured some of them of various ailments when she and Roger lived at Plymouth. They have long awaited her arrival at Providence."

Mary said clearly, "Taubotne aunanamean—I thank you for your love," and stepped out of the circle. She grasped Rebecca's arm, and drew her toward the Indians. Rebecca's eyes widened in fear, but she felt John's hand at her back, calming her as she moved forward.

Indicating Rebecca with a hand gesture, Mary said, "Naneeshaumo—There be two of us." Urgently, she bid Rebecca, "Bless them, as I did. It will take away your fear."

Blessing the Indians was among the hardest tasks Rebecca had ever faced. Before she stepped into the circle, John whispered, "Think of them as children." That helped some, and she was able to pronounce, "God Almighty bless thee," well over twenty times as she touched their heads. Roger looked at her sardonically when it was his turn, but she blessed him, anyway.

When she was done, Mary led her from the circle, repeated, "Taubotne aunanamean," and drew Rebecca out of the lodge into the fresh cold air.

As the skin over the lodge door fell behind them, Rebecca gasped, "What have I done?"

"You have purchased very cheap protection for your family from the Narragansett Nation. Every one of those Indians is a sagamore who commands many sannups, or braves. They will now defend you with their lives."

"But…"

"You are in the hand of the Almighty. This is one of His means for protecting you."

Rebecca had no more nightmares for a long time. John's reasoning and Mary's therapy had worked together to bring her peace.

The fires next door remained burning brightly all night.

"There goes the neighborhood," Rebecca commented to Goody. "I wonder how long we'll have to put up with this!"

Goody retreated to her tiny room, muttering about the derned heathens."

The chanting continued until dawn. Rebecca was scandalized to see Roger dancing with the sannups. John had to remind her of King David dancing before the Lord in the Old Testament.

"At least Roger usually keeps his clothes on," he told her.

"Usually?"

"Well, yes! Sometimes he works up a sweat, and…"

Rebecca had heard enough.

"I knew he was mad, but this is the worst yet!"

"He's a great man, 'Becca. Not many people can bridge so wide a cultural gap as he. If it weren't for the stubborn English at Massachusetts Bay and Plymouth, Roger might never have found his niche in life. This is definitely it."

"Hmph!"

The next day, Mary Williams began bringing a stream of sick and injured Narragansetts to Rebecca's back door.

"This is the best way to earn their good will, and to justify the wrongs we whites have done to them."

"What wrongs?"

"We have stolen their land, introduced deadly disease, eaten their food supplies…"

"If you say so. I find that helping them makes me feel stronger, somehow."

"They're like children, 'Becca. They need our love."

Just before dinner, they delivered a Narragansett baby. The mother appeared mystified when they handed her the infant, swaddled English style, but she smiled gratefully, anyway.

Mary told her, afterwards, "That was the sachem Miantunomi's wife. We are fortunate it was a strong male child; they have named him Canonchet. Now the whole tribe will be grateful."

Next day, all the Indians left. Rebecca, rising at dawn, watched them piling into canoes at the riverbank. Going out the back door to the privy, she was startled to find the new Indian mother and her baby on the step. Behind them stood fierce, proud Miantunomi, his handsome face alive with the shadows of his thought. Shyly, the young woman held out an exquisite shell bead necklace to Rebecca, who accepted it. Impulsively, Rebecca embraced the woman and kissed the baby.

"Taubotne aunanamean," she ventured, hoping they understood her accent.

Apparently, they did, for both the sachem and his woman smiled broadly before turning to go.

Later, Rebecca noticed that Mary wore a similar necklace.

"Roger says these bear symbols of the sachem's special favor."

"They are lovely. I shall enjoy wearing mine, now that I can do so without violating a dress code. I can even wear the gold ring John gave me for our engagement."

"I'd forgotten about dress codes," said Mary. "Strange, how easy it is not to allot time for five worship services per week, nor to comply with all the other foolishness."

"Is it freedom, Mary, or license? How do people behave in the absence of restraint?"

"We're all about to find out, 'Becca!"

What they found out during the following months was that people quarreled like children. Those attracted to the new colony begun by Roger Williams were such individualists that at times it seemed they had nothing in common.

One such was a recluse, the former Anglican minister William Blackstone who had built a house in the wilderness miles from the site of Providence in 1635. He visited town occasionally to purchase supplies from John, and Rebecca saw him riding to and fro on the back of a large white bull. Occasionally, he would lend John a book from his extensive library.

The heads of Providence families met formally every two weeks to consult about community needs, but there was also an informal town meeting in almost constant session at John Smith's mill. Every issue was discussed nearly into oblivion before any action would be taken, the men being extremely hesitant to impose restrictions upon individual liberties.

Trouble between Massachusetts Bay whites and Pequot Indians along the Connecticut River, to the west, continued, and by May there was out-and-out war. John said nothing to Rebecca about it, although she felt his tension and knew the reason for it because of information from Mary. Mary visited often, and was aglow with her third pregnancy.

On May twenty-eighth, John came home late, filthy, unkempt, his clothing stained and torn. Rebecca had never seen him so careless of his appearance, and opened her mouth to comment when she saw his face. She shut her mouth and went to him.

He held out his hands before her face.

"Look! Are these the instruments of a highly trained, civilized mind? Their color, under all the dirt, is it not white? Has not my tongue uttered English from infancy, and are not my knees used most to worship a loving and all wise God? It's all a lie, a hoax!"

Afraid, never having heard him rant so, Rebecca waited.

Softly, musing as if no one listened, he continued: "The face of war has ever been part of the human experience. I suppose that one becomes immune to its horrors after awhile. But I refuse to become the sort of beast which can do that."

His voice broke, and he sobbed, burying his face, dropping into his chair.

"Savages, we're just dressed up, self righteous, white savages, just as damned as any heathen on this earth…"

He looked up at Rebecca, an agony of guilt in his eyes.

"I contracted with the Bay to supply Captains Mason and Underhill on their Mystic River expedition. Their forces were to retaliate against the Pequots for their recent depredations along the Connecticut. I was originally ordered to deliver the material to mouth of Mystic, but found the signals scrambled. The troops had no food, but advanced upstream anyway, hoping to take the enemy by surprise. And so they did. When I caught up with them, two days ago, they had just slaughtered over seven hundred Pequot men, women, and children. Most were killed where they slept by being burned alive. I walked through their ashes, imagining the terror and the agony. The soldiers had searched their Bibles, finding justification for the action, and are apparently at peace about it."

Rebecca, horrified, nevertheless attempted to soothe him.

"It's not your fault, John—you didn't give the orders!"

"It's all our faults, don't you see? It's our greed, our willingness to defend with the sword that which we have stolen, which caused this. Even the European disease epidemics which wipe out thousands of Indians are our fault—we, the white, green eyed monster!"

Rebecca shook him by the arms.

"Enough! The men who perpetrated this outrage must answer to themselves and to God for it. The fact that you see connections between the honest reward of your hard labor and their cruelty does *not* make you personally responsible. If you bear witness to the massacre of innocents, and use the knowledge of it to prevent such in future, perhaps the deaths were not in vain."

He brushed her aside, and the hurt of it stabbed deeply.

Ignoring her own feelings, she said, "Here is hot water. Let's get your body back to normal with a wash and hot food and a long rest. Then you'll know if you want to change the course of our lives as a result of this horror."

The children being asleep, and Thomas and the servants having much earlier repaired to their own quarters, John suffered Rebecca to remove his clothing, scrub him in the tub, and feed him with her own hands as he lay, wrapped in a blanket, on cushions before the fire. Rebecca stayed there with John all night, replenishing the fire, trying with all her strength to comfort and lighten his spirit, but in the morning his face wore the same haunted look of the night before.

"I never want to get over this, 'Becca. I am unalterably opposed to the violent resolution of conflict. Reason must temper our actions, no matter what the circumstance. Did I tell you that Anne Hutchinson at Boston has led a resistance to this war?"

"No"

"I spoke with her when I was there a week ago. She sees these things, their causes and effects on the human spirit, more clearly than I. At her instigation, her brother in law, William Wheelwright, has convinced the Boston Church to oppose sending money for supplies or soldiers against the natives. Winthrop is fit to be tied; he has developed a particular antipathy toward her. He labels her ideas as both heretical and seditious."

"It sounds as if she treads a perilous path."

"Worst of all are the charges that she communes with Satan. I encouraged her husband to get her out of Massachusetts Bay, but he somehow does not feel the danger…"

"We must pray for them."

By the end of July, the Pequot War was officially at end. Roger facilitated the extended, complicated peace negotiations. John accompanied Roger on several of the visits to Sassacus, the Pequot sachem, but always came away sickened by the demands of the Massachusetts Bay English.

"They divide the conquered natives like cattle," he told Rebecca. "Even the holy Hugh Peter got a squaw out of the deal. Now they have taken away the Pequot tribal name. Never are they to call themselves by it again."

"How does Roger justify his part in all this?"

"He views his part as interpreter for the negotiations as his duty before God, Who gave him the gift of understanding them. He is as fair an advocate as the Bay officials will allow him to be for the Indians, and the Indians view Roger as their only hope."

Roger was away, with Sassacus, in November when Mary went into labor. Rebecca had prayed hard for this pregnancy to come to a safe end, and was overjoyed when baby Providence made his swift and easy appearance. Roger, returning a few days later in his canoe, was so happy to have a son that he declared a feast. The entire settlement, plus the nearby Narragansetts participated in this happy event.

It was after the celebration that John took Roger aside for a chat.

"You really must take better care of your family," he said.

"We are blissfully happy, Neighbor Throck," returned Roger, breezily.

"Have you looked at your wife lately? Rebecca gave her a gown for the feast, but most of the time she wears rags. You have no furnishings to speak of, and your Narragansett friends keep borrowing your livestock—I have been supplying your children with milk. When Winslow visited here last summer, he gave Mary a gold piece because he felt so sorry for her. I was chagrined that he thought the colony so poor that we cannot provide for the family of our founder."

Roger sighed.

"Such things have never mattered to me. But I suppose that appearances do matter to most people...I don't want their pity. What do you suggest I do, dig for gold?"

"Something like that. Why don't you claim some additional land, personally, then sell it off as more settlers arrive?"

Roger looked at John with scorn.

"The land isn't mine to sell. It belongs to the Indians."

"But Roger, you're living on it!"

"Only by Canonicus' leave."

"Then why don't you get his leave to sell a little of it to others? Winthrop is still waiting for word concerning his property. He would pay you in gold, I know!"

"Well, I sort of own Chibachuwest, or Prudence Island, out in the bay…"

"I didn't know you owned that!"

"Well, it was rather an odd deal. I bought it with wampum, from an old trader who thought he owned it, in order to return it to Canonicus."

"If you sell the half of it with the deep cove to me, I'll pay up immediately. I need dock space."

"I suppose that will be all right."

"Shall I send word to Winthrop? He can have the other half of Prudence; it's a prime location for investment. With the proceeds, I can help you get Dutch goods for your family so that they look nicer."

"Go ahead. I trust you; you are better at such things than I. I have negotiated my brains away this fall already. I care not to do any more."

"The other thing is, I have received a message from William Hutchinson that he definitely wants a place here for Anne's followers to settle. She was excommunicated and banished from Massachusetts Bay on November 8, but has been imprisoned until spring. The poor man is most distraught."

"Let me confer with Canonicus. He once offered me Aquidneck Island, but I refused. At the time it was just a game on both our parts, testing each other. He has no use for that land, and I believe would give it to me."

"Freely?"

"For love. I am very dear to his heart."

"And you are willing for the Hutchinsonians to settle there?"

"As long as they preserve the peace of our settlement."

"Roger, Anne is about as mellow and peaceable as you used to be, in Essex."

"Don't remind me of those days. If I met my old self walking down the road, I should disown him. Yet I recall, my dear friend, that you never did so. I owe the Hutchinsonians as much grace as I have received."

By February, 1638, William Hutchinson and a group of men who had sat under Anne's teaching were hard at work on Aquidneck, later called Rhode Island, founding the town of Portsmouth. Before they had constructed much more than a central meeting hall, however, on an afternoon in March, Rebecca answered a frantic pounding at her door.

It was Anne. Grey of face, weak and fainting, she stumbled inside. Quickly, Rebecca and Goody flung cushions onto the floor before the hearth, helping the woman lie down on them. Goody brought a shot of rum, which Anne gratefully drank.

When she could speak, Anne said hoarsely, "I walked here from Boston with the children...it took us six days."

"Through the snow?"

Anne did not reply.

"Where are your children?"

"I sent all seven up the hill to my sister Katherine's. I couldn't bear for her to see me like this; I have always been the one to care for her, since her childhood. Someone from the town went over to Aquidneck to find my William. I just want him to hold me..."

Goody brought some broth and corn meal bread, which she fed to the exhausted woman.

"Are ye with child?" Goody asked.

"I, I think so. I have been very ill, and the child may not be alive. This excommunication may kill us both."

Before long, William Hutchinson came in the door, followed by John. He sat, murmuring soothingly to his wife. When at last she fell asleep, he stood shakily and joined the Throckmortons at supper.

"She should not be moved, yet," said Rebecca. "I will be happy to care for her until she is stronger."

"Bless you, Neighbor. After so much cruelty, she will appreciate your kindness."

They nursed Anne for several days. In the meantime, all the men of the community pitched in to help William prepare her house on Aquidneck, and then move her and the children to it. In April, Anne miscarried, but after that grew stronger and began to prophesy as she had in Boston.

Before long, the new community of Portsmouth was seething with controversy, much as Providence had in the beginning. The experiment of liberty of conscience was receiving a thorough drubbing. Soon, part of the quarreling Portsmouth group departed to the south end of the island, founding Newport. They were led by William Coddington, who had been, with Winthrop, one of the first settlers at Boston.

John remained interested in Anne's views, and took Rebecca to listen to her whenever he was in port. His mercantile business was expanding, as he sailed the American coast as far south as Virginia. He put Thomas in charge of one vessel, then several, paying him handsomely for his efforts. One evening, Thomas came in Rebecca's door, leading a breathtakingly beautiful young Dutch woman.

"This is my wife, Antje," he announced. "She's from New Netherland, and speaks no English."

Rebecca did her best to make Antje welcome, using gestures much as she had with the Indians. She spent hours teaching her new sister in law English and, in return, learned to cook some Dutch specialties. Soon, Thomas bought Joshua Verin's house up the hill and moved his wife there.

Joshua was leaving the settlement because he thought his wife spent too much time at the Williams home. She had been captivated by Roger's prophesying, and Mary confided to Rebecca that she was glad to see the woman go.

"She was here every waking moment, 'Becca, and monopolized all Roger's time. I don't wonder that Josh was upset. And the town council refused to censure her for disobeying her husband, on the grounds that she was exercising liberty of conscience."

"Well, I hope you don't mind my coming over. I enjoy praying with you and Roger when John is away. It makes me feel not so, so cast off. You know, the church was an important piece of the person I used to be. I don't think anything can replace that."

"You are family to us, 'Becca, welcome anytime. Do you still experience nightmares?"

"Only rarely, and they don't involve fear of Hell. You and John helped me with that."

"I have prayed for you to be happy, and I think that my prayers were answered."

"Yes. I have likewise prayed for you. We are fortunate to have each other."

In 1639, Mary bore Roger's second son, Joseph. During that year, John received the news that his father Basingbourne had died. Rebecca comforted him in his profound grief.

In the following year, 1640, Rebecca had a daughter, Patience. Life was sweet except for the reminders of the hostile powers of Massachusetts Bay. Anne Hutchinson's son Francis and son in law William Collins were jailed, then banished from Boston for conscience' sake. The Bay authorities, alarmed by the spread of Antinomianism in England, sent emissaries to spy on Anne or to debate with her.

Antinomianism, a set of destructive ideas, was characterized as anarchy, encouragement of the breakdown of many systems and laws of civilization. Anne's ideas were more positive, and properly called Familism, the Family of

Love. Members rejected the concept of original sin, and were bound together equally, male and female, in an intimate relationship with God. The Bay authorities, threatened by any new ideas concerning the organization of society, inaccurately labeled Anne's ideas 'Antinomianism' in order to stir up more opposition to them. They continued to use their influence to attempt the eradication of these ideas wherever they found them, even beyond their borders at Portsmouth. Nearly everyone in the settlements at Providence, Portsmouth, and Newport was appalled by this.

1641 brought news; Hugh Peter was returning to England. In the same year, Mary delivered her third son, Daniel, with Anne in attendance.

In March of 1642, a visitor stood at Rebecca's front door. She looked into his face for several seconds before recognizing Francis Barrington. He caught her into a fond embrace.

"Come in! Come in! This is an excellent surprise! What has sent you across the sea?"

"There is nothing in England for me anymore. The place seethes with controversy—I fear that soon there will be civil war. Now that my older brothers have sons, I shall never inherit titles or lands. And dear Mama died in December."

Rebecca turned from him, sudden tears filling her eyes.

"I knew she could not live forever," she said, "but somehow I wanted her to do just that. She was a very great lady, the best I ever knew."

Francis wrapped an arm around her shoulders, and held out Lady Joan's silver dagger in its sheath.

"Here is a memento of her—I thought she'd want you to have it."

"Thank you my dear friend. I shall treasure it. Tell me, what are your plans in the new world?"

"I intend to settle on some property I own in the West Indies, on Jamaica. My physician believes the climate there will be good for my health. But first, I wanted to spend time here with you, in the "freest place on earth," to learn first hand about this great experiment you are conducting in Providence."

Francis visited for a month, then sailed away to his new home.

May of that year brought the Throckmorton's second son, John. His father was away at the time, and Rebecca quickly named the child lest her husband choose another odd moniker such as "Freegift."

In June, Rebecca attended a Familist service at Aquidneck with John. She normally spent the time at Anne's meditating, examining the varied colors of her own spirit, deriving solace from the usual atmosphere of joy. On this particular occasion, though, her attention was drawn outward by Anne's serious tone as she began to speak.

"I am wearied to death by these messengers from Bay Colony. What have they to do with us? If I were to be reduced from all my errors, as is their stated purpose, there would be nothing left of me. I earnestly desire to move to a location beyond their influence."

Rebecca glanced at John, saw his frown.

"What about New Holland?" asked Will Collins. "The Pilgrims found refuge with the Dutch before Plymouth—their religious tolerance is well known."

"That's a splendid idea!" said Francis Hutchinson. His eyes turned to John. "Can we get permission to live within their borders?"

"Are you sure you want to do that?" asked John. "They have no great liking for the English, especially since their quarrels with Bay Colony over trade on the Connecticut."

"Couldn't we explain that we are as opposed to Bay policies as they?" asked Anne.

John sighed, and said, "I'll want several of the men to accompany me to Vreeland, especially you, Thomas, since you have a Dutch wife. We'll visit Governor Kieft, convince him that our presence means more trade, or whatever other excuse we can dream up. We must not mention being banished—that makes us seem too much of a liability."

The men nodded.

Anne spoke, her eyes twinkling, "John, you said 'our presence.'"

"So I did. I confess I have been thinking of the advantages of living closer to my wharf at New Holland. I did not want to move my family there alone. I know we would not be permitted to live within their fortress, for security reasons, but perhaps in an outlying area…"

Anne continued, "But our dear 'Becca has nothing to say?"

Rebecca's eyes were clouded with worry as she said, "I hate to be the one to bring this up, but the Dutch are experiencing violent confrontations with the natives all about them—Mohegans, stray Pequots, Iroquois. Surely you do not propose taking our families into an unsecured situation."

Anne stood up, walked over, and embraced Rebecca patronizingly.

"Dear 'Becca, so practical, so weak in faith. Do you not trust my inspirations? God will protect us if we shower the natives with love."

Rebecca flushed, then kept silent. Anne was always less than supportive of those who expressed an opposing view. The next week, four of the men sailed for Vreeland. When they returned, William Hutchinson became quite ill, and soon died.

"An omen," thought Rebecca.

But no one else seemed to think of it in that way. She discussed her fears with Roger Williams, who sat, puffing his pipe, his children climbing over him.

"I've never believed in omens," he said, thoughtfully, "but you are right to worry about the natives. An Indian has a whole different approach to life from ours. I should never settle near them without first laying down a close, personal relationship with the sachems. And even then, I should watch my back. We forget that they have not been reared on the Ten Commandments. Murder, to them, is no crime unless they are caught. By the way, is there anything you particularly want to send or retrieve from England? I expect to be going there, soon."

Rebecca's eyes widened as she responded, "Neighbor, there is rebellion in England! The king and his Cavaliers are at war with Parliament. Going there is most dangerous!"

"Staying here is equally so. The Bay and Plymouth Plantation cannot tolerate the idea of us living outside their authority. If we want to avoid being peremptorily annexed, I must try to secure a patent for us as an official colony, from Parliament."

"Is that possible?"

"Anything is now possible in the turmoil of our homeland. Luckily, I have a few Roundhead contacts, Sir William Masham and Oliver Cromwell among them. John has promised to write letters to smooth the process."

"I hope that helps. I never thought the Puritans there would gain strength as they have."

"King Charles is a fool. He has paid less attention to popular opinion than any recent monarch—and he is paying the price."

In March, 1643, John transported Roger to Vreeland, from whence he would return to Europe on the next ship. Roger accompanied John to Governor Kieft's offices, where the two convinced the Dutch to grant permission to begin an English settlement within their territory.

Before long, John, with Rebecca's brother Thomas, Francis Hutchinson, and William Collins began construction of homes east of New Holland, north of Throg's neck, at the mouth of a little river they named the Hutchinson, in what later became Westchester County, New York. They named the place Anne's Hoeck. The site was crossed by a well used Indian trail.

In June, the moving began. Rebecca cried a little at leaving her lovely Providence home, but tried not to let her family see. The three older children were now able to be of some help. Joan, at fourteen, was quite capable and cooperative. Mary, twelve, was the most loving child Rebecca had ever known. She helped the bent, old Goody, who had declined to leave the family when her indenture was served, with every task. Freegift, seven, whom Rebecca had taken pains to teach responsibility, avoiding spoiling him, was the model of his father; he always seemed to know the right thing to do, and nearly always did it. Little Patience at three could fetch and carry admirably, while baby John, one, just smiled and played whenever awake. Rebecca felt very proud and pleased with them all.

Doing most of the packing was a married servant couple, Jan and Altje Hendrickson, whom John had hired out of New Holland several years before. They, as well as Thomas' wife, Antje, were excited to be moving closer to their home, where they had many friends and relatives. At last, moving day arrived. Rebecca had her doubts that everything would fit aboard the little pinnace, but it did. Besides instructing the servants, all Rebecca had to do was hold baby John and watch little Patience. She stepped aboard after kissing Mary Williams farewell, and they sailed toward their new home.

Anne's Hoeck

Characteristically, John had provided everything for his family's comfort. The servants unloaded the furniture first, and all was in place before Rebecca set foot on shore. A supply of food and firewood was on hand, and, again, all Rebecca had to do was instruct the servants and children as they arranged their belongings. By evening of her first day in Vreeland, Rebecca was settled and curious about the area surrounding her home. The house itself was quite similar to, but larger than the one in Providence. John explained that this had helped him judge whether their possessions would fit. The Dutch carpenters he hired followed his instructions exactly, even though they spoke no English.

"The credit for this house goes to my interpreter," John quipped.

As she stepped out the door, Rebecca again was struck by the symmetry and rightness of the house situations. John definitely had an eye for such things.

"That's what attracted me to you!" he responded when she complimented him. "You're so symmetrical."

Dodging her playful slap, he took her arm and propelled her toward the shore of their little bay. From there, she could see all four houses, spaced evenly in a semicircle. Thomas and Antje were located next door to the Throckmortons, with their two adorable blond children, Job and Elspeth. Tom was considering a return to England for his son, Edward. Next to the Cornells was Will Collins, husband of Anne Hutchinson's eighteen year old daughter, Anne, who expected her first child at Christmastime. The last house, nearest the little river and the Indian trail, was Anne's. With Anne dwelt six of her children: Francis, twenty-five; Samuel, twenty; Mary, sixteen; Katherine, fourteen; William, thirteen, and Susana, ten. One other of her children had remained at Aquidneck, three others at Boston, all with their spouses.

Wooded hills behind the homes framed them in green. From the shoreline, the little settlement appeared as a scene from an idyllic painting, lovely to see.

Life settled into a comfortable rhythm. The children played in the forest and at the shore as they had in Providence. Rebecca taught the older ones their lessons daily, having a horror of them growing up illiterate. John brought her paper and ink, and she made up textbooks for them, from memory, on various topics. Of course, they all read the Bible twice daily, following the morning—Old Testament, evening—New Testament pattern specified in Rebecca's old prayer book, which she had kept hidden all these years. Now she dug it out and used it, instructing her children to say, "Thus beginneth" and "Thus endeth the lesson," as she had done so long ago. She even taught them the catechism, sure that now it could do no harm, even if they foolishly prattled it in public.

"Freedom of conscience," she mused. "It is good that no one objects to my being comforted by old ways."

Rebecca even took to walking the beach with her three oldest, alone, by turns, teaching them lovingly as her father had done. The one thing she found impossible to do was to impose on them the burden of original sin. Anne taught against it, and Rebecca, remembering the childish terror of Hell which had never really vanished, refused to instill it in her own dear ones.

"They'll just have to grow up with God's love as a motivation to goodness," she thought. "I can't think of a better one."

So far, it was working.

The warmth of summer gave way to coolness by August. By early September, all the families were dressing more heavily than usual as they ventured into the forest, harvesting nuts for winter use.

One afternoon, Rebecca was sitting at her fireside, sewing, when she became aware of more commotion than usual from the direction of Hutchinson's house. Anne's children tended to be rather more undisciplined than her own. They seemed to be forever running through the house, splashing each other with water, and laughing uproariously. Today, though, the sounds did not sound happy. Idly curious, Rebecca rose, opened her door, and felt her heart stop. Anne's house was ablaze. Naked red men ran through the yard, seizing various family members, dispatching them with axes.

As she watched, frozen in place, Will Collins ran toward Anne's house. He fell, an arrow through his throat. Looking in Rebecca's direction, two dozen red men began running toward her, part of them stopping at Collins' and Cornells' houses. Rebecca backed up, not knowing what to do. She felt incapable of outrunning these athletic warriors. She closed the door, barred it, and picked up little John from the floor, hugging him tightly. She tried to think. The other children were in the woods with Goody and some of the Cornell and Collins servants. John was off with Thomas on one of their merchant voyages, due back today.

Just then, Altje, her maid, came out of the servants' rooms toward Rebecca, tried to speak, but fell, a spear through her torso. The front door was being splintered by repeated, heavy blows. Rebecca sat in a chair, prayer book in hand, young John in her lap. Determined not to die in hysterics, she began to recite, first the Lord's Prayer, then the Nicene Creed. Last, as a huge, horribly painted red man advanced toward her, she sang the *Twenty-third Psalm*, wanting its melody to be the last sound from her lips. The Mohegan, perhaps respecting her courage, let her finish her death song. Then his expression changed, and he reached toward Rebecca's throat, softly touching the Narragansett necklace which daughter Mary had hung there that morning.

"You must look nice, in case Papa returns today," she had said.

The Indian's eyes narrowed. "Miantu—nomi?" he asked.

Rebecca nodded. A moment later, she found herself being shoved out the front door, John and the prayer book still clutched tightly. Several other Mohegans ran toward her captor, but he held Rebecca and her child to his sweaty, red painted chest, angrily waving them away. For a time, he stood, watching his fellows ruin the settlement. The livestock were driven into houses, which were then set ablaze. Every wooden structure was burned, everything which moved was killed. With one exception. Rebecca saw Anne's ten year old, Susana, being held prisoner by another Indian. She was, miraculously, wearing Miantunomi's shell bead necklace, which Mary Williams had given to Anne for assisting her with Daniel's birth.

A Mohegan watching the shoreline called a warning, and the two female captives were swiftly dragged toward the river and up the trail, as all the Indians prepared to vacate the scene. Rebecca's heart had leaped at the hope of rescue, but then it seemed to stop entirely. Out of the woods, pursued by Indians, came her children and the servants. From her position among the trees, Rebecca could not see what became of Joan, Freegift, or Patience. But she clearly saw darling Mary, the one who so resembled her own brother Job, turn to assist old Goody over a fence. As Rebecca watched, a large Indian ran to them, his hatchet descending twice. She looked away.

Little John picked that moment to begin wailing, and she tried to shush him, fearful that her captor, who held her arm in an iron grip, would harm the child. Instead, the man pushed them into a raspberry thicket, from whence they were all but invisible, and vanished up the trail. Susana and her captor had already gone.

Rebecca sat there a long time.

"Why leave this nice, safe thicket?" she wondered.

She had little John and her prayer book. Surely God would listen to her from this place. There was no need to venture out where the butchered and burned bodies of her friends and relatives lay. Rain would fall so that she could drink; snow would come before long, as a blanket. Next summer, there would be berries to eat...She would just sit here.

Rebecca heard shouts from the distant shore, saw bare Mohegan legs running past. Then there was silence. Darkness fell. She nursed little John, wrapped him in her skirt, and held him, warm and safe through the night.

Dawn was not something she wanted to see. Sometime during that long night, she had realized that little John would not consent to sit in the thicket forever. If not for him, she would have. She had no desire to get up, move about, face the horror by the shoreline.

Nevertheless, in the morning light, Rebecca picked up her little boy and wandered back down the trail. The shore was deserted. A confusion of footprints marred the sandy beach, most coming from a central point in what had been the families' common front yard.

"That's odd," she said. "I didn't know we had a graveyard."

Then it hit her. She walked to the crude wooden markers. As she read them, she began to cry. First were Hans and Altje Hendrickson. Then Goodwoman Elizabeth Noakes, with the epitaph, "Well done, good and faithful servant." Anne Hutchinson. Francis, Samuel, Mary, Katherine, and William Hutchinson. Will Collins. Anne Collins. Thomas Cornell.

Rebecca fell to her knees, crying out, "No! Not Thomas! He wasn't even here!"

Then she remembered the Mohegans hiding by the dock, waiting for the boat to come...

She continued reading names. "Antje Cornell. Job Cornell. Elspeth Cornell...My dear nephew and niece! Now our branch of the Cornell family is nearly extinct, except for little Edward, in England..."

"Mary Throckmorton." The marker read, "Dear Daughter, Beloved of the Angels. Sweet Sister, We Shall Never Forget."

There Rebecca knelt and sobbed for a long time.

On hands and knees, she crawled to the last two markers.

"John Throckmorton, Jr. Rebecca Cornell Throckmorton."

On the last marker was written, in John's hand, "Heart's Lady, Sleep In Peace." Underneath that, in Joan's, was "Dearest Mother, Watch Over Us."

Rebecca slumped to the ground, confused. She watched little John crawling and stumbling around the markers.

"They must think we died in the fire. There were probably enough bones in the remains of the house, from the cattle..."

Feeling suddenly hungry, she walked over to the house, looking for meat. Finding a large, charred haunch of beef, she tore at it with her hands, eating until she felt full. Then she gave some to John before nursing him again.

"I'm so glad I put off weaning him," she said, laying the child down for a nap.

She returned to the graveyard.

"I must say the words," she thought. "John probably did so yesterday, but it will comfort me to repeat them."

Without opening her prayer book, in remembered bits and snatches, she recited in a clear voice:

> Unto Almighty God I commend the souls of my brothers, sisters, and children departed, and I commit their bodies to the ground; earth to earth, ashes to ashes, dust to dust, in sure and certain hope of the Resurrection, as our Lord hath said, 'I am the Resurrection and the Life; he that believeth in Me though he were dead, yet shall he live. And whosoever liveth and believeth in Me shall never die...' Therefore are they before the throne of God, and serve Him day and night in His temple: And He that sitteth on the throne shall dwell among them. They shall hunger no more, neither thirst any more, and there shall be no more sorrow, neither shall there be any more pain. For the Lamb which is in the midst of the throne shall feed them, and shall lead them into living fountains of waters: And God shall wipe away all tears from their eyes.

She then repeated the Lord's Prayer, ending by singing the *Twenty-third Psalm* which had helped to preserve her life.

As the day wore on, Rebecca walked the ruins, looking for more edibles, but finding little. She salvaged a few things which the fire had not consumed, among them Lady Joan's silver dagger. She dug for clams, as she had seen the Narragansetts do, but was not yet hungry enough to eat them raw. She took John to the shore line, washing him in the water, letting him play with the colored rocks and shells. At late afternoon, she prepared a bed of dried grass against one of the still standing walls of her house, and laid John there to sleep. She dragged a piece of charred blanket out from under a roof timber, intending to use it as a cover. Then she glanced toward the water.

A lone boatman was rowing a small shallop to the shore. As he approached, she saw that it was John. He fastened the boat to a dock piling and disembarked, walking slowly toward the little cemetery. He carried flowers. He passed all the other markers, then fell on his face, sobbing, before Rebecca's. She dropped her blanket and ran to him, kneeling at his side. He did not notice her at first, because he was venting his inner torment. She touched his shoulder.

He raised his head, face sand covered, and looked at her.

"'Becca? Are you real, or imaginary?"

"I'm the most real woman you'll ever have," she replied.

He lunged at her, knocking her over, covering her face with sandy kisses. He lay on top, nearly crushing her for a long time, tears of relief mingling with incoherent confessions of his guilt at having left her in danger.

When he seemed more calm, she said, "Let's get the baby. Then you can take me back to civilization. It gets cold here at night…"

"The baby? Do you mean that John is alive?"

"Yes. Miantunomi's necklace saved us. And Susana Hutchinson, though they took her away…Are my other children well?"

"Yes, yes, they are safe, except for sweet Mary. But they are mourning for you. Let us go to them."

They collected their sleeping son, climbed into the shallop, and rowed out of the bay to the pinnace which lay anchored offshore. The children embraced Rebecca ecstatically, and she cried as much for them as she had at Mary's grave.

Providence

A few days later, they stood at the Williams door in Providence, where Mary took them in.

Unfortunately, Edward Cope had bought the Throckmorton's house, and was living there with his family. Since Rebecca had no interest in living anywhere else, John soon moved his family to furnished rooms he had used for visitors. These were located over his store near the Providence docks. He hired several servants to care for the household, and watched his wife carefully during the following weeks for signs that the horror at Anne's Hoeck had damaged her emotional health. He did not realize that she, wanting so much to comfort him, had buried her feelings deeply until she should have opportunity to express them. She knew, as he did not, that this must occur while he was absent.

On the first night John was away on one of his boats, Satan returned to Rebecca's dreams. He, of course, was dressed as a Mohegan, but spoke English, and smirked when Rebecca hurled her prayer book at him.

In Endecott's silky voice, he began:

"I'm sorry if I startled you, Mistress…I trust that we shall become close friends…I came to enquire how I may serve you…Pray do not be alarmed, Mistress, I mean you no harm…I am merely trying to comfort you…Loneliness is too great a burden…We can find Paradise together…"

The lies continued all night, and there was no escape this time. She saw his skull ring as his hand reached to caress her cheek; she struggled against his sweaty red chest.

At dawn, she was at Mary Williams' door.

"Satan has returned for me," she told her friend.

Mary looked at Rebecca's white face and frightened eyes and said, "We're going on a little journey, 'Becca."

Within the hour, Mary had found a neighbor to oversee the children, as well as a pinnace willing to transport the women down the bay. On the way, Mary explained that the Mohegans and Narragansetts had been in conflict all summer. Miantunomi had been captured and murdered by Uncas, sachem of the Mohegans.

"When the Mohegans saw your necklace, they knew you were special to the Narragansetts. They probably intended to hold you for ransom. One way to strike back at the Mohegans is to let the Narragansetts know what has happened. Perhaps we can also facilitate Susana's release."

By early afternoon, they had reached Narragansett, and stood before Canonicus' lodge.

"Summon your sagamores," Mary told him. "The wife of Trader John Brown Eyes is here to thank and bless them. The Mohegans' fear of their strength has saved her life, although they killed her daughter."

After the brief ceremony, the women presented the tribe with a fifty pound bag of sugar which they had brought from John's warehouse. Then they departed, sailing back up the bay.

Rebecca spent the following nights at Mary's, where her sympathetic friend prayed with her after every evil dream.

"'Becca, you will feel safer after Canonicus has retaliated against the Mohegans," promised Mary.

A week later, Rebecca was surprised but not frightened to find a Narragansett sagamore at her door.

"Those who harmed the family of Trader John Brown Eyes have paid in blood," he said. "Their souls are banished from the council fires."

"What about the white girl they stole?"

"Uncas wants many pounds of wampum for her, more than she is worth."

"I will pay much. I want her back!"

"It is a difficult thing."

He left.

When John returned, Rebecca said nothing to him about her problem, but the children must have, because he soon confronted her.

"Where were you sleeping while I was away?"

"I don't see that as your concern."

His eyes widened, surprised at her tone.

"Everything about you is my concern. What were you doing at Narragansett?"

"Unlike your other property, I do not just sit, waiting while you are away. I go on living, breathing. I have needs; I find ways to satisfy them. Sometimes I take journeys."

"Rebecca, this isn't you speaking. I am going down to my office. When you are ready to talk reasonably, come to me."

She didn't go to him, and he slept downstairs that night. The next afternoon, he came to her sitting room.

"All right. You slept at Mary's because you had nightmares. I'm not completely sure why you and Mary went to Narragansett, but you gave Canonicus a huge gift of sugar, which somehow sent his sagamores on a killing spree. Why couldn't you just tell me these things, instead of making me check on you?"

"You need not have checked. I told you: This is not your concern. If you do not believe my word, there is no point in discussion."

"'Becca," he pleaded, "you are half of myself. Anything which distresses you causes me pain."

"I am well acquainted with pain, yet I'm not the one who slept down in the office. I did not sleep last night, but rather waited for you in our bed. I dare not sleep there when you are gone…it is a punishment reserved for the damned."

"Heart's Lady, come to me…"

Firmly, he took her hand and drew her toward him. At first, she resisted, but from long habit soon gave in, letting him hold and caress her, gentling away the fear until she slept.

When she woke, it was night, and John's arms were still around her. She stirred, but his muscles tightened.

"I'll not let you go," he whispered, "until you tell me everything."

She told him. When she was finished, he said,

"Endecott was long ago; I understand that you were frightened by him, yet you are blameless. But why did you send the Narragansetts down the warpath? Did you not know the Mohegans killed Miantunomi?"

"Yes, but that happened last summer. Mary and I did not cause that. And neither she nor I requested the vengeance taken on the Mohegans. John, can you not imagine what poor Susana Hutchinson must be enduring, after watching the slaughter of her family? I believe Mary was trying to facilitate her return, more than anything, as well as to speed my inner healing. But you know how the Narragansetts are—they cannot be commanded, only influenced indirectly."

John sighed deeply, "Of course, you are right. Mohegans and Narragansetts have always used any excuse for killing one another. To them it is no crime. By the way, I have set up a large reward for Susana's return, and advertized it both at New Netherland and at Massachusetts Bay. I only hope that she still lives. I abhor the idea of any more death resulting from my bad judgment."

"There were more forces at work at Anne's Hoeck than your judgment, John. The Dutch surely bear much of the blame because of their massacres of Indians last spring. I believe we must accept that the evil perpetrated there was part of God's overall plan for us."

"That is a very hard acceptance for me."

"And for me. What I need is to feel I have overcome the terror myself, that I have the strength to face the evil alone, in the dark."

"You ask much of yourself. The events you faced so calmly in September would have driven many strong men into hysterics. In the mean time, sleep anywhere you are able while I am away; but please refrain from inciting the natives to violence."

In early December, 1643, Mary Williams delivered another daughter, Mercy. The next spring, Rebecca bore a girl child, Deliverance.

"For," she said, "I have finally been delivered from the hand of Satan into the hand of God."

At that point, her nightmares ceased.

In September, 1644, Mary Williams received the joyous news that Roger had returned to Massachusetts Bay with a safe conduct pass through their territory. He bore a charter for his new colony, to be called, "Rhode Island." Among the eleven signatures on the charter appeared those of Sir Thomas Barrington and Sir William Masham. The authorities of Massachusetts Bay were less than pleased.

John was able to find out exactly when Roger would return, overland, to Providence, and organized a reception and feast. As Roger reached the Seekonk River, a fleet of fourteen canoes filled with friends and neighbors came across to meet him. They sent up a ringing shout of welcome. He was given a seat of honor in the center canoe, and brought downriver to Providence, where the celebration continued.

Roger greeted Rebecca among the women at the feast, but, occupied with his new daughter and many guests, did not speak to her. Late that evening, when nearly everyone had gone, he took Rebecca's hand and walked with her to one of the dying bonfires.

"Neighbor Throckmorton, you have the look of one who has wrestled with Satan and won!"

"He came for me, Neighbor Williams. But he could not pry me our of our Father's hand. He did, though, kill my precious daughter Mary, and my brother Thomas with his family, and Anne Hutchinson, and six of her children…it was an evil time."

Roger's eyes filled with tears.

"I'm sorry you had to witness his power. But I see that you are no longer afraid."

"I am no longer afraid…of anything! But tell me about the evil during the sojourn to England. Were you able to overcome it?"

"All except for the sea sickness," he grimaced ruefully. "That was as bad as before. Did you realize that Massachusetts Bay was attempting to officially annex Providence? When I arrived, they were in the process of submitting their own charter for 'The Territory of Narragansett.' Hugh Peter and Thomas Welde were at London, representing the Bay interests, but Sir William Masham, Sir Thomas Barrington, and Sir Henry Vane accomplished God's will against them. Having John headquartered here to represent Sir Thomas' interests hurt us not at all. John wrote an introduction for me to his friend, the scrivener for Parliament who copied both charter documents, the Bay's and ours. That fact alone explains why ours was properly signed and sealed and theirs wasn't. Ours, therefore, passed the table with ease."

"God has blessed you, Neighbor. Now we owe you our freedom, twice! I heard you saying that you did some writing and publishing of your thought."

"I did. Immediately on arrival at London, I published my *Key Into the Language of America*, which I wrote so long ago at Plymouth. Quite unexpectedly, it became a bestseller on the newsstands. It got me instant name recognition as well as sympathy for our charter.

Later, I published old letters from John Cotton with my responses. I exposed him as the self righteous opponent of religious tolerance I know him to be. I then proceeded to publish tracts and books against the notion of a state church. My last book, *The Bloudy Tenent of Persecution*, which slipped past the censors, may actually gain the distinction of being burned at London—they hadn't decided by the time I left."

"Busy, busy, Neighbor! You couldn't resist stirring the waters, could you?"

"John was saying that you and Mary did a little stirring, yourselves. Don't you know that, with Canonicus, a little sugar goes a long way?"

"We know it now. We'll need your help, to get Susana Hutchinson released, though. The sugar wasn't enough for that. I was told tonight by one of the sagamores that she still lives."

"I'll do all I can; Susana is a dear child. Uncas is not my particular friend, unfortunately."

"I know you are fatigued, Neighbor Williams, so I'll find John and head for home. We live over the store at the docks; don't be a stranger!"

"Neighbor Throckmorton?"

"Yes."

He kissed her brow, saying, "You are dear to our hearts. I praise God that you have escaped the Evil One and remain with us!"

One morning in early summer, 1645, Rebecca had taken baby Deliverance, as well as John, then two, for a stroll down river, past the common meadow. A fair path ran along the river bank, and she often walked it when she wanted to think. As she was passing Smith's Mill, she was surprised to be politely approached by a well dressed, handsome young man who she vaguely recalled seeing in John's store and around town.

"Neighbor Throckmorton? My name is John Taylor, and my father is a physician of Newport. I wish to speak with you...could I help with your little boy?"

John was tugging energetically at Rebecca's hand, nearly pulling her over. When she nodded, the young man stooped down, holding his hands out to John. The child responded fearlessly, so the man boosted him high, settling him on a broad shoulder. He then proceeded to bounce a little, making John squeal in delight. Rebecca walked beside them with her baby, wondering what this fellow wanted.

At last he turned to face her, saying, "I have seen your daughter, Joan, and find her most attractive. I realize that she is very young, but I seek your permission to make her acquaintance with the intent to court her."

Rebecca was stunned. She had never thought of Joanie as being old enough for such things. She cast her mind back to Hatfield Broad Oak, remembering herself at the same age, trysting with John in the chapel...

Seeing that young Taylor was anxious for her reply, she said, "Joan's father and I treasure our daughter. We also treasure the chance to meet considerate neighbors such as yourself. Would you be our guest at dinner today?"

By the time they returned home for dinner, Rebecca had the young man carefully evaluated. He had been educated in England, and expected to return there to read the law. He seemed kind and thoughtful, yet held some interesting political/religious views which differed from her husband's. With some amusement, she listened during dinner as the two men disagreed, while watching Joanie's eyes change from disinterest to awe. There were not many men around who could hold their own in an argument with John Throckmorton.

That night, Rebecca served her husband his favorite supper, with wine, and afterwards led him to her sitting room for a pipe of specially blended Virginia tobacco. She sat on the floor, her head on his knee.

Rubbing her neck, he asked, "What's afoot, Heart's Lady? We don't sup this well every night."

"I believe we shall soon have to give up our daughter to some young man, such as young John Taylor."

"I don't think so."

"Why not? He is a good man, well off. Don't you want her to be happy?"

"Not with a supporter of that shower, Will Coddington. Besides, she's too young for marriage."

"Have you looked at her lately?"

"Yes. I see big brown eyes and a woman's body. But I know that her mind, though quick to learn, does not always separate information from emotion."

"Whose mind does? We're not discussing the education of a future monarch, John. Have you not watched the young men practically drooling over her as she passes through the store, or takes a turn around the common on her horse?"

"They had all better put their tongues back in their mouths, and look elsewhere. Joanie cares not for any of them."

"For how long? Do you realize what a great risk we take in allowing them all to run after her? Sooner or later, she will fall in love with some charming lad without any good sense or prospects. We must encourage her to associate with those of good character. And I thoroughly approve of John Taylor."

"Did you not listen to me at dinner today? Will Coddington does not have the good of the colony at heart. He seeks to make Aquidneck a separate colonial unit, with himself as governor for life! Unless we find a way to unify all the towns of Rhode Island into a cohesive unit, we shall lose our charter, as well as our land, piece by piece, to the colonies at Plymouth, Massachusetts Bay, and Connecticut. Then we shall surely lose our hard won freedom."

"I refuse to debate with you. But the point John Taylor made was clear: Coddington has the leadership skills necessary to unify the people. Without that, we shall still lose the charter. Perhaps we must give up a little of our freedom, to Coddington, in order to avoid giving up all of it to the other colonies."

"Never to Coddington."

"I am trying to discuss the character of John Taylor. Did you not notice how reasonable he was, how controlled, and how intelligent? Most of the Aquidneck men would have been foaming at the mouth during that discussion, but he was thinking, even agreeing with you at times."

"I noticed. So what makes you think he is interested in Joanie?"

"He asked permission to court her today."

"WHAT!"

"I talked with him for an hour. He seems to be a kind, decent man, and I believe we should encourage him. Perhaps Joan will not respond, but just knowing him will give her an idea of the sort of person she should be looking for."

John shook his head. "She's older than you were when I found you at Broad Oak. And yet I see her as such a child. Perhaps you're right. But if he harms her in any way, I'll…"

"You'll what, my nonviolent husband? Your options for retaliation are extremely limited. Why don't you just make up your mind that it is good for Joan to be courted in a civilized way by a respectable man, and let it go at that?"

"I'll try."

John Taylor became a frequent visitor at the Throckmorton's, and the activities of Will Coddington a major topic of discussion. By August, 1645, an order arrived from Winthrop, Sr., as President of the New England Confederation of Colonies. It forbade the Rhode Island Council to exercise authority over Aquidneck, Pawtuxet, or Mishamet. In violation of the legal charter, these three areas were being claimed by the other colonies. Coddington was beginning to appear as one cause of this problem, while Roger seemed noble and more wise.

The superiority of Roger's judgment became even more obvious as he negotiated a treaty of neutrality with the Narragansetts, even after an officer of the Bay military, Captain Atherton, had stupidly enraged them by dragging their war sachem, Pessicus, from his lodge by the hair.

John Taylor graciously acknowledged Roger's ability when dealing with natives, but stood by his assertions that Coddington's personal charisma as perceived by the English settlers was necessary to the future effectiveness of Rhode Island government.

Rebecca was more interested in Taylor's campaign for Joanie's affections. He began with an older brother style companionship, teaching Joan advanced concepts of any academic topic in which she showed interest. Rebecca would happen upon them at odd times, to find John's arm around Joan, her head on his shoulder or knee, both of them absorbed in reading and understanding a work on natural history, geography, or astronomy.

In the spring of 1646, the girl came to her mother, asking the questions Rebecca would have loved to ask her own mother, had she survived the plague at Chelmsford.

"What is the difference between friendship and love, Mama?"

Rebecca tried to explain that friendship was the best foundation for a marriage, and that sexual passion was only a small but important piece of that foundation. Love was the magical combination of the two.

Afterwards, Rebecca noticed that the young couple disappeared for whole days, after which Joanie appeared dazed with bliss. Soon she came to her mother.

"I can't live without him, Mama. What shall I do?"

"Has he proposed, yet?"

"No. He says he cannot until I am ready, whatever that means. Mama, how can I show him that I AM ready?"

"That would depend on his criteria. But perhaps we can find a way to convince him…What would happen if you were unavailable to him for awhile?"

"I should die, missing him!"

"And what else?"

"He would realize how much a part of him I already am…Oh, thank you, Mama! Where shall I go?"

"How about visiting Roger and Mary Williams at their trading post at Cocumscussoc? It's only six miles distant, perfectly safe, and I could explain that you have gone away to seriously contemplate your future."

"How long must I stay?"

"When young Taylor begs your father for your hand, we shall send him to you. Roger, as Chiefe Officer, will marry you. I guarantee that it will not take long for young Taylor to reach the point of desperation. Is the man not here nearly every day the sun shines? A week without you will seem an eternity to him."

"And to me."

"My precious daughter, will you consider the days apart well spent when he casts himself at your feet, pleading for you to become his wife?"

"I'll pack immediately. Will Papa's boat take me down the bay tonight?"

"I'm sure of it. Now let's speak with your father."

Reluctantly, John agreed to the plan, kissed his daughter farewell, and signed the letter to Roger and Mary which Rebecca had written. Next day, Rebecca sent a servant to the door, telling John Taylor that Joan was not at home. The young man stayed long enough for a chess game with ten year old Freegift, then departed, disappointment showing in his posture. After three days of being denied access to Joan, he begged to see Rebecca, who acted the innocent party to perfection.

"I believe Joan is showing a great deal of maturity, Neighbor Taylor. She is spending some time in fasting and prayer, considering the direction her life should take. We would all benefit from doing the same, surely."

"Neighbor Throckmorton, I have become more attached to your daughter than I realized. Perhaps I could assist her in answering some of the questions she is asking herself."

"Joan specifically requested that she be allowed this time, undisturbed, for contemplation. I would never betray her trust. If you return tomorrow, perhaps there will be some message from her for you…"

John Taylor returned next day, but Rebecca had no message.

"Is your husband in his office?"

At her affirmative nod, he raced downstairs and knocked urgently at John's door. A few minutes later, Rebecca saw her future son in law racing for the dock, a note from Joanie clutched in his hand. Rebecca murmured its message to herself.

"My love, come to me at Cocumscussoc."

Two weeks later, the newlyweds came to call, identical looks of wonder on their handsome faces. Since John Taylor already owned a house on Aquidneck, his new in laws bought the indentures of several servants as a present, to ease their daughter's early married life.

In May of the next year, 1647, the forty representatives of the four main towns of Rhode Island Colony finally reached an agreement which bound them together. They codified a set of laws, wrote a bill of rights, and ended the document with this statement:

"These are the lawes that concern all men, and these are the Penalties for the transgression thereof…and otherwise than this, what is herein forbidden, all men may walk as their consciences persuade them, every man in the name of his God. And lett the Saints of the Most High walk in this Colonie without Molestation in the name of Jehovah, their God for ever and ever."

In June, John came to Rebecca saying, "Walk with me."

The two walked down the river path, occasionally greeting neighbors out enjoying the warm weather.

Presently, John asked, "'Becca, do you want your house back, the one I made for you?"

"I have told you many times that I want no other."

"It has come up for sale. Old Ed Cope is going to live with a daughter, and must liquidate his assets."

"That house means a great deal to me. I learned many hard lessons before and after I lived there. The time actually spent within its walls remains a cherished memory."

"Thinking of our dear Mary there will not distress you?"

"No. I think of her as dwelling with angels now, watching over us. Living in the house where we were happy together will make me feel close to her, even more content."

"Very well. We shall move soon."

And so they did. A few days afterward, Rebecca had a morning call from Roger Williams.

"Come in, Neighbor! What a pleasant surprise!"

"Pray with me, Neighbor. I am much cast down in spirit."

As they prayed, Rebecca discovered that Roger had suffered the loss of his Narragansett father, Canonicus, who had begged Roger to attend his death. When they finished, Roger's face still wore an expression of distress.

"Is there anything I can do, Neighbor? You seem quite unhappy."

He looked at her.

"It's the words of the Anglican burial service. I have preached, debated, written against them as a vestige of popery, and now they are outlawed in England. Since Canonicus' death, they run continually through my mind. Could I ask...when your daughter was killed, what did you say over her grave?"

Rebecca walked to a Dutch style cabinet, opened a drawer, and withdrew her prayer book.

"I have no faith in the power of this book, Neighbor, but when its words ring true in my soul, I find comfort in them. Is that so evil? Yes, I said the burial service over Mary. And John did, too. I suspect we are not the only ones to be comforted by old ways."

Roger took Rebecca's hand and pleaded, "Would you repeat the words with me now, for the peace of my own spirit? There is no one else on earth who I would trust to understand, to do this with me."

When they had finished, he seemed much relieved.

"Words," he said. "They have power of their own over our spirits."

"Only when we allow them to. But there is no evil in being comforted by these words."

"Neighbor, you are the kindest heretic I ever met."

"And you are the boldest. Imagine having one's own words burned in London!"

"A high point in any career, surely."

"John will be home, soon. Can you stay to dinner?"

"It would be my pleasure. Living at Cocumscussoc, I find I miss the opportunities I used to have to debate with John."

But there would be no debate that noon. John came in wearing an expression of anxiety.

After greeting Roger, he said, "I must leave for New Holland right after dinner. Susana Hutchinson has just been released to Governor Stuyvesant by the Mohegans."

"Praise God!" exclaimed Rebecca. "I have long prayed for this."

John's eyes were deeply troubled.

"The reason for the delay was Uncas' great hatred for the Dutch chief officer, Governor Kieft. He has waited until a new administration to release the girl. In the meantime, Susana has become so attached to the tribe that she has resisted being ransomed, preferring to remain Uncas' slave."

Rebecca announced, "I'm going with you. Let us dine, then pack and be off. Neighbor Williams, we especially covet your prayers while on this mission."

New Netherland

The Throckmortons disembarked at John's wharf in New Holland, walking swiftly over spotless cobbled streets to the governor's mansion near the town center.

Shown in by a servant, they were soon greeted by the elegantly dressed, peg legged governor. After the usual inconsequential pleasantries, he took both Rebecca's hands and looked deeply into her eyes.

"I see that the story I heard is true," he said. "You are a brave lady. Is the little boy with whom you faced the savages well?"

Rebecca answered, "He is, indeed, a typical busy five year old. But surely you understand how anxious I am to see Susana…"

Stuyvesant turned to John.

"I hope the two of you do not expect too much. There is no doubt that this is the right girl. But we have not been able to get her to respond to any of us. She seems to view us as her captors, the Mohegans as her family. She is most confused."

"Take me to her!" exclaimed Rebecca.

A servant led John and Rebecca down a long corridor, and unlocked a door at the end. The room was small, clean, but illuminated only by a small, octagonal window set very high in the wall. The only furnishing was a cot, on which sat the fourteen year old Susana. Recognizing the Throckmortons at once, she leaped up with a glad cry, flinging herself into Rebecca's arms. After a minute of being held and gently rocked, Susana stepped back and turned to John. She held out her hands, imploringly.

"Neighbor Throckmorton, no one understands me here. I want to go home…please, please take me home, to Uncas!"

John pulled her to his chest for a hug.

"Little Miss, we are here to help you. Do you believe that?"

"Y-yes."

"Then trust us. We only want you to be happy." Turning to Rebecca, he said, "I must talk a little more with the governor. Then we will leave. If you'll excuse me…"

Rebecca sat on the cot with Susana, trying to comprehend all that had happened to this girl's mind during the four years of captivity.

"Uncas calls me his White Dove," she said. "I am his most precious possession. He would never give me up, never, not for any money. There has been a mistake. I must return to him, finish beading his new moccasins…"

"You know how to make moccasins?"

"Of course. And many other articles of clothing. I would show you mine, but that nasty Dutch maid burned them all, holding her nose. And she washed all the goose grease out of my hair…It won't shed rain anymore, and I shall stay wet, become ill…"

Rebecca said, gently, "I believe you'll be living indoors, now, for a time. The roof will keep the rain off. Do you remember how we all rinsed our hair in rainwater, to make it soft and shiny?"

Susana sniffed scornfully.

"In my village, soft shiny hair means that a person is weak, and will soon sicken and die."

"There must be many things you love about your village. Can you tell me about them?"

"The best part is the feeling of unity. Everyone helps everyone else, nearly all the time. I felt so necessary, not like here. Here I am a prisoner."

"I'm sure it seems that way, but with your permission, John and I will take you for a ride today, on our boat. We want you to explore your options for the future."

"Options? I only want to return home, to Uncas."

"But surely you recall that you have other homes, with your real family."

"Uncas is my real family."

"I meant with your original family, the Hutchinsons."

"Hutchinson? That seems an ill name. Once a white man came to my village from Massachusetts Bay. He asked if my name were Hutchinson. I couldn't remember. He said I'd be better off without that name, since those people were damned to Hell. He seemed very sure of it. Neighbor Throckmorton, what is Hell?"

Tears in her eyes, Rebecca replied, "Susana Hutchinson, the King of Hell passed right over you, four years ago, in all his power, and was unable to touch you. Hell is the worst evil place, but you shall never see it."

"I am glad of that. Is my name truly Hutchinson?"

"Yes. Do you remember how you came to live with Uncas?"

"I remember running, then being carried, a long way through the forest, with Mohegan sannups. We moved about for weeks. One morning, our camp was attacked by most wicked Narragansetts. They killed all the men while I hid in a thicket, under the edge of a log. When they had gone, the next day, I followed a little stream to the village of Uncas. I have lived there ever since. Many times Dutch, English, and Indians have come to try to buy me, but Uncas always refused. I don't understand why he let them take me this time…"

"Susana, you have two brothers and two sisters who love you very much, and want you back. Do you not remember Faith, Bridget, Richard, and Edward?"

"I don't think so. Do I have parents?"

"They have died. But you have an Aunt Katherine, who is a neighbor of mine."

"And who are you, exactly? I recalled your faces and names, but I don't remember whether we are related, or…"

"My husband and I were friends of your parents. Your mother helped me deliver two of my children. I was with you the day the Mohegans took you away…do you not remember it at all?"

Susana shook her head.

"Perhaps that is best. If ever you begin remembering, come to me, and I will help you. It took me a long time to recover from the events of that day."

Providence

Rebecca and John returned with Susana to Providence. She did not recognize her sister, Bridget Sanford, or Aunt Katherine Scott at all. She therefore remained at Throckmorton's until she felt comfortable enough to live with her relatives. Four years later, she married John Cole, a good man who tried hard to understand and allow for the trauma his wife had endured.

Shortly after bringing Susana back to Providence, Rebecca and John bid a tearful goodbye to daughter Joan. She and her husband, as yet childless, were leaving for England, where he would read the law at Gray's Inn, London. They did not expect to return during the seven year course of study, and Rebecca was grieved at the parting. Joan promised to look up old friends and relatives of her parents in England, and to write often with news.

During the next year, 1648, William Coddington took Roger Williams' place as President of Rhode Island.

In England, Oliver Cromwell's Puritan and Scot (Roundhead) forces had prevailed over those (Cavaliers) of the king. Charles was imprisoned at Windsor, then tried at Westminster Hall for treason. On January 27, 1649, Charles was sentenced to death as a tyrant, murderer, and enemy of the nation. Oliver Cromwell signed the death warrant. A stunned Europe looked toward England in disbelief.

In early June of that year, Rebecca and John received a letter from daughter Joan:

Dearest Mama and Papa,

We are well and John is studying hard. Sometimes he forgets I'm alive, but I have found friends among the other wives, and we entertain each other pleasantly.

I visited Aunt Elspeth in Essex, and cousin Edward. Mama, he looks just like Uncle Thomas, and is so brilliant! They want him to read the law when he is older.

The most horrid event I have witnessed here was the execution of the king at Whitehall on January 30. John, of course, did not know I was going, but at the last minute several of the other wives came by for me with a coach. The crowd was at first rowdy, then savage, then ashamed at what passed. Charles was very brave, requiring no restraint. I heard they had to prevent his little spaniel from following him to the block. I did look away when they raised the king's head aloft. I believe you knew at least one of the regicides, Sir Richard Whalley, brother of Lady Jane Hooke.

I dearly hope that now England will see peace and prosperity. Civil war was so destructive to the civilian population—the poor have suffered terribly.

Have you heard of a man named George Fox? He has begun a Society of Friends at various locations in England which causes much controversy. Strangely enough, he preaches many ideas which I would expect to come from you, Papa, such as nonviolence, and reliance on the guidance of one's own conscience, or "Inner Light." The most heretical thing he teaches is that the Bible is not the Word of God, but only contains the words of God. He encourages his followers not to pay tithes, support the military, or swear oaths. This has resulted in many Friends, including Mr. Fox himself, being jailed. I never realised how free we were in Rhode Island until I came to England. Liberty of conscience is indeed a treasure worth guarding.

I must close this now if I am to get it to the boat before it sails. Oh, yes, I shall be delivered of a child in October if all goes well.

Love and kisses,

Joanie

When she shared the letter with Mary Williams, seeking only to inform her friend of the events described therein, Rebecca was dismayed at the response.

"That's where this all leads. It's where we all will end up, dead!"

"Did you expect some other end to your life, Mary?"

Her friend turned strange, angry eyes on Rebecca.

"We have sacrificed our all for liberty of conscience. You lost a daughter; my husband lost all semblance of a normal life, all for this grand notion which drew us across the sea. Now those who claim to support liberty and toleration in England have descended to the level of beasts, killing God's annointed king."

"Mary, this was a political thing. Charles ignored the needs of his subjects. If he had provided for them rather than continually stealing their money, they would have protected him!"

"'Becca, in England, politics and religion are one. The side we have been supporting all our lives has committed regicide. What hypocrites we all are, to claim the love of Christ, yet kill a Christian king!"

Mary withdrew into a shell of mourning. She wore only black, neglected her children and house, saw no one. At last, her daughters, Mary and Freeborne, sixteen and fourteen, came to see Rebecca.

"What can we do to help Mother?" they asked.

"These things take time," she answered. "You two know how to keep the household running. Do that, and I'll try to think of something to draw her out..."

But nothing worked. Mary remained as steadfastly melancholy over the death of King Charles as she had over that of Job Cornell so long before.

One March noon in 1650, John brought Rebecca a letter from Joanie in England. Having read it through already, he was astounded when Rebecca burst into tears.

"Did I miss something," he asked, "or does news of a healthy grandson sadden your heart unnaturally?"

Rebecca looked at him accusingly.

"It's bad enough that you smugly bring me news of being an old granny. But you also had to get me with child again."

Shocked, he nevertheless wrapped loving arms around his wife.

"'Becca, you did not tell me! Do not grieve. Are not our other children all blessings from God? Surely you do not regret bearing any of them."

"It's not that, John. I just assumed that I was through bearing. I'm sure that I've not been pregnant since Deliverance, nearly five years ago. Another pregnancy just seems so hard! I'm forty years old, too old for this!"

"We'll get a wet nurse for the child, and an extra lady's maid for you, as well as the best midwife in the colonies. I'm delighted that I have a strong wife who is still able to conceive at forty. I love you, 'Becca."

In October, 1650, Rebecca took her new son, Job, to visit Mary. When she told her friend the name, she saw Mary smile for the first time in many months.

"Your uncle is an angel of God," she told the infant. "Carry his name proudly. Have I shown you this, 'Becca?"

Curious, Rebecca lifted the sheaf of bound papers Mary held out and leafed through them.

"Did Roger write this?"

"Yes. He wrote it to comfort me, and indeed, it has helped immeasurably. Of course, I cannot read it myself, but the children read to me."

Rebecca read the title, *Experiments of Spiritual Life and Health*.

"Here he says that he and others have discerned in you, Mary, the marks of a joyous Christian life, and prays that you may rejoice in them. Do you remember what Roger was like back at Otes? Do you recall Lady Joan instructing you to surround him with love? The sweet and gentle spirit which characterizes Roger Williams today is your creation, with the help of God. You can be very proud of him, Mary."

"Indeed, I am. And now I know that I shall be well again, soon. My family has been very patient with me."

"I am glad. You have fine children, Mary."

"They may be all I have, before long. Roger is contemplating another trip to England to renew our colony charter. He must sell our trading post and all our possessions except for the house and furnishings to pay for his ship's passage."

"You will miss him."

"Very much. I shall depend heavily on your friendship while he is gone."

That fall, Rebecca noticed unusual occurrences in her backyard. Every morning, the barn door or that of the corn crib was found to be hanging open. Nothing was missing, but sometimes tools or other items had been moved, and often the hay and horse blankets had been rearranged, as if someone were making use of them for a bed. Rebecca at first scolded Hans, the Dutch servant in charge of their farm, for carelessness, thinking that perhaps he had a sweetheart who was trysting with him on the property, or that he had taken to drink.

The honest Hans, indignant that his employer should think ill of him, protested in his broken English, and began keeping a watch that very night. Next morning, he reported to Rebecca.

"Is Chon Sayles und yoong Mary Villiams," he said. "Dey meet in da barn."

That night, Rebecca waited up to see for herself, and discovered that Hans had told the truth. Much concerned, she lay awake, wondering what should be done. Considering her friend Mary's emotional state and Roger's impractical attitudes, she decided to speak to the sixteen year old girl, herself. Next day, she sent Patience with a message to young Mary that she wished to see her.

Greeting the girl at the door, she said, "Let's go for a stroll, shall we?"

As they reached the common meadow by the river, Rebecca leaned against the fence, and indicated the beasts grazing and wandering about.

"They have vastly increased their numbers since we first arrived here. Have you not watched them mating in the spring?"

Mary flushed and mumbled, "Yes."

"You are aware, of course, that mating leads to the production of offspring. The more frequent the matings, the more likely is pregnancy…"

The girl hid her face in her hands.

"Is there any way I can help you, Mary? It would grieve me to hear your name being spoken by others with contempt."

Mary began to cry. Between sobs, Rebecca could understand most of her story. The girl's mother was too melancholy to be of any help. Roger had done nothing to inform or guide his daughters in such matters except to read Biblical warnings against the sin of fornication. He had forbidden both the older girls to so much as speak to men, for fear they would be tempted…Young John Sayles had seemed so understanding, so gentle until one night when he had hurt her. Since that time, they had been together often, each meeting ending in the same way…

"He has no property, no prospects. He hires himself out as labor, and never saves a shilling of his wages…But I am his, for good or ill. I could never give myself to anyone else…God help me, I am so sinful!"

Rebecca slipped an arm around Mary and hugged her gently.

"If you continue your present course, I see disaster ahead. We must get your young man to marry you, and your father to give his blessing. Do you object if I ask my husband to help?"

"N-no. Oh, Neighbor, do you really think he could?"

"He has remarkable powers of persuasion."

Within the week, John hired young Sayles and took him on one of his boats, to Virginia. Several times during the voyage, he spent an hour with the youth, discussing his future and the steps necessary to ensure a comfortable life. In January, 1651, he sold the young man a house and lot in Providence, in exchange for labor. Then he accompanied him to visit Roger, begging for Mary's hand in marriage.

Rebecca, in the intervening time, had softened Roger on the topic of marriage for his daughters, and the Williamses soon had a son in law. Rebecca breathed a sigh of relief that Mary Sayles' pregnancy had not become obvious before the wedding. Her son was born in late June, 1651, and called John, Jr.

One morning in early June of that year John sent a message home that he would bring a guest to dinner. When the men entered the house, Rebecca saw that the guest was Dr. John Clarke, one of the first settlers of Portsmouth, on Aquidneck. He was both a physician and Baptist minister.

Apparently, he and John were in disagreement concerning a prospective course of action. After politely greeting Rebecca, the man put his case before her.

"You have lived here as long as I, Neighbor. Tell me what you think. Roger Williams, William Dyer, and I intend to sail to England in November, in order to reverse the damage done by the Council of State. They gave Will Coddington a commission for life, to govern Aquidneck and Quunungate. This divides the territory of our original charter, and leaves our colony open to depredations from the greedy tyrants who run the neighboring colonies.

In order to be most successful in England, we three need to appear in the public eye to have suffered for our beliefs. Roger has his sad tale of being hounded from England by Laud, then banished from the Bay Colony through the snow. But we need a current example of the intolerance, preferably to be told in first person, to make it most convincing. My thought is to make a journey into Massachusetts, violate some ridiculous, minor law, then suffer one of their usual inappropriately harsh punishments. I shall write up my experience, then publish it on arrival in England."

Rebecca took a deep breath.

"Have you considered how many things could go wrong with this plan?"

"Your dear spouse has spent the morning acquainting me with most of them."

"And you have an irresistible urge to be flogged? I understand that the officers of the Bay Colony delight in the screams of Baptists."

"They'll hear nothing but God's praises pass my lips."

"Let's feed this man dinner, John. He's going to need all his strength!"

Rebecca prayed earnestly for John Clarke, but heard that he suffered much in Lynn, Massachusetts. Clarke, Obadiah Holmes, and John Crandall went to visit friends there, where Clarke preached a sermon against infant baptism, insisting that the doctrine was a false one. Then the three attended church with their hats on. The hats were knocked off, and the men jailed. Holmes was fined thirty pounds, Clarke twenty, and Crandall five, in default of which they were publicly whipped.

Outstanding quotes of the occasion, later published by Clarke in his *Ill Newes From New England*, were Holmes' statement:

"I bless God I am counted worthy to suffer for the name of Jesus."

and Pastor John Wilson's, delivered with a slap in the face:

"The curse of God and Jesus go with thee."

John Cotton's comment on the affair, given much later, was this:

"Better be a hypocrite than a profane person."

Rebecca merely shuddered and prayed that the mission to England would succeed. She never wanted her children to be forced to live under such a harsh and punitive system of government.

It was November of 1651 when Roger Williams came over to bid the Throckmortons goodbye. The three prayed together, earnestly entreating God that this mission to preserve the liberty allowed by the colony's 1644 Charter would be successful. Roger seemed cast down in spirit, and John assured him:

"Do not fear for your family. They shall want for nothing while you are away. If the Almighty does not permit you to return, I will care for them as if they were my own."

Roger said, "I shall never be able to repay your kindness, Neighbor Throck."

Rebecca said, "We and our children owe you our precious freedom, Neighbor Williams. We shall never forget that."

The three wept as Roger left.

The two and one-half years of Roger's absence passed swiftly, it seemed, for everyone except Mary Williams. When Rebecca presented her new son, Joseph, in spring of 1652, Mary mourned that she probably would be unable to have any more babies, since she was nearly past the age of bearing.

"Now it is time to rest and enjoy your grandchildren," Rebecca told her. "It's much easier than rearing your own. And you have three strong sons to provide for your old age."

"Yes. But I shall always long for just one more baby of my own. Roger misses me so much that he wrote, asking me to sell the house and join him in England...If I did that, we might have another child. But I would not risk the sea voyage again, with or without the older children. He left it up to my discretion, so I decided to stay here. Rebecca, is it worth the sacrifices, knowing that our children and grandchildren may have to continue the struggle for liberty when we are gone?"

"You are the only one who can answer that for yourself, Mary. My own thought is that they will 'rise up and call you blessed.'"

John Cotton died in Boston that year, leaving a legacy of Puritan intolerance.

In 1653, Anne Hutchinson's son in law, John Sanford, was elected President of Rhode Island. The following summer, 1654, Roger returned from England. He had accomplished the confirmation of the 1644 Charter, plus the overturn of Will Coddington's commission as Governor for Life. But a new charter seemed beyond reach, since the Lord Protector, Oliver Cromwell, had dissolved Parliament and the Council of State, which issued charters. John Clarke had, however, remained in England to continue the effort.

Returning on the same boat with Roger were Rebecca's daughter Joan, with her husband John Taylor and sons, Edward and Samuel. The Throckmortons rejoiced, seeing their grandchildren for the first time.

Rebecca's daughter, Patience, had never lived up to her name. She was one of the more impetuous, active young ladies of the colony, riding her horse and canoeing wherever and whenever she chose. Rebecca struggled to keep track of her, but, with her babies demanding so much attention, was unable to restrain the girl as she wanted to.

One hot afternoon, in August, 1654, Rebecca glanced out the window to see a procession of men carrying Patience up the hill to the house. Alarmed, she flung open the door to admit them.

"Do not be distraught, Neighbor," said one of them. "Her canoe was over-turned by a passing pinnace in the channel. She held onto her boat, and is merely exhausted. John Coggeshall, here, rescued her."

They had laid the dripping Patience by the hearth, and the hero, a wealthy gentleman as well as a strong athlete, was supporting her head and shoulders. The other men left, but John Coggeshall had not moved, and seemed mesmer-ized by the beautiful girl he held in his arms.

After Rebecca finally shooed him out the door, Patience nimbly leaped to her feet, saying, "Gracious, I thought you'd let him stay all night! I was grateful for the rescue, but truly, I'm no invalid."

Rebecca released an exasperated sigh, and said, "Then why did you lie there so long, letting him hover over you?"

"Because he's the horseman I've been trying to beat when racing down the river trace. He always gloats mercilessly that he owns the better animal, and it intrigued me to see the softer side of him. Now I shall feed my mare more oats and molasses, and try again to win, once the weather cools…"

"Patience, your father is going to be very upset when he hears of this. You must not compete against the men that way. They take their sports quite seri-ously, you know. It is a part of their lives not open to females."

"Nonsense. I can ride and paddle with the best of them. I refuse to become idle and fat just to please the men."

"Well, I saw Coggeshall's eyes, and if you do not care for him in a romantic way, you had better not play games with him. He is not a man with whom to trifle."

"Mother, I'm only fourteen, and John is well over thirty. He's even a father, by his first wife. There is no romantic attachment between us."

"I saw what I saw this afternoon, Miss, and you had better watch out! If you tease Neighbor Coggeshall any more, you may not be able to get rid of him."

Next day, Rebecca sent her trusted servant, Abrams, to Aquidneck to investigate the personal life of John Coggeshall. The man returned with a discouraging report: Coggeshall and his wife of thirteen years had divorced, citing irreconcilable differences.

"That isn't enough information, Abrams!" Rebecca was frustrated. "Why did they separate? Did he beat her, or lie with other women, or drink to excess…"

Abrams, who disliked speaking of anyone's personal matters, replied delicately, "I interviewed all the servants. It is possible that Neighbor Coggeshall did not watch his wife closely enough…she seemed to need more excitement than one man is able to provide."

Exasperated, Rebecca demanded, "Is there any evidence that John Coggeshall did anything to cause her unhappiness?"

Abrams fixed her with a look which informed her that this was his final word on the subject.

"None!"

A month later, the man in question was at Rebecca's door.

"Neighbor Throckmorton, I am hopelessly enslaved by your daughter, Patience. I worship the ground she treads. But she does not respond to me as I would like. How can I get her serious attention?"

"Neighbor Coggeshall, I have been trying to get her serious attention for the last five years or so, since she first learned to ride and canoe with her brother, Freegift. She cares nothing for any of the normal feminine pursuits, preferring the outdoor life. I confess that I understand it not at all.

Neither do I understand how a man could divorce the mother of his children, as you have, and seek the affections of another. Without this understanding, how can I trust you near my daughter?"

He, looking directly into Rebecca's eyes, replied, "I was granted a divorce decree by the Council more than a year ago, before I met Patience. To protect my family name, I sought the court's action and convinced the deputies that my wife and I parted because of mutually exclusive religious beliefs. But that was all a lie."

He paused, gulped, and continued.

"It is extremely humiliating for me to admit that I was unable to make my wife happy. I am accustomed to humiliation, however, for I spent most of our thirteen years together castigating myself for the many faults she found in me. As to our five children—although I claim them all and love them dearly, I know I did not sire them all. Now my ex-wife has married the most recent of her many lovers. Neighbor Throckmorton, it is not good for me to live alone, or for the children to be reared by my servants. Because my parents have always been happy, I have faith that I could yet find peace with a fine person such as Patience. I swear to you that I would treat her with the respect she deserves."

Rebecca gazed into the hearth fire for a time, weighing the man's words, feeling his anguish. She recalled attending a feast, years before, on Aquidneck, where a woman had shamelessly flirted with her husband. John had been greatly amused at Rebecca's jealous reaction.

"Over the years, I have been offered the intimate companionship of many women, white, red, even black…most were much more attractive than Neighbor Coggeshall's wife," he had told her. "But none of them could make me want to debase the precious bond you and I share. For good or ill, 'Becca, I am yours alone."

Suddenly, she felt strong compassion for this young man who had been cruelly denied the happiness she had enjoyed for so many years.

"Neighbor Coggeshall, my husband and I owe you Patience' life. We can never forget that. If you are able to find a way to win her heart, we will not oppose you."

Fortune smiled on Neighbor Coggeshall. In December, it was he who discovered Patience, her forearm broken after falling from her horse ten miles from home. He carefully splinted and wrapped the arm, meanwhile soothing her tears of pain with kisses which went beyond the intensity absolutely necessary. He carried her home on his horse, though hers was nearby and would have served as well, kissing her often along the way to make sure of his privilege. He visited Patience every day until she was able to ride again in the early spring, and on that first ride convinced her to marry him.

"Mama, he is the best outdoors man in the colony. He has promised that I shall be able to ride and swim and do all the things I love, even after marriage. Surely not many men would permit that!"

"Probably not, my darling daughter. But you will find that caring for his needs and those of his children will limit your activities."

"I know, Mama, but he is a good man, and I shall be happy with him."

The pair was married in December, 1655, and went to live at Newport, on Aquidneck. John Coggeshall later served as Deputy Governor of Rhode Island.

During the following spring, 1656, John came home for dinner one noon, his eyes clouded with concern. Rebecca took his hand and waited for him to speak.

"A ship arrived this morning, loaded with passengers. They had been denied permission to land at Boston and at New Amsterdam, and Roger is trying to decide whether to permit them here."

"Are they bearing some dread disease, such as smallpox?"

"'Becca, they are Friends."

"What do you mean?"

"They are followers of the famous heretic, George Fox."

"And that's their only problem?"

"It's problem enough. The spokesmen for the other colonies already describe Rhode Island as a 'moral sewer.' Accepting their cast offs will confirm that view."

"So what? These are human beings who need our help."

"Their views may cause dissension in our colony."

"John, it would be impossible to incite more dissension than exists here already. Besides, the Quakers are said to be nonviolent, hardworking, thrifty...their presence would probably benefit our community!"

"That's what I told Roger."

"And?"

"He's still thinking about it. He won't admit a religious sect for no other reason than that they may benefit the colony."

"But he will admit them because of liberty of conscience?"

"I believe he's working himself around to that position."

"I believe I'll take a stroll after dinner. Is Roger holding forth in the tavern?"

"Yes."

Rebecca let John escort her to the tavern, but she did not permit him to follow her inside. Roger sat at the back of the large room which doubled as town meeting hall. An empty tankard of ale was at his elbow, and his face was buried on his crossed arms as he slumped over the table.

"We're getting old," thought Rebecca. "Perhaps Roger lacks the will for this struggle."

He raised his head as she sat on the bench across from him.

"Good afternoon, Neighbor. I see that I am about to feel the other side of the Throckmorton pincers of persuasion."

She flushed.

"God forbid that I should cause an error in your judgment, Neighbor Williams. If you prefer that I not speak, I shall withdraw."

"I would rather hear your voice than any of those rabid individuals to whom I listened all morning."

"I only came to remind you of something you once told me."

He groaned.

"I hope I was being lucid at the time."

"It was one of your better moments."

"Then remind me. There were all too few of those."

"You said that liberty of conscience is not an end unto itself, but rather the means which makes possible the Christian pilgrimage."

"I did?"

"Yes. And since the Friends consider themselves Christian..."

"So do the damnable papists."

"Yes, but the Friends are quite thoroughly Protestant."

"They are a cult. They have invented peculiar manners and speech patterns to keep themselves apart. They are said to quake in ecstasy when communing with the Spirit of God."

"So what? They are Saints of the Most High. Let them walk in this colony without molestation in the name of Jehovah, their God for ever and ever."

"I hate having my own language quoted back to me."

"Then you must stop being so quotable. Neighbor, think of those poor people on that ship, longing only for a breath of free air. You were in their position a mere twenty years ago..."

"Neighbor Throckmorton, will you consent to house one of the families until they build their own residence?"

Rebecca gulped. These were strangers, heretics.

"Yes, Neighbor Williams. I owe them as much grace as I have received..."

"Will you not stop quoting me?"

"...and I feel sure that my two daughters will, likewise, each house a family over on Aquidneck."

"This feels like a decision, Neighbor, one I am sure to regret."

"It surely will not be the first or last of those for you, Neighbor. I consider you to have become a truly kind and gracious man."

"Only because I agreed with you."

"No. Because my dearest friend, Mary, was able to teach you the love which Jesus bears for sinful men."

That very afternoon, John brought a family of ten Friends to stay at the house. Rebecca immediately set her servants to work, helping the Quakers bathe and wash clothing, feeding them a huge meal, and settling them for the night.

When he got the opportunity, John whispered to his wife, "What did you say to him? Roger seemed to take particular glee in selecting the largest and noisiest group for us."

"I quoted things I remembered him saying in the past. It makes him crazy."

"Indeed."

During the following days, Rebecca acquired a clear conception of the Quaker beliefs, and of why she could never join their ranks. For one thing, they believed that the return of Christ to earth has already occurred, creating the Kingdom of Heaven within each believer. From this idea, they extrapolated the notion that each individual is taught the gospel directly by the Lord. This inner teaching took precedence over all other instruction, including that of the Bible. By following the Inner Light, through constant self evaluation and discipline, the Friends believed that they could overcome sin and be free from its power.

This sounded good to Rebecca until she realized that the Friends had not left the self evaluation and discipline entirely to the individual, but had been unable to resist setting up a code of disownable offences for members. In addition, these Quakers seemed unable to keep their convictions to themselves, but considered themselves the Publishers of Truth, proclaiming the Day of the Lord. They were particularly obnoxious about this, and after being addressed as "thee" for a week by the lower class family who infested her elegant home, Rebecca had had enough.

"The rooms over the store were good enough for us, all those years," she told John. "They're good enough for our Friends."

The family remained grateful for the Throckmorton's help, especially since John was able to employ the man and his older sons in his business. They seemed to have a knack for merchandizing, and no Puritan style compunctions about acquiring riches.

Thinking the Quaker crisis nearly over, Rebecca was shocked when, weeks later, her daughter showed up, dressed as a Quaker, thee-ing and thou-ing her mother.

"Stop that, Joanie! I'm you mother, not some tradesman who has ill served you."

"I must practice speaking this way, Mother. If I make exceptions, my tongue will become confused."

"Thee is confused in more than just tongue…Now you've got me doing it! Surely you do not plan to become a Friend!"

"I have done so, already. I was convinced by the wife of the couple we took in off the ship. I have never felt such inner peace!"

"Wonderful. Just keep it to yourself. I have worked a lifetime to achieve the inner peace I now enjoy, and I do not wish it to be disturbed."

"Oh, Mama! Know thee not that such overflowing happiness as I now have must be shared? I could no more keep this to myself than I could keep the river channel from flowing."

Rebecca groaned, and asked, "What does your husband say about this?"

"He is thinking it over. Perhaps he will be convinced. And Papa, likewise."

"Your papa has been living according to his Inner Light for his whole life. He needs no one to teach him how to do so."

"Perhaps it will comfort him to join with others of like mind."

"I've not noticed that he is in need of comfort."

"Surely we all need that."

Rebecca began to watch John carefully, but noticed no changes except that he tended to spend the last hour before bedtime in prayer. She attributed this to his need for solitude, as the bustle of his work and family life left little enough time for reflection.

Freegift, tall and lean at twenty-one, had learned his father's business from the ground up. He was now running several of his own vessels as far south as the West Indies. Rebecca heard rumors that he had a sweetheart in every port, but as yet he had not confided any information to her.

John Jr., at fourteen, accompanied his father everywhere, and made his parents proud with his every word and deed.

Twelve year old Deliverance, shy and introspective, seemed determined to be the scholar of the family; she read everything she could get her hands on, memorizing her favorite literature.

Little Job and Joseph, at six and four, were so active that Rebecca spent most of her time just keeping them from mischief. Their mother was grateful that they both showed early ability to read, which calmed them somewhat, inducing them to sit still occasionally.

By the year 1657, many more shiploads of Friends had come to Rhode Island to escape persecution in England. They built a meeting house on Aquidneck, and Joan attended regularly. Many of Anne Hutchinson's former followers became Quakers, as some of their beliefs were quite similar.

1657 was the year of Patience' first childbed. She named her son Freegift, after her favorite brother.

England continued in turmoil as Lord Protector Cromwell sickened and died in 1658. His son, Richard, attempted to take his place, but by 1660, Charles II ascended the throne, restoring the monarchy. Several of the regicides of Charles I were tried and sentenced, and Oliver Cromwell's body was exhumed to be displayed with them. Rebecca heard that Hugh Peter, though innocent of regicide, had suffered the traitor's fate of being half hanged, disemboweled, and beheaded at Tyburn.

"The worst part," she thought, "must be knowing what will happen ahead of time, imagining it in advance. No matter the anguish Peter caused me, surely justice was not truly served by such a horrible sentence."

In February, 1660, Patience presented her mother with another grandson, James.

In early June of that year, Rebecca went into mourning when she learned that an acquaintance, Mary Dyer, had been hanged in Boston as a Quaker. A former patient and follower of Anne Hutchinson, the woman had been safe at Rhode Island, but had fatalistically returned to the Bay, where the heresy of the Friends was not tolerated. Rebecca's mourning was not so much for the foolish woman as for the Bay officials who had learned so little about toleration from the stark pageant enacted by the monarchs of their homeland.

In March, 1662, Patience had a daughter, Mary. Rebecca was shocked to learn that her daughter had continued to ride her horse throughout her pregnancy, and was already teaching her young sons horsemanship. She decided to say nothing, knowing that Patience would not listen to her advice, anyway.

During that summer, John came home unexpectedly one mid afternoon. Hearing the door close, Rebecca walked downstairs.

The man standing next to John turned and suddenly lifted Rebecca, whirling her around.

"I have prayed for you all these years, Mistress. It is delight to see you once again!"

When he set her down, Rebecca recognized John Winthrop, Jr. She flushed in embarrassment, remembering her emotional state at their last meeting in Salem.

"I have longed for the opportunity to apologize to you for my rudeness..." she began.

"It is I who should apologize," he rejoined, gallantly. "When last we met, I had no concept of how much you were giving up, how deeply the decisions of the Boston Council were cutting into your life…But it seems that you have found the bitter gall which you drank sweet in the end."

"Life is sweet, no matter what I drink. I have avoided rum since that time, however. It made me quite ill!"

John said, "We were saddened to hear of your father's passing, several years ago. His seemed the only voice of reason in the Bay, at times."

"His great regret was that the lines drawn by the Bay officials drove people of good will, such as yourselves, out of fellowship and into the wilderness. My father loved Roger Williams until the day he died, and I believe he sincerely mourned the Hutchinson family."

Not wanting that topic pursued, Rebecca said, "I heard you have been elected Governor of Connecticut again."

"Yes. It is an honor for me to serve in that capacity. But I dare not tarry. My ship's captain threatened to cast off without me if I returned not quickly. I must bid you farewell."

He kissed Rebecca twice, saying, "This one is from Endecott!"

She grimaced. Then he laughed, and was gone.

Later, John told her, "Winthrop was surprised to find us living civilized lives here. The popular concept is that we live as beasts—in chaos."

"Sometimes we do! Sometimes I think that no two residents of this place agree on anything. But I prefer chaos to tyranny!"

"Indeed. Winthrop, however, will never see things that way."

In November of 1663, Dr. John Clarke returned in triumph from England with the royal charter for Rhode Island, secured from Charles II. It was the most liberal charter issued by England during the colonial era. It provided for self governing autonomy, the maintenance of earlier territorial claims, and "full liberty in religious concernments." On November 24, the freemen of the colony gathered "at a very great meeting" to hear the charter read. It was a day of great rejoicing. Later that same week, Rebecca and John entertained Neighbor Clarke at dinner.

"How fare the common people of London?" asked Rebecca. "I heard from my daughter that the coal and food shortages during the civil wars and Protectorate had caused great suffering among them."

"You heard correctly, but conditions are now improving, slowly, because of the confidence and stability inspired by the restoration of monarchy. The renewed legalization and use of the Book of Common Prayer was well received;

it seems that most people missed the old ways and resented the repressive Puritan regime. London is at last beginning to breathe and live merrily again."

"Except for the persecutions, of course."

He sighed, and said, "The Quakers seem honor bound to offend people. They make it hard even for those who support religious toleration to grant them the liberties they demand. How are they received here?"

"You have surely noticed, because of their peculiar dress, their large numbers here. They remain active in proselytizing others, and have constructed a meetinghouse on Aquideck. They have many fine qualities which benefit our colony. I'm sure that Roger Williams' influence is responsible for the welcome the Friends have received here. He has preached toleration so long and so hard that our entire population takes great pride in owning the "Freest place on earth."

"But surely Roger does not tolerate the Quakers' precepts, himself. He remains unalterably Calvinist in many of his views."

"That is true. It takes a great man to make allowance for the views of one's opponents, just as it takes a great man to sacrifice years of his life to the service of his colony, as you have done, Neighbor Clarke. May God richly bless you!"

In September of the following year, the English, under Colonel Richard Nichols, drove the Dutch from New Netherlands, renaming the place New York. John's wharf and warehouse at New Amsterdam were damaged during the conflict, but he was able to rebuild afterwards and continue trade there almost as profitably as before.

In the next year, 1665, Rebecca's daughter Patience bore her fourth child, Joseph, in May. News came from Salem; Endecott had died, incorrigibly womanizing to the end.

In June, John came to Rebecca, entreating her to walk and talk beside the river with him.

"My darling wife, your old husband is waxing greedy again. As you know, the land area of Rhode Island is extremely limited; all of it is spoken for and therefore difficult to acquire. But, thanks to the late British action at New Netherland, land is being opened for settlement, to the south, in an area known as New Jersey. I should like to get in at the onset, by virtue of which our sons may become quite prosperous."

Rebecca's face clouded, and she stopped beside a huge tree, gazing up into its branches. She thought of the bright prospects at Boston, at Salem, at Anne's Hoeck, which had so swiftly turned dark. She began to cry.

"John, we've had this discussion before, with terrible results."

She felt his arms slip round her from behind. His lips found the back of her neck, and lingered there.

"Heart's Lady, I'll never ask you to move away again. Providence is the only place both safe and free enough for your spirit. New Jersey can be settled by our children if I buy the land now."

She turned, burying her face over his heart, and sobbed, "I've become such a coward in my old age!"

"'Becca, for me you are forever young. And you know, better than most, the reasons for being fearful. That is called wisdom, not cowardice!"

"Then give me reasons why I should not fear sending our sons to New Jersey."

"For one thing, New Jersey is being established with the help and protection of the British army, under Philip Carteret. I have spoken with him; he is being very careful not to leave himself open to attack either from the Dutch or from the natives. I am impressed with his plans for defense; otherwise I should never risk our sons."

"And what else?"

"Have you looked at our boys as I have? They are strong, capable, adventurous. Freegift is in love with the sea; I do not expect him to settle on land. But John and Job will never be content without this sort of challenge. This is the opportunity they need in order to focus their energies."

Rebecca said, "At least I still have Deliverance and Joseph by me...I know I cannot keep the children at home forever. Do what you think best, John. But for right now, just hold me. Before many years have passed, we shall only have each other."

In the following year, 1666, Rhode Island received the great Quaker missionary, John Burnyeat. Many were convinced, and Rebecca was glad that her sons John and Job had safely removed to New Jersey, remaining Baptists. John attended Burnyeat's meetings with Joanie, who pressed her father to become a member.

"Thee agrees with us, Papa. Why do thee resist joining our fellowship?"

"I am old and stubborn, my dear. It is hard for me to make changes at this point in life. Besides, if I suddenly began to thee and thou your mother, I'm not sure she would still allow me in her bed!"

"Oh, Papa! Those aren't reasons, only excuses! Why resist the overwhelming joy of the Spirit?"

"Joanie, I will be convinced when I am ready, and not one moment sooner."

He kissed her farewell.

In the following spring, 1667, a ship unloaded at Aquidneck, and Joanie, as was her habit, took in a Quaker family from it. Rebecca found this out when her eighteen year old Quaker grandson, Edward Taylor, arrived at her door.

"Can thee put me up for a while, Grandmama? Home is in chaos, children everywhere."

"Of course, honey! Just put your things in Joseph's room. You're welcome for as long as you want to stay."

Edward was soon off, looking for Joseph, then fifteen, at the wharf. The pair quickly began looking for ways to annoy the local girls. Rebecca and Deliverance actually didn't see much of them, except at mealtimes, and therefore were surprised, a week later, when John brought the two home in mid afternoon.

Edward was crying, Joseph appeared frightened, and John more worried than Rebecca had seen him in years.

Wrapping protective arms around Edward, Rebecca seated him in a chair, then stood beside, holding and rocking him gently.

"John Taylor's dead," Joseph blurted. "That family of Quakers brought plague off the ship...Joanie and Samuel are very ill."

Rebecca straightened her back, turned to the cabinet, grabbed a shawl and headed for the door. It was blocked by her husband.

"Excuse me," she said. "I must go to her!"

"No, darling," he murmured.

She tried to pass by him, but his hands seized her arms. His tears began as she struggled against his strength.

"Let me go! Joanie needs me..."

"I need you. And I am not ready to let you go. Being with Joanie now could mean death for us all..."

"John! Please!"

"No. You have vowed to obey me in all things. And I insist that you stay here. Joanie and Sam are being tended by the Quaker woman, and have every appropriate physic to succor them. Going there will serve no purpose but to make you ill."

John saw the stubborn light in Rebecca's eye.

"Promise me," he commanded.

"No."

"Promise me you'll stay here!"

She collapsed into his arms, sobbing, and he lifted her easily, as if she were a child, carrying her into the parlor. John held her for a long time, his heart breaking because he had been told that Joanie was very near death.

Next day, word came that the suffering of Joan and Samuel was forever ended, and the family grieved together. John, Joseph, Deliverance, and Edward Taylor sailed to Aquidneck, where they joined other friends and relatives, including the Coggeshalls, at the Quaker style burial. Rebecca, knowing that no formal service would be read, and still angry at being denied the chance to see her daughter one last time, remained at home just until John's pinnace left the dock. Somberly, she walked next door.

"Pray with me!" she begged.

Roger and Mary prayed, but noticed that she remained restless, unsettled.

"Do you want me to accompany you?" asked Roger.

"I hate to ask. You are so miserable with arthritis…"

"I rowed to Aquidneck, myself, only last week."

"Yes, but I need to come straight back here so that John does not worry…Let's use a pinnace this time. I long to say the words over the grave, since no one else will do it."

"All right."

"Mary, will you come with us?"

"No. I prefer to remain at home. I shall be in prayer for you."

Aquidneck

At sunset, Rebecca stood in the empty Quaker burial ground, gazing at Joanie's plain wood marker, a clod of earth in her hand. As Roger compassionately intoned the words of the service, Rebecca crumpled the dirt, sprinkling it on the grave. Kneeling, the two prayed, and then rose to return to the boat. Roger leaned upon his ever present staff, and Rebecca supported his other arm.

John, his children, and his grandson stayed that night with Patience, who had recently born a fifth child, named Rebecca.

Providence

Satan made his first visit to Rebecca Throckmorton's bed in many years. First he showed the image of Mary being tomahawked at Anne's Hoeck, then that of Joanie, screaming, her lymph nodes swollen, bursting, her face turning black.

"I have your daughters," he laughed. "Soon I'll have you!"

Rebecca refused to become alarmed. Calmly, she woke herself, then spent the remainder of the night drinking herb tea by the hearth downstairs.

"My daughters are angels of God," she told the flames. "Satan cannot touch them, and he shall not touch me!"

Her family returned, midmorning. John was dressed as a Quaker, and approached Rebecca hesitantly.

"Will thee have a Friend as thy husband?"

"My husband has always been a friend. Will you have a heretic to wife?"

"My wife has always been heretical. It's what I love most about her."

Their two children and their grandson gathered around, surrounding John and Rebecca in an embrace expressing both tolerance and love.

When Roger encountered John and realized he had joined the Friends, there was a heated discussion.

John: "Thee founded this sanctuary as a haven for the oppressed. Now thee are angry that the oppressed have come here."

Roger: "No. I am angry that intolerant fanatics have come to the citadel of toleration. They may not be violent of deed, but are certainly violent of thought and word."

John: "As are thee!"

Roger: "I never claimed to be nonviolent, only tolerant of others' thought. And I shall be nonviolent toward the Friends only when they learn toleration toward me!"

John: "Thee is speaking to a tolerant Friend at the moment."

Roger: "I know it well. Perchance you can teach toleration to the others; I have been unable to do so."

The two parted, agreeing to disagree.

Newport

In August of 1669, Rebecca was present on Aquidneck for the birth of baby Patience Coggeshall.

"I'm trying to equal your record, Mama! Only two more children to go!" exulted the mother, Patience.

"You have ever been competitive of nature," responded Rebecca. "My thought was that you should live up to your name."

"I'm learning, Mama. The children are teaching me."

"Indeed."

Providence

Upon her return home, Rebecca was greeted at the dock by John, whose tears were streaming down his face.

"Freegift," he choked, barely able to speak. "He was lost off his ship in a storm, and never recovered."

Rebecca cried against John's chest for a time, then turned, walking with him up the hill toward home. She passed their door, heading for Williams', intending to make Roger recite the service for burial at sea with her.

"Wait," begged John. "I'll come with thee!"

After relating their latest family tragedy, John and Rebecca knelt as Roger and Mary prayed, laying loving hands on their heads in blessing.

On the way home, Rebecca nervously asked, "Are you going to be in port for awhile?"

"I am leaving in a week."

"Oh…"

"Is Satan bothering thee again?"

"He tried. I defeated him after Joanie died. But after this…he could even bring back Way Peirce to torment me. We never said a service for him, you know."

"Well, let's do so when we get home. It can't hurt. And why not make Deliverance sleep in thy room while I'm gone?"

"She, she doesn't know about this. I didn't want the children to know I am so weak in faith…"

"'Becca, thee has stood alone against Satan both in the flesh and in dreams. Thee are stronger in faith than any one I know!"

"I was never alone; God was with me. But I have learned that the Evil One always returns when my faith is weakest. The battle is ongoing, and shall never cease while I live. This is the heretic's special torment. I have no church behind which to hide."

"Would becoming a Friend help thee? I should be glad to show the way…"

"John, I am not convinced."

"Then I shall pray for thy spirit. It is truly the most beautiful one I have ever known. Perhaps that is why Satan covets it so."

The next week, Rebecca again defeated Satan, calling on the name of Jesus to banish the tempter from her dreams.

In September, Rebecca's servant came into the parlor, a peculiar look on his face.

"A Reverend James Ashton is here to see Miss Deliverance. Should I disturb her?"

Deliverance spent most of every day in prayer, study, and writing in the library.

"Show him in here, Abrams."

The Baptist minister entered the parlor, hat in hand, peering myopically at Rebecca.

"Miss Throckmorton?"

"I am Mistress John Throckmorton; Deliverance is our daughter."

"I had hoped to speak with her; I have traveled from New Jersey for the purpose."

"I should like to help you, but my daughter does not like to be interrupted in her studies. Could you give me some notion of your errand?"

"Of course! I have read her treatise on mutual toleration between opposing religious sects, which she sent to her brother, John. I wanted to check one of the references she cited, and hoped that she had a copy of it here…"

"She may. Deliverance has done research at several privately owned libraries in the colonies. The work could be from one of those. I will determine if she is ready for her mid afternoon break."

When Rebecca, behind closed library doors, informed Deliverance of the caller's name, her daughter's eyes grew round with astonishment.

"James Ashton is a famous scholar, Mama! I must see him right away!"

"Don't you want to adjust your hair? It looks as if you have been twisting it round your fingers, again."

"Oh, Mama, he didn't come here to see how I look!"

Deliverance strode past her mother, opened the door, and headed for the parlor. The two were still talking at supper and at bedtime, when Deliverance put Ashton up in the guest room for the night. He departed after dinner next day, and Deliverance acted quite strangely afterwards.

Rebecca held her peace. Was not the woman twenty-four years old? When she wanted advice concerning men, she would ask.

The next week, when John was home, Rebecca heard Deliverance asking her father to take her for a visit to New Jersey.

"I long to see my brothers, Papa. John and Job have been there too long without any feminine guidance."

Amused, her father asked, "What makes thee think they'll accept thy guidance? When I saw them last, they were quite content without being ordered about!"

"I shall not make myself obnoxious, Papa. I just need to breathe sea air and to view new territory."

In bed, John asked Rebecca, "What's gotten into our Dee? She's never wanted to travel before, except for her studies."

"It has to do with her research, I believe. She wants another in depth interview."

"Of whom?"

"The Reverend James Ashton, of Middletown."

"Oh, ho! Why didn't she say so? Women are so devious!"

"You're just discovering this?"

"Come to me, my devious one!"

When Deliverance Ashton returned from New Jersey, it was to collect her belongings and remove to Middletown with her husband.

At Christmastime, 1670, Rebecca and John had a visit from their son, John, with his new wife Alice Stout. Rebecca was much impressed with the lively, intelligent girl chosen by her son, and wished them well.

In early spring of 1672, John came home one evening exuding a satisfied glow.

"What's amiss?" teased Rebecca.

"Plenty, if thy name be Roger Williams! George Fox is coming to town."

"No! Not the inventor of the Inner Light!"

"'Becca, a little respect, please. This may be our only chance to meet this man who has brought joy to so many."

"And led so many to jail and death."

"Would thee consider entertaining him at dinner while he is here?"

"I suppose. To what do I owe this honor?"

"Thy husband is the wealthiest Quaker grandee of the colony, of course!"

"And the only one with an heretical wife!"

"Perchance meeting Fox will convince thee."

"You forget that Satan himself has been unable to convince me of anything lately."

"For that I'm grateful, but not for the comparison."

One noon in April, George Fox came for dinner. Rebecca noticed that the man was quite self involved, or involved rather with his own role as missionary. He spoke of the natives he had met during his journey, with whom he had shared crosscultural revelations from God. He was one of the few white men Rebecca had ever known to consider the Indians' religious experiences to be as important and valid as his own. Unfortunately, the Indians, having met too many white men, were less than fascinated with him. Rebecca let the men do all the talking, and was a little hurt when Fox left her home without saying much more than "Hello" and "Farewell" to her.

Gazing moodily into her looking glass, she mused, "In my youth, no man ever ignored me that way. I wonder if it was my appearance, or my obvious lack of membership in the Society of Friends which failed to attract his interest."

She pushed back a strand of gray hair, smoothed the skin which sagged from her high cheekbones. Trying a smile, she watched wrinkles spring into place. Losing patience with her self pitying attitude, she turned from the glass and laughed.

"It's probably his Inner Light which dims the glow from lovely creatures such as myself!"

But she remained miffed.

Roger was more than miffed by George Fox's visit. Each of the two great men was unable to humble himself to call on the other. Their potential for civilized conversation, or even formal debate was therefore lost. The two settled for writing and publishing books against each other's views.

Roger's was called *George Fox Digged Out Of His Burrowes*. George's was *A New England Firebrand Quenched*. Both authors descended into name calling and insulting language.

After reading Roger's book, John felt constrained to write several sharp letters, upbraiding Roger for his ill manners during Fox's visit, as well as the crude form of his written attacks on the man.

Roger sent John a brief message: "I have discharged my conscience; so have you. This time it is I who forgive first."

In July of 1672, Patience bore her seventh child, Benjamin.

In August, 1673, during war with Britain, Dutch forces recaptured New York, and held it until November, 1674. John's trade with the area was curtailed during this time, and he was not pleased. Luckily, their sons' mercantile exchange in New Jersey was not much affected.

In April of 1674, Patience and John Coggeshall sadly buried their eighth baby, Content, who had been born prematurely, too weak to survive.

In June, 1675, Mary Williams came into Rebecca's parlor, saying, "Pray with me, Neighbor!"

As usual, from Mary's prayer, Rebecca discovered what was distressing her friend; messengers had come that morning to Roger from Josiah Winslow, Governor of Plymouth and Commander in Chief of the combined English colonial army. Roger had gone with them to Narragansett, to secure new promises of neutrality from the sachem, Canonchet. But Mary's agitation was caused by the news they brought: The English were fearful because of the ten thousand warrior, intertribal alliance formed by Metacomet. He, called King Phillip by the English, was the Wampanoag sachem, son of Massasoit. To prevent the surprise attack they feared, English forces would attack the Indians at Swansea on the following morning.

When their prayers were ended, Rebecca turned to Mary.

"This is it, the war we have dreaded most."

"Yes. Roger has feared and tried to prevent this for over forty years. Because of the wide distribution of the allied tribes, no English settlement in Massachusetts is safe. If the Narragansetts join Metacomet, even Rhode Island towns are at risk."

Within a few days, Roger was back, and consulted worriedly with John in the parlor.

"The Bay officials have never trusted the Narragansetts," he said. "Canonchet assured us he has not allied with Metacomet, but only sheltered the Wampanoag old men, women, and children."

"And of course, Winslow wants Canonchet to surrender the helpless ones."

"Yes. He would sell them into slavery, to the West Indies, to break the spirit of the Wampanoags."

"Such hate, such cruelty! It makes me ashamed to be English."

"When among the natives, I have felt that way many times. However, Winslow will never understand. He suspects me of disloyalty, when all I desire is justice and peace."

The conflict between English and Indian forces intensified through the summer and into fall. The fighting at Swansea in June and at Pocasset in July caused Roger, who was in charge of the colony's militia, to make plans for evacuation of women and children to the island towns. He planned for the defense of Providence, using Neighbor Field's house, set high on the bluff, as a small fort.

In August, the war action moved farther away, to Brookfield, Hopewell Springs, then to Deerfield and Northfield, Massachusetts. But in December, as the English commanders hardened in their resolve to force Canonchet to surrender the Wampanoag civilians, Roger wisely insisted that the Providence and Warwick evacuation plans be implemented. His son, Providence Williams, assisted, taking Mary and many others away on his sloop. John and Joseph

Throckmorton had loaded their boats with people, making several trips before Joseph came to fetch Rebecca.

"Why aren't you packed, Mother?"

"Because I'm not going anywhere. This is my home."

Her handsome son, then twenty-three, advanced upon her. He was tanned from months at sea, his muscles hard from joining his sailors at the work he loved so much. He gently gripped her shoulders in strong hands.

"Mama, Patience is expecting you over on Aquidneck. Think of it as a visit."

"I don't usually leave my house empty to go on visits...I prefer to have someone here to look after things. Now you run along. I have already sent the servants down to the ship."

Joseph evidently went straight to his father, who came striding up the hill with an energy which belied his seventy-four years. Rebecca saw him, and threw a few things into a canvas bag. Meeting him at the door, she handed it to him.

"Put this on your boat for me," she said, "I'll be along, with Joseph, directly."

When she saw Joseph, later, she repeated her performance, saying, "I'll be along, with your father."

As evening came, she saw that both pinnaces had left the harbor, the evacuation complete. Rebecca walked to the Williams house, where Roger sat alone, gazing into the fire.

"Will you sup with me, Neighbor?" she asked.

Looking up in surprise, he replied, "With pleasure! All I have is cold bannock bread."

Leaning on his staff, the little man limped painfully beside Rebecca as she clung gently to his free arm. She seated him close by her fireside and brought a bowl of hot beef stew, some crusty bread, and a mug of ale for each of them.

"Truly, I have lived too long," he said. "Had I died before June, I could have stood before the Lord, making good account of my allotted time. I could have faced my Indian father, Canonicus, on the other side, satisfied that I had kept my word to his people. Tomorrow, much of my life's work—forty years' worth—will be destroyed."

"What do you mean?"

"I received word from Winslow to be prepared for retaliation. One thousand of his men, united with the Mohegans under Uncas' son, Oneko, will attack the Narragansetts at their headquarters in the Great Swamp at dawn."

"Neighbor, tomorrow is the Lord's Day!"

"The Narragansetts know this well, and will be unprepared."

"The sins multiply on themselves."

"Indeed."

Roger stayed with Rebecca for three days, sleeping on a couch before the hearth, eating the food she prepared, praying and reciting scripture with her. At last, John came home, his face a mixture of sorrow and rage.

"I bring ill tidings. Even though our own families are safe upon Rhode Island, our Narragansett and Wampanoag brothers, sisters, and children have been massacred in the Great Swamp."

His face flowed with tears as he added, "It was Mystic River all over again. How can we continue to destroy the helpless ones?"

Roger and Rebecca took his hands, leading him to the fireside.

"It is the human condition," said Rebecca. "We are impelled to evil by forces we do not understand."

"We must await a further manifestation of God's perfect will," said Roger. "He will explain all when we meet Him face to face."

John sank to his knees, sobbing, as they wrapped loving arms around him.

The three remained together in the house all winter and into early spring.

In March, 1676, they received word that the remnants of the Narragansetts had joined the Wampanoags and were on the move against all English. Warwick, ten miles south of Providence, was burned on March 17. When the messenger had gone away, John turned to Rebecca.

"Darling wife, thee has stayed long past the point of safety. Will thou not allow me to transport thee to the island?"

"John, you and this house are all that is truly mine in this world. My conscience bids me stay to protect you both."

She fingered Miantunomi's shell necklace which hung at her throat on its leather thong.

John stared at her, then asked, "Will thee stand against Satan again, in the flesh?"

"I have met him before, many times. I am not afraid."

For a week, John, Roger, and Rebecca thought that the marauding Indians had passed Providence by. Led by their sachem, Canonchet, they had in fact circled away to the north, attacking English soldiers and civilians wherever they found them. They burned William Blackstone's elegant home and priceless library. In the dawn of March 26, they appeared at the top of Providence hill. Roger, leaning heavily on his staff, slowly made his way up there, to parley. For an hour, Rebecca peered out her upstairs windows, watching Roger attempt to negotiate the salvation of his town. At last, he turned back, entering the Throckmortons' door.

"Since we had no part in attacking them, they have agreed to harm no one. But they will burn the town."

Rebecca looked out to see three homes already ablaze.

John said, "That's it. Let's head for the wharf."

Rebecca said, "Wait, John. Isn't that Canonchet with his sachems?"

"Yes."

"I will speak to him!"

Before they could stop her, she ran nimbly out the door, heading for the grouped Indians. Rebecca was quickly surrounded by sannups, who seized her arms roughly, dragging her away from the chiefs.

"Stop!" she ordered. "Take me to Canonchet!"

She showed them the shell necklace.

Seeing that she was unarmed, they let Rebecca walk toward their chief. Recognizing his father's symbol in the beads, the haughty red man folded his arms and glared at her.

"Why do you wear my father's blessing? He is dead, and can no longer protect you."

"Miantunomi's blessing was given because I assisted at your birth. It has protected me all these years, even against the Mohegan. It has protected my house, where you were born."

"How is it that his blessing protects you, but nothing could protect my mother in the Great Swamp?"

"Perhaps his spirit longed for hers to join him."

He seemed to regard this answer favorably, then said, "Perhaps the Great Spirit longs for those of all my people. They have suffered much in order to join Him."

Canonchet lifted his chin and began to stalk past Rebecca when she turned, saying, "Taubotne aunanamean."

He froze, and turned his head to look at her. Unspeakable sadness shone in his eyes. He then led his small group of sachems down Towne Street. As he passed the Throckmorton home, where John and Roger stood in the doorway, Canonchet raised his spear, shouting a command. The sannups ran past the property, firing the other homes on down the hill. Of one hundred three homes, only twenty-three, including Rebecca's, were saved.

Not long after, they heard that Canonchet was captured by the Mohegans. He was given the choice of submission to them or death. Choosing death, he said:

"I like it well. I shall die before my heart is soft, or I have said anything unworthy of myself."

He was killed by Oneko, son of Uncas, who was the killer of Miantunomi.

On March 31, the officials of Massachusetts colony, hearing that Roger's house was destroyed, and that he himself was disabled, revoked their edict of banishment against him, giving him "liberty to repayre into any of our Towns..." as long as he behaved himself peaceably and inoffensively, "not disseminating and venting any of his different opinions in matters of religion to the dissatisfaction of any."

Roger, however, and John stayed with twenty-five other men to salvage what they could of Providence. They began rebuilding. Unfortunately for the colony, John Clarke died that year. He was later honored as "the Father of American Baptists."

In May, 1676, Patience was delivered of a girl whom she named Content after the baby lost in 1674. This child was strong, but Patience herself did not recover her former vigor after the birth, and began wasting. John Coggeshall, distraught at the prospect of losing his dear companion, sent for Rebecca to comfort Patience.

Newport

Rebecca summoned all her resources in order to manage the active Coggeshall household during that time. She knew that the whole family was likely to need spiritual nurturing in the near future. Therefore, Rebecca began reading the lessons from her prayer book to the younger girls, Patience, seven, and Rebecca, nine. Before long, the other children and their father sought the solace of family worship.

In late August, news came that King Phillip's War, as the Indian conflict was called, had ended. Estimated losses were three thousand natives and six hundred English. King Phillip, or Metacomet, himself met death by treachery in a swamp near Swansea. Never would the Wampanoags or Narragansetts regain their former strength.

During that year, John Winthrop, Jr. died in Connecticut.

On September 10, 1676, Rebecca stood in the cemetery on Aquidneck with John, crumbling a clod of earth onto Patience' coffin. She thought of her daughter's words, whispered the week before:

"When he is ready, Mama, encourage John to marry again. I cannot bear to think of him alone, and the children...they need a mother's love. Promise me...and let them know I shall watch over them all."

Providence

Therefore, Rebecca managed to be happy for John Coggeshall when, a year later, he married a young widow with a child of her own. Rebecca remained close to the grandchildren, enjoying their frequent visits to her home.

John Throckmorton continued in service to his community. Over the years he had held the positions of Moderator and Town Council Member. Between 1661 and 1675, he had been elected Deputy ten times. In 1677, in recognition of his honesty and financial knowledge, he became Town Treasurer. At seventy-six, he was not only one of the wealthiest, but also oldest and most respected men of the colony.

One morning in 1679, Rebecca was summoned urgently next door to the Williams' home. It had been rebuilt and was being maintained by Daniel Williams and his wife, Rebecca. Roger and Mary had lacked the physical strength to operate their own place for some time, and by then depended on the support of their children.

Mary had aged gracefully, her hair snowy white, her dark eyes young and sparkling in a serene face. This morning, however, she had suddenly been unable to rise or speak, and was frantically trying to communicate with her husband and children. Her eyes increased their intensity as Rebecca Throckmorton entered the chamber. The others left them alone.

"Mary, my dearest friend, I see that our Lord is calling for you!"

A tear trickled from a large brown eye in the lovely, pallid face, and Rebecca wiped it away.

"Your daughter in law told me that they think there is something you want, but they cannot figure out what it is. If I guess it, can you blink twice for me?"

Mary blinked twice.

"It must not be Roger or the children, since they are all with you...here is a Bible, which someone has open to *I Corinthians*, Chapter 13...was that Roger?"

Mary blinked twice.

"You taught him love, Mary. He would surely have died of rage by now without that. I know! Is it Roger's book that you want, the one he wrote for you? I could read from it!"

Mary blinked twice, and more tears flowed onto her pillow, this time from relief. She slept, but when she woke, Rebecca read to her from *Experiments of Spiritual Life and Health*. She seemed content. John came by that evening to fetch Rebecca home, and held their dying friend's hands in his.

"The love that founded Providence came from thee," he said. "This town will ever be thy monument."

Before leaving, Rebecca whispered, "Greet them all for me, on the other side...Job, Lady Joan, my Mary, Thomas, Freegift, Joanie, Patience...let them know I am coming..."

Then she sang the *Twenty-third Psalm*, knowing she had given all the comfort in her power.

For three days, the Throckmortons mourned Mary's passing with Roger. At last they laid her to rest in the orchard behind the house. Together, the three friends repeated the Anglican burial service, commending her gentle spirit to God.

For four years afterward, John and Roger remained the antithesis of each other. John, physically strong and vigorous, ever remained gentle and reasonable of nature. Roger, wracked with multiple infirmities, hobbled about Providence in good weather, prophesying to and debating with whomever would listen. Rebecca loved them both for what they were, and gathered them to her fireside frequently for long talks which often included reminiscence of times gone by.

In early 1683, as soon as the ice melted in the harbor, John came to Rebecca.

"I long to see our children and grandchildren of New Jersey," he said. "Joseph is due to arrive with his ship any day, and could transport us."

Rebecca pictured them all in her mind. By that time, John and Alice had six children: Joseph, Rebecca, Sarah, Patience, Alice, and Deliverance. James Ashton and Deliverance had five. Job had not yet married. He was desperately in love with twenty-three year old Sarah Leonard, who insisted that God had told her to wait for a sign from Him before marrying. Job had yet to figure out how to make her see the light.

Thinking of the cold, tiring journey as well as the hubbub caused by so many active grandchildren, Rebecca answered him, "I prefer to remain here, but I will let you go, if you promise to be careful."

John laughed, "I am far past the age for being careful. When the Almighty wants me, He need only call, for I am ready!"

Two weeks later, she recalled his words as her children, Joseph, John, Job, and Deliverance entered her parlor, tears in their eyes.

"Papa is gone from us. He lay ill for only two days. His last words were of you. He said, 'Heart's Lady, come to me...'"

Rebecca rose from her chair, surprised at the sensation in her stomach. She felt as if a hole had opened there, growing, pressing on her lungs; she found it difficult to breathe.

"Help me, children," she gasped. They surrounded her, assisting her to the couch.

When she could talk, she asked, "Will someone call Roger Williams? He was John's best friend..."

Roger prayed and recited scripture with Rebecca all afternoon. At sunset, the two old people went out the door, over to the orchard where Mary Williams lay. There they recited the service for John Throckmorton, who lay under the sod at Middletown.

A few days later, Deliverance addressed her mother, "We would all like you to move to New Jersey, with us, so as to be close...we love you so, Mama, and do not want you to be alone."

"Your father said that Providence is the only place safe enough and free enough for my spirit...I know that he was right. I have sacrificed much for the freedom I enjoy here with every breath, and I will not give it up!"

"I was afraid you'd say that. Mama, would you let my oldest daughter, Patience, live here to look after you? She is a good girl, quiet, and not given to causing trouble. She could be for you as you were to Lady Barrington so long ago."

"I shall try that for six months. If the girl and I get along well, she may stay."

So it was settled, and Patience Ashton became a resident of Providence. Joseph lived with them when in port, and various grandchildren were frequently at the house. Seeking land, however, many of them settled in New Jersey.

In April, 1683, Rebecca Williams, Daniel's wife was at the Throckmorton door.

"Father Williams is asking for you," was all she said, but Rebecca saw her tears.

Entering Roger's chamber, Rebecca knew at once that he had not long to live. His lips were blue tinged, and his breaths came in shallow, noisy gasps. Roger's famous ice blue eyes had never seemed more intense, as he concentrated on his next effort to obtain air. When he saw Rebecca, he seemed to relax, as if he had been afraid he could not stay until she arrived.

Summoning all her strength, Rebecca smiled down with love at this once despised man and took his cold hand. She began to recite:

"I have fought a good fight, I have finished my course, I have kept the faith; Henceforth there is laid up for me a crown of righteousness, which the Lord, the Righteous Judge, shall give me at that day; and not to me only, but unto all them also that love His appearing."

Between gasps for air, Roger tried to smile.

"The liberty of conscience, was it worth the fight?" she asked.

Roger, with great effort, said, "Ecstasy, ecstasy..."

Then all his painful struggles ceased, and he slid into death.

When she was sure he was gone, Rebecca closed his eyes and turned away. As she left the house, she could hear Daniel and his family crying over their beloved patriarch.

Days later, Rebecca stood, more alone than ever before, in the Williams' orchard. She had watched the parade of Rhode Island soldiers marching to Rogers' grave, had been startled by the volley of muskets fired in his honor as founder of the colony. But she had waited to come here alone to utter the powerful words which no one would expect to hear from a heretic at the grave of a Seeker. As the sun sank, she said them, sure that they would be understood in Heaven by those she had loved most.

Before long, Rebecca induced a grandson to build her a bench beside Roger and Mary's graves. She went there often to pray and to talk with them, wrapped in John's loving spirit, which she felt constantly around her as if it were a warm cloak. It was on this bench that Patience Ashton found her one evening, forever asleep with her dear friends.

Notes for Rebecca of Providence, Rhode Island

Page 3 Rebecca's maiden surname is in dispute. Some researchers have it as Colville, others suggest Cornell. I chose Cornell because of the Thomas Cornell who later joined the Throckmortons in Providence, Rhode Island, and who died with some of them at Anne's Hoeck.

Page 4 The location of Rebecca's family in Bradwell and Chelmsford is speculative, based on a possibly unrelated Edward Colville being located there.

The given names of Rebecca's family are my own invention, except the above guesses about Thomas and Edward. I chose the name Job because Rebecca named one of her sons Job, and there were no Jobs in the Throckmorton family. As far as I know, Rebecca had no actual brother named Job.

Page 5 The association of Rebecca with the Barrington family is my own invention. I made this connection because I needed to attach Rebecca and John Throckmorton to Roger Williams, who had an historic, documented association with the Barringtons.

Page 7 The descriptions of Hatfield Broad Oak are as accurate as I could make them. The names, activities, and situations of the Barrington family members are a matter of historic record.

Page 8 All information about John Throckmorton, especially his education, his family, and his activities in the Americas is based on my compilation of many sources, among them *Throckmorton Family History with Cognate Branches* by Frances Grimes Sitherwood and *History of the Throckmorton and Allied Families* by Charles Wickliffe Throckmorton.

Page 12 The imprisonment of Francis and Joan Barrington in Marshalsea prison is historically accurate.

Page 32 The Barrington's association with the various Puritans I mention, including the Winthrop family and Oliver Cromwell is a matter of record.

Page 52 Most information about Roger Williams is based on *Master Roger Williams, A Biography* (The Macmillan Company, New York, 1957) by Ola Elizabeth Winslow. Other sources, including histories of the various locations where he lived, were used. The descriptions I give of his violent behavior toward women are my invention; his violent personality is a matter of record.

Page 57 The letter to Lady Barrington from Roger Williams was found in the Winslow book.

Page 59 The given names of the Throckmorton's first two children, Joan & Mary, is my invention.

Page 74 The imprisonment of Richard Chambers for mouthing off to the King is a matter of record.

Page 84 The description of the Lyon, her passengers and crew, and the events which took place during the voyage are very close to accurate.

Page 93 The descriptions of the Winthrop family, their names and manner of their deaths are a matter of record, quite a bit of it contained in Governor John Winthrop's famous journals. And yes, he does mention the Throckmortons.

Page 98 The descriptions of early Salem and of John Endecott are accurate. His social behavior is my invention, except that he *did* have an illegitimate son in Europe, he *did* wear a skull ring, and his various political struggles are a matter of record.

Page 122 The description of Anne Hutchinson and everything which happens to her is as accurate as I could make it.

Page 124 There was a hurricane at this juncture which affected the settlers of early Boston.

Page 126 The accounts of Roger Williams' defiance of the Massachusetts Bay authorities, and his excommunication, along with that of the other founders of Providence, are accurate.

Page 145 The description of early Providence, is based on diagrams and printed histories of the town.

Page 148 The relationship of Roger Williams to the Native Americans is factual.

Page 151 The Mystic River massacre is historically accurate.

Page 161 The events at Anne's Hoeck are mentioned in Winthrop's Journal. My description is as accurate as I could make it. The necklace is my invention, of course.

Page 179 Anne Hutchinson's daughter Susana was rescued. Involving the Throckmortons was my invention.

Page 184 Mary Williams apparently did suffer from depression, and Roger wrote *Experiments of Spiritual Life and Health* to comfort her, but it is believed that she could neither read nor write.

Page 192 Roger Williams' struggle with the policy of admitting Quakers to Providence is accurate.

Page 207 George Fox did visit Providence, and did quarrel, in print, with Roger Williams. Because John Throckmorton was such a wealthy and influential Quaker, it is likely that they interacted.

Page 209 The descriptions of King Phillips War is accurate. Rebecca's involvement is my invention.

Page 216 John Throckmorton died in New Jersey. It is thought that he did not settle there.

Page 218 There is no record of the date of Rebecca's death.

0-595-30392-7